Praise for *Requiem for a Lost Empire*

"[E]pic in scope . . . shocking [and] enlightening, *Requiem for a Lost Empire* is a war novel, elegiac in tone, but also immediate and intense in presence."
—*The Boston Globe*

"Powerful and compelling . . . shocking, harrowing, beautiful and in many ways profound. . . . With immense poignancy, it captures the complex and contradictory tangle of memories, thoughts, and emotions that the demise of this empire has engendered in the hearts of its people."
—*Washington Times*

"[L]uminous, beautifully crafted. . . . Makine writes lyrically, baring his struggling characters' emotions and vivifying their oft-chaotic backdrops with equal brio."
—*Publishers Weekly* (starred review)

"The 'lost empire' of the title obviously won't let Makine go— much to his agony, one suspects, but also much to our benefit as readers still sorting out the whys and wherefores of the East-West showdown that shaped half a century of our history."
—Michael Upchurch, *Seattle Times/Post Intelligencer*

"A splendid haunting and haunted novel."
—*The Providence Sunday Journal*

"*Requiem for a Lost Empire* is a worthy lyrical addition to Makine's Proustian tapestry depicting a vanished country's deeply conflicted past and present."
—*Kirkus Reviews*

. . . and for *Dreams of My Russian Summers*

"One of the great autobiographical books of this century."
—*Los Angeles Times Book Review*

"Skillfully constructed and elegantly written . . . a major novel."
—*The New York Times Book Review*

Translator's Note

Andreï Makine was born and brought up in Russia but *Requiem for a Lost Empire,* like his other novels, was written in French. Part of the book is set in Russia and the author uses some Russian words in the French text, which I have kept in this English translation: these include *agitprop* (political propaganda, especially in art or literature); *gulag* (the system of forced-labor camps in the Soviet Union in the period 1930–55); *izba* (a traditional wooden house built of logs); *kolkhoz* (a collective farm); *kolkhoznik* (a member of the *kolkhoz* collective); *kulak* (a peasant farmer, working for his own profit); *muzhik* (the somewhat contemptuous historic word for a peasant); *shapka* (a fur hat or cap, often with ear flaps); *soviet* (an elected local or national council in the former U.S.S.R). The nickname "Shakhmatov" ("the Chess player") derives from the Russian word for chess, *shakhmaty.*

G. S.

REQUIEM FOR A LOST EMPIRE

A NOVEL

ANDREÏ MAKINE

Translated from the French
by Geoffrey Strachan

WASHINGTON SQUARE PRESS

New York   London   Toronto   Sydney   Singapore

WSP WASHINGTON SQUARE PRESS
1230 Avenue of the Americas
New York, NY 10020

ISBN: 0-7434-5362-X

First Washington Square Press trade paperback printing April 2003

10 9 8 7 6 5 4 3 2 1

WASHINGTON SQUARE PRESS and colophon are
registered trademarks of Simon & Schuster, Inc.

Manufactured in the United States of America

For information regarding special discounts for bulk purchases,
please contact Simon & Schuster Special Sales at 1-800-456-6798
or business@simonandschuster.com

1

"Wicked men have no songs. How come the Russians have songs?"

—Friedrich Nietzsche, *The Twilight of the Idols*

"There are only two peoples now. Russia is still barbarous, but it is great. . . . The other young nation is America. . . . The future of the world is there between these two great worlds. Some day they will collide and then we shall see struggles of which the past can give no idea."

—Sainte-Beuve, *Cahiers* 1847

"The other day I turned up the pages of an address book from before the war. I had to mark crosses and grim notes on every page: 'Exiled . . . Disappeared . . . Dead . . . Killed in battle. . . . Shot by the enemy. . . . Shot by his own side. . . .'"

—Alfred Fabre-Luce, *Journal d'Europe* 1946–1947

It has always been my conviction that the house that sheltered their love, and later my own birth, was much closer to the night and its constellations than to the life of that vast country they had managed to escape without leaving its territory. The country surrounded them, encircled them, but they were elsewhere. And if, in the end, it discovered them, hidden deep in the woods in the Caucasus, this was the chance outcome of a game of symbols.

For it was a symbolic tie that, in one way or another, linked every inhabitant of the country to the mythical existence of the master of the empire. In their mountain refuge they believed they were free of the cult the country, indeed the entire globe, had built up around an old man who lived out his days consumed by the fear that he had not killed those likely to kill him. Adored or hated, he had a place in everyone's hearts. By day he was acclaimed, when night fell he was cursed in feverish whispers. But these two had the privilege of never bringing his name to mind. Of thinking only about the earth, the fire, the swirling waters of the stream by day. Of loving one another, loving the constancy of the stars by night.

Until that moment when the dictator, now almost halfway through the last year of his life, called them to order. Despite his morbid obsessions, irony was no stranger to him: he often smiled through his mustache. They did not wish to come to him? He would go to them. The mountain that towered above the narrow valley where their house lay hidden reverberated with explosions. Was the construction of a dam that would bear his name being embarked on? An artificial lake created to his greater glory? A power transmission cable set up that he had decided should bring light to remote villages? Was a mineral deposit being uncovered that would be dedicated to him? They only knew that, whatever the nature of these works, the master of the empire was making his presence felt.

After each explosion, fragments of rock shot up above the mountaintop then hurtled down the slope, now sticking fast in the tangles of the underbrush, now parting the smooth surface of the stream. Some of the slabs came to a halt just yards short of the fence that screened the house. Each time they caught sight of a fresh stone missile, the man and woman would leap up, holding out their arms instinctively, as if they could block the bounding fall that snapped tree trunks and tore up broad swathes of the forest floor.

When the explosions fell silent they exchanged looks and had time to say to themselves that their presence had not been discovered, so the place was really safe, or perhaps (they dared not believe this) their clandestine, criminal way of life was finally going to be accepted. The last salvo was unlike the others: it sounded to them like a stray echo that had been delayed. The slab of rock that detached itself from the mountaintop was different too—flat, rounded, and, in a manner of speaking, silent. Its fall was almost soundless. It struck a tree, stood on edge, and revealed its true nature. It was a granite disk, sliced off by the whim of the explosion, rolling faster and faster. The man and woman made no move, mesmerized both by the speed of its rotation and the improbable slowness with which the action was unfolding in front of their eyes. A tree trunk barring the path of this stone wheel was not smashed but sliced, like an arm by a saber. The thickets that might have stopped it seemed to part to let it through. It avoided another tree with the sly agility of a big cat. The dusk veiled some of the stages in its descent—they heard, before seeing it, the dry shattering of the fence.

4

The disk did not destroy their house. It embedded itself in it, as if in clay, plunging into the heart of it, tearing up the floor and coming to a halt, still bolt upright.

Standing about a hundred yards away from the house, the man lashed out in the direction of the mountaintop, threatening someone with raised fists, and let fly an oath. Then, walking like an automaton, approached their home, which still seemed to be mutely quivering from the impact. The mother, nearer to the door, did not step forward but fell to her knees and hid her face in her hands. The silence had returned to its original essence—the incisive purity of the peaks against a sky still radiant with light. All that could be heard now was the man's halting footfalls. But almost audible in its intensity was the unknowable prayer, silently murmured by the woman.

Making their way into the room, they saw the granite disk, even more massive there under the low ceiling, embedded between the deeply furrowed floorboards. The child's cradle, which hung in the middle of the room (they were wary of snakes), had been grazed and was rocking gently. But the cords had not given way and the child had not awakened. The mother held him tight, still incredulous, then allowed herself to be convinced, heard the life in him. When she looked up, what the father saw in her eyes was the trace of a dread that was no longer related to the child's life. It was the echo of her terrible prayer, the vow she had made, the inhuman sacrifice she had offered in advance, to the one who would keep death at bay. The father did not know the name of this dark and vigilant god. He believed in fate or, quite simply, chance.

Chance willed it that the explosions did not start again. The man and woman, who accepted each day of silence as a gift of God or of fate, were not to know that artificial lakes were no longer needed, since the one to whom they were dedicated had just died.

The news of Stalin's death would be brought to them, three months later, by a woman with white hair, a lithe and youthful step, and eyes that did not judge. The only one who knew their secret refuge, she was more than a friend or relative. She came as night fell, greeted them, and spent several seconds stroking the surface of the granite slab, whose presence in their house no longer amazed the couple and seemed as natural to the infant as the sun at the window or the fresh scent of the clothes hanging up outside the wall. The word "rock" would be one of the first he learned.

It was from that infant, no doubt, that I inherited both the fear of naming things and the painful temptation to do so. An infant, borne away one night by the white-haired woman who, as she made her escape, did her utmost for him not to be aware of it. At first she was successful, until she came to cross a narrow suspension bridge above the stream. The infant was dozing with open eyes, and did not seem surprised. He recognized the warmth of the woman's body, the shape and strength of the arms holding him tight. Despite the darkness, the air had the same scent as usual, the pleasantly sharp tang of dead leaves. Even the mountains, now black, and the trees tinted blue by the moon did not amaze him: often the sun's fierce light at noon would seem to turn the ground and the foliage around their house black.

But halfway across the little bridge, as it sways on its ropes, suddenly everything changes. The infant does not see the worn slats on which the woman is moving falteringly forward, nor the gaps left by the missing ones, nor the phosphorescent foam on the stream. But he senses, without knowing why, that the woman carrying him is afraid. And this fear in an adult is as strange as the abrupt maneuver by which she grips the collar of his little shirt in her teeth, reaches out with her arms to cling to the ropes and leaves him dangling in the dark air. Her stride—almost a leap—over the broken slats is so long that the child feels as if he is flying. The pebbles on the bank crunch under the woman's feet. She unclenches her jaw, takes the infant in her arms again. And hastily puts her hand over his mouth, anticipating the cry that this being, who is beginning to understand, was about to utter.

For the infant their nocturnal escape coincided with that unique moment when the world becomes words. Only the day before everything was still fused together into a luminous mixture of sounds, skies, familiar faces. When the sun went down, his father would appear on the threshold of the house—and the joy of the setting sun was also joy at seeing this smiling man whom the sun brought home, or was it, perhaps, the father's return that sent the sun plunging into the branches of the forest and turned its rays copper? His mother's hands smelled of clothing washed in the icy waters of the stream, a fragrance that scented the first hours of the morning, mingling with the breeze that blew down from the mountains. And this flow of air was inseparable from the quick caress with which his mother's fingers strayed into his hair when she woke him. Occasionally, amid this tissue of lights and scents, a rarer note: the presence of the woman with white hair. Sometimes her coming coincided with the retreat of the last snows toward the mountaintops, sometimes with the blooming of those great purple flowers on their tall stems that seemed to light up the underbrush. She would come and the infant would notice an extra clarity in all that he saw and breathed. He came to associate this mysterious happiness with the little suspension bridge that the woman used to cross when she spent a few days in their house.

On that particular night it was the same woman, gripping his shirt collar in her teeth and carrying him over the little bridge as it set snares for them with its broken slats. When she collapsed amid the thickets she just had time to stifle the infant's cry. He struggled for a second, then froze, alarmed by quite a new sensation: the woman's hand was trembling. Silent now, he observed the world disintegrating into objects he could name, and which, once named, hurt his eyes. This moon, a kind of frozen sun. This bridge, a secret herald of happiness no longer. The smell of the water, no longer associated with the coolness of his mother's hands. But above all, this woman, sitting in the darkness, her anxious face turned toward impending danger.

He recalled that their whole journey, begun well before sunset, had been nothing other than a slow slide toward a world riven by strangeness and fear. They had started by walking through the forest, up hill and down dale, at a pace too fast for an ordinary stroll. The sun had gone down without waiting for his father's smile. Then the forest had thrust them out onto a level, open space and the child, not believing his eyes, had seen several houses lined up along a road. Before that there had only been one house in the world, theirs, hidden between the stream and the wooded flank of the mountain. The house, unique, like the sky or the sun, impregnated with all the scents given off by the forest, in tune with the yellowing of the leaves that covered its roof, attentive to changes of the light. And now this street lined with houses! Their multiplicity hurts his eyes, provokes a painful need to respond. The word "house" forms in the infant's mouth, leaving an insipid, hollow taste. They spend a long while in an empty courtyard behind a fence, and when the child grows impatient and utters the word "house," to indicate that he wants to go home, the woman hugs him to herself and stops him from speaking. Over her shoulder he becomes aware of a group of men. Their appearance leaves him totally baffled. To himself he says "people," the word he had heard spoken at home with a slight anxious hesitation. People, the others, them . . . Now he sees them in flesh and blood, they exist. The world is growing bigger, teeming, destroying the singularity of those who hitherto surrounded him: his mother, his father, the white-haired woman. By saying "people," he feels he has done something irreparable. He closes his eyes, opens them again. The people disappearing at the end of the street all look alike in their dark jackets and pants and their long black boots. He hears the woman heave a deep sigh.

★

8

During the night, after crossing the little suspension bridge, words assault him, force him to understand. He understands that what was missing from the houses in the village, where they have just seen "people," was the great stone disk. These houses were empty, their doors were wide open and no glint of mica shone in the gloom of their rooms. A sudden doubt assails him: what if the house has no need of the gray rock at its heart? What if their own house was not a proper house at all? The conversations between adults that he used to retain in his memory as simple rhythms now bristle with words. He understands scraps of these words, remembered in spite of himself. The story of the rock, its appearance, its strength. They often spoke of it. So, it was an aberration: even his mother's action one night when she fixed a candle in the long fissure on the slab of rock.

All at once his family's life seems to him very fragile in the face of this threatening world, where the houses get by without granite disks and the inhabitants all wear black boots and vanish up a road that has no ending. The child senses confusedly that it is because of these "people" that their family has been obliged to dwell in the forest and not in the village where the others live. He goes on deciphering the words he recalls from the adults' conversations and is more and more afraid. He has not seen his parents since the sunshine of the afternoon, a separation, he senses, that could last indefinitely in this world without limits.

The hand smothering his cry seems unfamiliar, for it is trembling. He remains silent for a moment. In the darkness below their hiding place footfalls can be heard on the pebbles at the stream's edge, voices, a brief metallic grating sound. The infant struggles, he is about to free himself from the hand restraining his sobs, to cry out for his mother; he has recognized his father's voice down there. He wants no more of this world where everything is booby-trapped by words. He does not want to understand.

Through the breathlessness of his struggles he suddenly hears a melody. A hardly audible music. A soft, almost silent singsong that the woman murmurs in his ear. He tries to grasp the words. But the phrases have a strange beauty, devoid of meaning. A language he has never heard. Quite different from that of his parents. A language that does not require understanding, just immersion in its swaying rhythms, in the velvety suppleness of its sounds.

Mesmerized by this unknown language, the child falls asleep and hears neither the distant gunshots, multiplied by echoes, nor the long-drawn-out cry that just reaches them, laden with all the despair of love.

Had it not been for you, I would have left behind forever that infant falling asleep in the heart of the Caucasian forest, as we often abandon and forget irretrievable fragments of ourselves that we judge too remote, too painful, or simply too difficult to acknowledge. But one night you made a remark about the truth of our lives. I must have misunderstood you. I was certainly mistaken about what you meant. Yet it was this misapprehension that caused the forgotten child to be reborn in me.

Later on I attributed my confusion to the stress of all the dangers, long-term and immediate, that made up our existence at that time. To our wanderings from country to country, from language to language, to all the masks that our profession imposed on us. And, still more, to that love we superstitiously refused to name, myself knowing it to be unmerited, you believing it had already been declared in instants of silence in cities at war, where we might well have died without ever experiencing such moments at the end of the fighting that restored us to ourselves.

"One day it must be possible to tell the truth. . . ." These were the words, uttered with a mixture of insistence and resigned bitterness, that misled me. I pictured a witness—myself! Confused, lost for words, stunned by the enormity of the task. To tell the truth about that age whose course our own lives had here and there stumblingly followed. To testify to the history of a country, our country, that had succeeded, almost in front of our eyes, in building itself up into a formidable empire, only to collapse in a cacophony of shattered lives.

"To tell the truth one day." You were silent, half lying beside me, your face turned toward the rapidly maturing night outside the window. The netting of the mosquito screen could clearly be seen against the hot, dark background. And in the middle of this dusty rectangle a zigzag tear was becoming more and more visible: the blast from one of the last shells had cut into this fabric that separated us from the city and its death throes.

"To tell the truth . . ." I did not dare object. Uneasy at the role of witness or judge you were assigning to me, I mentally ran through all the reasons that made me incapable or even unworthy of such a mission. Our age, I told myself, was already receding and leaving us on the shore of time, like fish trapped by the ebbing of the sea. Bearing witness to what we had lived through would have meant speaking of a vanished ocean, evoking its ground swells and the victims of its storms, while faced with impassive undulations of sand. Yes, preaching in the desert. And our native land, that crushing empire, that Tower of Babel cemented together by dreams and blood, was it not disintegrating, story by story, vault by vault, its glass-lined halls turning into batteries of funhouse mirrors, its vistas into dead ends?

The weariness of sleepless nights gave substance to these words. I saw the desert and the tiny puddles of water sucked in by the sand, the colossal ruined tower, drowning in long red banners, a liquid red, a whole river of purple.

You slipped off the bed. I woke up, ready, when suddenly awakened, as for many years now, to abandon our current dwelling, to reach for a gun, to reply calmly to anyone who might be hammering at the door. This time the reflex was unnecessary. The silence of the city was broken only by occasional uncoordinated shots, and a brief rumble of trucks, swallowed up at once by the density of the night.

You went over to the table. In the darkness I saw the pale touch of your body, colored by reflected light from a fire at the other end of the street. "To tell the truth . . ." All my waking energy became focused on this impracticable notion. As I watched you moving through the dark room I resumed my silent refusal.

You speak of truth. But all my own memories have been falsified. Ever since my birth. And I could never bear witness for other people. I don't know their lives and I don't understand them. As a child I never knew how they lived, all these normal people. Their world stopped at the door of our orphanage. When one day I was invited to a birthday party in a normal family—two little girls with long braids, parents brimming with goodwill, all as it should be, jam in little silver-plate dishes, table napkins I didn't dare touch—I thought they were making fun of me and at any minute they were going to admit it and kick me out. I still remember it with morbid gratitude, you see, as if by not dismissing me they had performed an act of superhuman generosity. Just think of it, tolerating this young barbarian with a shaven head and hands nearly blue with cold, sticking out of sleeves that were too short. And to top it all, the son of a disgraced father. So how can you expect me to be an impartial witness?

You switched on a flashlight, I saw your fingers in the narrow beam, the glint of a needle. "To tell the truth about what we have lived through." I raised myself on one elbow, wanting to explain to you that I understood nothing about the age that was already slipping away beneath our feet. And that the whole shambles of it made me think of the innards of the armored vehicle I had seen the day before at the center of the city, when taking refuge from bursts of gunfire. Ripped apart by a rocket, it was still smoking and displayed a complex mixture of dislocated machinery, twisted metal, and lacerated human flesh. The force of the explosion had made this chaos astonishingly homogeneous, almost orderly. The electric cables looked like blood vessels, the dashboard, battered and splashed with blood, was like the brain of a rare creature, a futuristic war beast. And, buried somewhere in this lava of death, the radio, undamaged, blared forth its quavering rallying calls. Such a scene was not new to me. Only the sudden, sharp realization that I did not understand was quite new. Sheltering in my hiding place, I said to myself that these men who were killing one another under a cloudless sky lived in a land where epidemics were palpably more efficient at this than armaments; that the cost of one rocket would have sufficed to feed a whole village in this African country; that the money spent on that vehicle would have funded the sinking of hundreds of wells; that the blame for this war must be laid at the door of the Americans and ourselves, for we were fighting each other through intermediary nations, and also of the former colonial powers, who had corrupted the Eden-like state of these lands. But that primitive paradise was a myth, too, for men had always fought, with lances in the past, with rocket launchers today; and the only thing to distinguish the deaths of the occupants of the burned-out armored car from the carnage of their ancestors was the complex fashion in which their deaths, deaths both so individual (beneath a layer of torn-off armor I saw a long, very slender, almost boyish arm with a fine leather bracelet on the wrist) and so anonymous, were swallowed up by the interests of remote powers, their thirst for oil or gold, the cut and thrust of their bureaucratic diplomacy, their demagogic doctrines. And even by the petty concerns and anticipated pleasures of that arms dealer I had seen, two days before the fighting broke out, getting onto the plane for London. He had given his name as Ron Scalper and seemed like a very ordinary sales representative. He sought to accentuate his ordinariness by handing over his briefcase to security with a tourist's naive clumsiness, mopping his brow in front of the person checking his passport. Yes, that soldier's death was insidiously linked to the relief this man feels once he is seated in the plane, turning up the ventilation control and closing his eyes, already transported into the antechamber of the civilized world. By the same tortuous routes, that wrist, with its leather bracelet, reaches out into the life of the woman whom the man on the London plane can already picture, offering herself naked, yielding to his desire, the young mistress he has earned for himself by taking all those risks. Our age, I thought, is nothing more than a monstrous organism that digests gold, oil, politics, and wars, and secretes pleasure for some, death for others. A gigantic stomach that churns up and blends together things that, in our shame and hypocrisy, we keep separate. The young mistress, at this very moment moaning beneath her arms dealer, would utter a cry of indignation if I told her her happiness (for, no doubt, they call it happiness) is inseparably linked to that childish bracelet stained with grease and blood!

I got up, wanting to confide these thoughts to you in all their despairing simplicity: no, I do not begin to understand this grotesque organism, for there is nothing to understand. I crossed our room in the darkness streaked with reflections from the flames, I joined you at the window.

"One day it must be possible to tell the truth." I was going to give you my reply: the truth about our age was a young body steeped in beauty creams, the human flesh the arms dealer treated himself to, in exchange for his rocket launchers. And this trade, the tragicomic outcome of global maneuvers, had ordained that today, in that precise spot, a soldier, wearing a leather band on his wrist, should be blown to pieces by an explosion. The truth was absolutely logical and absolutely arbitrary.

Just as I was about to say this to you, I noticed what you were doing. Hands raised halfway up the window, you were darning the torn mosquito screen. Long stitches of pale thread, movements very slow, guided by the needle as it felt its way in the darkness, but there was also another slowness, that of a deep reverie, of a lassitude so great that it no longer even sought rest. It seemed to me that never before had I happened on you in such a relaxed state, at a moment in your life of such perfect harmony with yourself, with what you were

15

to me. You were the woman whose shoulders my hand caressed lightly when they seemed cold in the sweltering heat of the night. A woman whose infinite singularity and troubling uniqueness, as the being I loved, I was aware of as never before and who, that night in this ravaged city, inexplicably found herself living so close to death, whether accidental or intended. A woman who was drawing two edges of fabric together on a night when the fighting had stopped. And who, noticing my hand at last, inclined her head, letting my fingers rest beneath her cheek and was already becoming utterly still, in a half sleep.

Your presence was one of total strangeness. And at the same time of completely natural necessity. You were there and the murderous complexity of this world, this tangle of wars, greed, vengeance, and lies found itself face to face with a truth beyond dispute. This truth was poised in your gesture: a hand closing up two pieces of fabric against a night glutted with death. I sensed that all the testimonies I could have offered were overtaken by the truth of that moment, snatched from the madness of men.

I did not dare, and in any case I would not have known how, to question you about the meaning of your words. I kissed the back of your head, your neck, the start of the fragile rosary of your vertebrae, transfixed by the tenderness a woman's body inspires when she is totally absorbed in a task she cannot interrupt. And so it was as a simple response to your desire for truth that I began telling you about the birth of the world in the eyes of that infant lost among the mountains. His fear of understanding, his refusal to name things, his life being saved by the music of an unknown language. He hesitated for a moment on the brink of our games of pleasure and death, then let himself sink back once more into the fraternal intimacy of the universe. The woman who held him in her arms went on softly singing her lullaby, even as the sound of gunshots reached them from the other bank of the stream. The unknown language was her mother tongue.

I embarked on this story beside the window, beside the rectangle of netting you were darning, I finished it in a whisper, leaning toward your face relaxed in sleep. I thought you had dozed off and missed the ending. But after my last words, without saying anything, you gave my hand a gentle squeeze.

There were times, long before I knew you, when I did go back to that night in the Caucasus and the sleeping child. These returns to the past allowed me to take refuge from sudden excesses of grief, horrors that were too overwhelming. They marked a dotted line of brief resurrections along the course of my life, following each of the temporary deaths that punctuate our lives. One such death had assailed me on the day when a fellow pupil, the leader of one of the little gangs that were rife at our orphanage, spat some crumbs of tobacco from his cigarette stub in my direction and hissed with explosive scorn, "Look, everyone knows about your father. The firing squad shot him like a dog!" Or another time when, out for a stroll, I chanced upon a woman deep in the long grass of a gully, half naked and drunk, being taken in brutal haste by two men, who puffed and panted with little false laughs and oaths. Against a dark background of lush June vegetation, her rotund, obese body was blinding in its pallor. She turned her head, and I recognized the simpleton whom the townspeople called by a little girl's pet name, Lyubochka. And then there was that birthday party with dishes of silver plate. Everyone tried to behave as if I were just like the others, tried not to notice my clumsy actions or to anticipate them. And their kindness was so evident that there was no longer any doubt: I would never be like them, I would always be that youth whose hands were red with cold, dogged by his past, who, if asked about his background, would sometimes stammer out truths that people took for wild lies and sometimes lie to reassure the curious. And there would always be, as there was that day, a very young child who would tug at his sleeve and ask him, "Why aren't you laughing with us?"

After each of these deaths I would once more find myself in my Caucasian night: I would see the face of the white-haired woman, her eyes fixed on my eyelids; I would listen to her song, crooned in a language whose beauty seemed to stand guard over this moment in the darkness.

Later on, when studying medicine, I tried to put an end to these returns to the past, seeing them as a sign of sentimental weakness, shameful for a prospective army doctor. I stopped being ashamed of them when I realized that night had had nothing in common with the soft-heartedness wrung from us by a happy childhood. For there had been no happy childhood. Only that night when, venturing across the frontier into the world, the child took fright and, through the magic of an unknown language, was able to retreat for a little longer into his earlier universe.

This was the universe I always returned to in my flights from the suffocations of life. And when, having joined the army, I found myself looking after soldiers in the undeclared wars waged by the empire at all four corners of the globe, little by little this night of the child became the sole remaining trace that allowed me to go on recognizing myself.

One day this trace was obliterated.

At first I convinced myself that the very last wounded man did exist. At the end of the very last war. Wars, I told myself, were small now, local, or so the diplomats said. So, logically, an end to them was thinkable. But I discovered soon enough that it was the big wars that came to an end, not the little ones; these were simply a continuation of the others in peacetime. For the first few months, perhaps a whole year, I kept a diary: customs of the country, characteristics of the inhabitants, scraps of life stories that wounded men confided to me. Then on to another country, another war, and I perceived that the differences in terrain and customs were increasingly blurred by the routine of fighting, with its monotony of suffering and cruelty, which is the same under every sky. Ethiopia, Angola, Afghanistan . . . Now the pages of my diary disgusted me, with their tone of the nosy tourist and the detachment of the observer who plans to leave tomorrow. By now I knew that I would not be leaving. My dreams were no longer peopled with human faces but with the gaping grins of wounds. Each had its singular smile, sometimes broad and fleshy, sometimes with an indented gash blackened with burns. And, like the filter on a camera, the same light colored all these dreams, the color of dirty blood, of rust on the carcasses of armored vehicles, of the reddish dust raised by helicopters bringing fresh wounded to the hospital. Often the same vision woke me: what I was stitching up was not the gaping grin of a wound but lips trying to speak. I would get up and, for several seconds after being switched on, the light seemed to alleviate the raging furnace where an old electric fan kept churning away. My watch showed it was the hour at which soldiers returned from night operations. Standing at the mirror, I would try to reassemble the man I must once more become in the morning. I would make the effort for several seconds, then return to the child hidden in the mountains of the Caucasus.

One day this refuge lost its power. A soldier who had had both arms amputated escaped during the night, loomed up in front of the sentry with a threatening cry, and was killed by a burst of gunfire. The authorities preferred to call it an attack of madness rather than suicide. That evening, after a day in which there had been two men seriously burned and another amputation, I realized I had almost forgotten the suicide of the night before. When I went to bed I had to wait for the blissful weightlessness of morphine before admitting that within me there was no longer any place, no longer any moment, where I could hide.

Thus I lived, letting each new day obliterate the anguish of the previous one in the panic-stricken looks of the newly wounded. The only measure of time left to me was the all-too-evident progress in perfecting the weapons used by our soldiers and their enemies. I no longer remember in which war it was (it may have been in Nicaragua) that we first encountered strange bullets with a displaced center of gravity. They had the appalling characteristic of traveling through the body in an unpredictable way and lodging in parts that are the most difficult to reach. Some time after that cluster bombs appeared, ever more ingenious shells filled with needles that seemed to be dragging us into a macabre competition in which our normal surgical instruments frequently turned out to be ill adapted. And then one morning, the helicopter that was due to pick up the wounded and dead following a battle did not return. We learned it had been shot down by a new portable missile. From that morning onward what our ears detected in the throb of the propellers was a dull vibration of distress.

I had no time to reflect on the underlying causes of these wars. Besides, all the discussions I had with other doctors or with officer-instructors always used to end up in the same little geopolitical dead end. The world was becoming too small for the two vast, over-armed empires that shared it between them. They collided with another, like two icebergs in the bottleneck of a strait, they disintegrated at the edges, breaking countries in half, tearing nations apart; avoiding the worst while in disputed zones there was continual friction. Hiroshima and Vietnam sufficed to establish who was the aggressor: America, the West. Some of our number, the most prudent or the most patriotic, left it at that. Others would add that America, this convenient enemy, justified a good many absurdities in our own country. In return, our baleful existence helped the Americans excuse their own. This, they concluded was the price of global equilibrium. These sober conclusions would often be swept away a few hours later by an armored vehicle in flames whose steel shell echoed with the cries of people being burned alive or, as on the last occasion, by the death of the wounded man reaching out with his stumps toward bursts of submachine-gun fire. I made an effort not to comprehend these deaths, lest I make light of them in our discussions of strategy.

Curiously enough, it was thanks to a man who adored warfare that I was able to keep this salutary incomprehension intact.

A professional instructor, short, robust, and impeccably turned out in his elite mercenary's uniform, he introduced soldiers to new weapons and engines of war, explained how to handle them, compared characteristics. The room in which he gave his classes was separated from our operating theater by a fairly thin wall. His voice, in my opinion, could have cut through the roar of a whole column of tanks. I heard every word.

"This assault rifle has a tremendous rate of fire: seven hundred and twenty rounds a minute! It can easily be dismantled into six components and, as it's very light, you can fire it from a vehicle. And there are cartridge clips that take fifty rounds. . . . This is a guided missile. It carries three warheads with an explosive charge that detonates after entering the target. . . . With this caliber you can use armor-piercing rounds, explosive rounds, or even incendiary rounds."

His voice was only interrupted by the much softer one of the interpreter and occasionally by questions from the soldiers. I ended up detesting his tone, which tried to be authoritative and informal at the same time.

"Now look, my friend, if you don't tighten this fixing screw in properly, you'll be dead with the first shot. . . ."

It was as if, still in theory, he were forecasting the results that would soon turn up on our operating table, in the form of human flesh lacerated by all these brilliant explosive, incendiary, and armor-piercing devices. Thus it was that I formed a part of a single chain of death, linking the politicians who decided on the wars, this gallant instructor who provided training, and the soldiers who would die or be stretched out naked beneath our busy gloved hands. And I did not have the classic humanitarian's feeble excuse, for I was often healing people just to put them straight back into the chain.

The notion of bursting into the lecture room and slitting this military man's throat in front of his listeners often occurred to me. It was a scene of rebellion from a movie about colonial wars, I would tell myself at once, for I perceived that the routines and lazy compromises of real life would gradually reconcile me to the voice on the other side of the wall.

"Now this is what you might call a flying tank. . . . The cockpit has a titanium shield. . . . It can be used both for daytime and night fighting."

So there I was, listening to him with my former anger gone. Like all talented speakers, he had a favorite topic. It was combat helicopters. He had flown several models before becoming an instructor. On this subject he waxed poetic. Through repeating the same tale to generations of soldiers, he had ended up creating a whole mythology in which he traced the birth of the helicopter, its teething troubles, the daring exploits of its youth, and, above all, the technical feats of recent times. This fabulous machine transported trucks, destroyed tanks, was loaded with equipment that protected it against missiles. I had the feeling that at any moment the voice on the other side of the wall might break into metric verse.

"The Americans thought they had us beaten with their Stinger, but they don't have a prayer in hell. We're installing infrared jammers and decoy-projectors there, at the ends of the blades. And that's not all! Even if a piece of shrapnel punctures the fuel tank, no need to panic: from now on the tanks are self-sealing! And even if the copter goes into free fall, you're still okay. The seats will withstand a fall rate of a hundred and twenty feet per second. Just think: a hundred and twenty feet per second! And what's more, the self-detonating bolts blow off the doors, a moment later a chute inflates, and you can bail out without being carved up by the prop."

There was a moment halfway through this epic poem where the officer-instructor's sincerity became beyond doubt. I ended up learning this episode by heart: at the height of the Yom Kippur War, in a sky riven by chopper blades, a helicopter from the Syrian army (a Soviet Mi-8 whose pilot had been trained by the instructor himself) was confronted by an Israeli Super-Frelon. And it was the very first dogfight between helicopters in human history! No one had ever foreseen that this machine could attack one of its own kind. With unprecedented perfidy the Israeli soldier opened wide the side door, aimed a machine gun, and riddled the Syrian helicopter. It crashed in front of the instructor's very eyes. . . . When describing this battle the instructor sometimes said "Jewish," sometimes "Israeli": in his mouth the latter term became a kind of superlative of the first, to indicate the degree of spite and malignancy. However, like a true poet, he acknowledged the value of this evil genius, without whom History might have marked time and possibly lost one of its finest pages.

The voice booming out on the other side of the wall, which exasperated me so much to begin with, was on the point of lulling me into amused indifference when suddenly I got to the heart of its secret. It was from poets like this that wars derived their effectiveness and staying power. This pure passion, this believer's enthusiasm, was essential: no geopolitical strategies were a substitute for it.

The military lectures that I listened to, bent over the bodies of patients undergoing operations, drove me to reflect, in a way that was simultaneously very direct and somewhat oblique, on the stunning poverty of my experiences with the women I had met and believed I was in love with. Mentally I made facetious comparisons between the technical ingenuity of the weapons whose praises were sung by the instructor (all those self-sealing fuel tanks and decoy-projectors) and the rudimentary mechanics of my own love affairs. I was not yet thirty at the time and my cynicism sometimes had a thin skin. "I've had what I chose to take from those women," I told myself, though not believing it. "What they wanted to give me . . . All we could have expected from affairs like that . . ." As I worked away at my phrase-making, I was striving to compete with the perfection of those machines, at least through my combinations of words.

"Curiosity!" All at once the word, long sensed subconsciously, suddenly rang harshly true. The woman who had returned to Moscow three days earlier had been curious about me. And this curiosity had led us into an intense affair in which we played our parts to perfection from start to finish, without any risk of love. Like a deep-sea diver she sounded me out with her body, explored the man who had intrigued her, storing up memories, like those of an exotic country seen for the first time. On the last night before her departure she had not come to me, she had "too many suitcases to pack." I had a sneaking suspicion that already I missed her. But with no great effort of cynicism I contrived to reduce this sense of loss to one for the tactile softness of her breasts, the angle of her parted knees, the rhythmic breathing of her pleasure.

"What the instructor would call technical features," I now thought, recalling that the women who had preceded her (one had worked at the embassy, the other I'd met in Moscow . . .) had also had the same curiosity, like women explorers. The very distant memory returned that had pursued me since childhood: the birthday party with a family who are generous enough to invite a young, shaven-headed barbarian to join them, two little girls studying me with curiosity, taking minute soundings. Their parents have doubtless warned them that this would not be a child like the others, one without a family, without a home of his own, and who has very likely never tasted jam. Sometimes all these "withouts" seem to the two fair-haired sisters like inconceivable privations, sometimes like a vague promise of freedom. They observe me with the feigned nonchalance of a zoologist walking around an animal with his head in the air, so as not to frighten it, while scrutinizing its every movement out of the corner of his eye.

I translated the curiosity of those little girls into the language of women. I was still the same strange beast who did not behave like the others, that is to say did not save up the pay he earned in all those countries at war, did not aspire to a career, had no plans. For women this life "without" held the promise, now clear, of an affair without the burden of love, of a swift zoological exploration that would have no sequel in their main lives. With somewhat acid irony I told myself that, when it came down to it, I was very like that instructor bellowing away on the other side of the wall ("Four smoke grenade projectors are placed at the front of the vehicle, here and here. . . .") who, apart from the uniform that was never creased, had nothing in his one and only suitcase other than an old suit and a pair of shoes from another era.

It may well have been her youth or her lack of experience (she was just twenty-two and found herself abroad for the first time) that had led me to emerge from my zoological carapace. An interpreter at the embassy in Aden, she had a touch of sunstroke one day, they brought her to us at the hospital. I felt I could be of service, I already knew the Yemen well and, moreover, her vulnerability gave me a pleasant sense of being old and protective. It was an impression that felt like affection. And in making love her body still had the same resigned and touching frailty as on the day of her sunstroke. I came to hope that this attachment might continue, even though at the start of the civil war the embassy was leaving. "We'll meet again in Moscow," I told myself. "It's really time I settled down." It was the first occasion in my life that such thoughts had occurred to me.

She left on one of the first planes to evacuate the embassy personnel and volunteer workers. What shocked me most was not her refusal to meet me again in Moscow but rather the sudden discovery that I dreaded such a refusal, a dread several days old.

"It would be diplomatically delicate," she pronounced, smiling, but with an air of firmness that already transported her into a future where I did not exist.

"Delicate as regards your fiancé?" I asked, in a poor imitation of her irony.

"It's more complicated than that."

She intercepted my retort ("What could be more complicated than a fiancé?") by asking me to help her down with her suitcases. At the bus I saw her as she would be on arrival: a suit (the days in Moscow would still be cool), dress shoes in place of her sandals, the air of a young woman who has worked abroad, with all that this implied in a country it was difficult to leave in those days. I racked my brains for a polite but wounding remark that might, if only for a second, have rendered her weak, childish, surprised once more—the way I had loved her and dreaded losing her. Sitting by the window she was already eyeing me in a quite detached way, observing my shoes, gray with dust. "A man I made love with," she must have said to herself, and no doubt she experienced the moment of pity that grips us at the sight of a part of ourselves preserved in the body of someone who will henceforth be a stranger to us.

"I'll write you. . . ."

"But . . ."

We spoke that "but" in unison, she, straightening up in her seat, I, dodging the dust thrown up by the bus as it moved off. In the place where she was going I had only this vague address of a room in a communal apartment long ago rented to someone else. Here the crackling of gunfire on the outskirts of the city was already audible.

I returned to the hospital on foot. Around the embassies people were gathering, the cars were all heading off in the same direction, toward the airport. It was amusing to see that, in spite of this turmoil, each nation remained true to itself. The Americans were blocking the road with the multiplicity of their means of transport and the ponderous, blithe arrogance of their preparations. The English were leaving the place as if this were merely a routine move, the banality of which did not merit a single extra word or gesture. The French were organizing chaos, giving one another orders, all waiting for the one person without whom departure was impossible, but who had already left. The representatives of the small countries sought the understanding of the big ones.

I did not succeed in gaining entry to the hospital. The soldiers were creating defensive positions around the building, sealing the main entrance, it was hard to know exactly why, and directing their mortar barrels skyward. I was to hear their noise on my own return journey. During the night, spent at the embassy, I tried to identify by ear which district of the city was the worst hit, picturing the empty wards at the hospital, my suitcase in a room on the first floor and, in a drawer, a seashell from the Red Sea, planned as a gift for the woman who had just left. Cynicism not being an attitude that flourishes at night, I failed to see the ridiculous side either of this shell (which ended up the next day beneath the rubble of the bombarded hospital) or of our leave-taking by the bus. And when I finally ventured to revive this mirthless mockery, I would see that nothing else was left in my life, just this exhausted irony and the shreds of useless memories.

In the morning the city was in flames and as the fire advanced it seemed to be driving the last of the foreigners back toward the sea. I found myself on a beach among a crowd of my compatriots who were waving their arms in the direction of several small boats as they came toward us. Out at sea a massive white liner could be seen, a red flag stirring slightly in the wind. The little boats appeared motionless, stuck fast in the oily blue of the sea. A few hundred yards away from us, in the streets that led to the coast, soldiers were running, shooting, falling. Their deadly game was advancing toward us and at any minute now would compel us to join in. Hands reached out toward the to-and-fro of the oars, anguished and exasperated shouts stuck in people's throats. This desire not to be killed, idiotically, on the sun-drenched beach took hold of me, contagious like all mass hysteria. I was on the brink of following the men heaving enormous suitcases onto their shoulders and walking into the water so as to increase the distance between lives that were suddenly feverishly precious to them and death. It was my lack of any luggage that brought me to my senses. What little I possessed had burned in the hospital destroyed by shells during the night. That morning a member of the embassy staff had lent me his razor.

I sat down on the sand, observing the scene with an almost absentminded gaze. The number of suitcases the men were loading onto the boats astounded me. So somewhere there must exist a life, I said to myself, where all these things it was so difficult to transport were irreplaceable. I pictured this life, for which my own past had left me ill suited. I guessed at its delights: when augmented by the contents of the suitcases, it seemed to me quite legitimate and touching. As I stood up to assist in the loading process, I ran into a man, trying to climb on board alongside his luggage, who took me for a competitor. I drew back, he clambered up, avoiding my eye. Beyond a jetty a shell hurled up a thick geyser of sand. The man, already on board, quickly ducked, pressing his forehead against the leather of the suitcases. Someone yelled, "Quick, quick, we're leaving!" Another, who was still staggering about in the water, swore at him. People were jostling one another now, not hiding their fear.

Just after that explosion I saw a man who had no luggage either, standing slightly behind me, apparently watching a quarrel between two candidates for departure. His first remark was not addressed to anyone in particular, "At moments like this one becomes quite

29

naked." Then, turning to me, he added, "Since you have nothing to load on board, I should like to ask a service of you. On the express instruction of the ambassador . . ." He uttered these words in a tone that was at once respectful and jocular, thus conveying to me that his own authority needed no support from that of the ambassador, who had already left for home. I stared at his face, with a memory of having glimpsed it at an embassy reception. His features had stuck in my mind because he looked like the French actor Lino Ventura. I had forgotten him for the same reason, mislaying his face among images from films. Anticipating my question, he explained, "We shall leave together a little later. . . ." He then threw a final glance at the boats overloaded with suitcases and I thought I saw in his eyes a brief flash of irony, which faded at once into a neutral expression.

The jostling on the beach made us invisible. He led me toward a structure made of cement blocks, beyond which a four-wheel-drive vehicle was parked. We headed toward the city, which looked as if it were being drawn up into the sky by the smoke from the fires. As he drove along he told me his name (one of the names that I would come to know him by) and asked me to call him "counsellor" in the presence of the people we were about to meet. For a good few moments now I had been living as if at one remove from reality. The simplicity, almost indifference, with which the counsellor explained to me the task that awaited me only served to accentuate the strangeness of the situation. "Your presence at these negotiations, or rather at this bout of haggling, will be doubly useful. One of the parties has been wounded and, well, in view of his age, the heat, the emotion . . . You see, we need to keep his old heart beating until the final agreement. Furthermore, if I'm not mistaken, you speak his language."

At first I thought his detached tone was a pose, a bravado he was assuming for my benefit (his resemblance to the film actor was partly responsible for my misreading of this). But when we encountered crossfire in one street and he managed to avoid the bursts of gunfire by squeezing the vehicle close to a wall without abandoning his air of indifference, I grasped the simple fact that he was long accustomed to danger.

We arrived in a district I did not know, and which, though only a few streets away from the fighting, seemed asleep. Only the traces of smoke on the ocherous surface of the houses and the cartridge cases we slipped on as we walked betrayed the presence of war. We crossed a courtyard and another linked to it, stopping before a narrow passageway that made one think of the entrance to a maze. Half a dozen soldiers who were sheltering there from the sun emerged, searched us, then allowed us to pass inside.

The windows, protected by metal screens, sliced through the darkness with long rays of sunlight. These blinding blades cut into our eyes. After several seconds of sightlessness I made out two guards, one squatting beside the door, his submachine gun laid across his knees, the other watching the street through the slit between two sheets of steel. Two other men faced one another: seated with his back to the wall, a Yemeni with a glistening brown face and a multi-colored turban that hung down onto one shoulder like a ponytail and, at the other end of the room, half reclining in an armchair, a very pale man, with a swathe of bandages across his brow—like a strange replica of the turban. His angular features, sharpened by weariness, seemed almost transparent beneath glistening sweat. Despite his white hair there was in his face the kind of youthfulness that surges up in elderly men at the moment of a mortal challenge. Our arrival interrupted their discussion. All one could hear now was the furious drumming of flies caught between the glass and the steel, the distant sounds of shooting, and the breathing of the wounded man, short gasps, as if he were about to burst into song but could not bring himself to do so.

It was he who greeted us and began speaking, forcing his breathing to adopt a regular rhythm. The counsellor asked me to translate. The man stopped, to give me time to do this. But I remained silent, feeling myself to be at a vertiginous distance from this stifling room.

The wounded man was speaking the same language that the sleeping infant had heard amid the mountains of the Caucasus, on the darkest night of my life.

The man I had to keep alive and whose remarks I had to translate knew that his death would have simplified the bargaining. He told me this with an imperceptible smile, as I was giving him a further injection. "I feel like a fabulously rich old man, whose stamina is the despair of his heirs. . . ." This was one of the sentences I chose not to translate. And indeed, from his very first words, a kind of double translation had become established between us: I did my best to interpret the arguments he put and those of his adversaries, but parallel to this, I was noting the revival within myself of this language that had remained mute for so many years.

The object of their laborious verbal struggle quite soon became apparent to me in the form of a conundrum. The man in the turban, one of the military leaders of the rebellion, had captured three westerners. The wounded diplomat was trying to obtain their release. The counsellor was able to put pressure on the Yemeni because his troops were being armed and supported by us. In return for this service the diplomat was to guarantee the neutrality of France, which would turn a blind eye to our military involvement in the conflict. The deal was on the point of being concluded ten times but suddenly the Yemeni would lose his temper and begin to denounce the perfidy of the West and the great Satan of America. Each time his rage—sometimes expressed in blunt and rudimentary English, sometimes in a propagandist Russian that was no doubt learned in Moscow—

seemed to sound the death knell for the negotiations, I was ready to get up. But neither the Frenchman reclining in his armchair, nor the counsellor, listening with his head tilted slightly toward me, seemed impressed by these crises; they waited in silence for them to come to an end, each one with his own manner of being politely indifferent. An aide de camp would come in and spend a long time whispering into the ear of the chief, who kept nodding as he gradually abandoned his air of fury. The discussion resumed and followed its already familiar circular course: the Yemeni liberates the hostages, the counsellor arranges the delivery of arms, the diplomat gives his word that his government will be discreet. I now understood that success depended not on the logic of the arguments but on some ritual of which only the Yemeni knew the secret and that the Frenchman and the Russian were trying to grasp. An "open sesame."

This round of more or less identical sentences left me the leisure to feel the texture of the words I was translating, as one fingers the grain of the pages of an old book. The diplomat must have been aware of this subterranean translation and spoke in a more and more personal style, abandoning the eroded vocabulary one uses when faced with an interpreter whose command of the language is in doubt. For me, some of his words were more than twenty years old, dating from the period when I had learned them and they had lodged themselves in memory, very rarely used. As they rang out in this low-ceilinged, overheated room, barricaded with plates of steel, the sound of them opened up long, bright, windswept vistas. Mingled with this recollection, there was even a sense in me of childish pride, still intact, at mastering this uncommon language. During a further break in the negotiations the Frenchman referred ironically to a "*navicert,*" the navigation certificate the counsellor and I would need in order to leave the city by sea. Hearing this word, I felt a child's comical triumph, for I knew the term thanks to Pierre Loti, and what the sound of it introduced into the stifling heat of the room was both the sea breezes of his novels and the chill of a long snowy evening cadenced by the rustling of turned pages.

From time to time the discussion broke off because of the Frenchman. He would close his eyes for a few seconds, then open them wide in sockets that were becoming increasingly hollow: they were sightless, or at least did not see us. Beneath the trickles of sweat his face resembled a fragment of quartz, now milky, now translucent. I would treat him, knowing only too well that all these injections only served to prolong this absurd bargaining by one more round. I said this to him. His face of quartz lit up with the ghost of a smile: "You know, here in the Orient they often practice expectant medicine. . . ." Again I had the impression of being face to face with a man from another era. Not so much because of his French, which was that of my books, but because of the calm, at once ironic and haughty, with which he confronted the cruel farce of the present, as if he were observing it from the height of a long and great history filled with victories and defeats.

He resisted to the last, until the final accord late in the evening. Sensing that the game was won, he sat up a little in his armchair and even hurled a little dart at "Monsieur le conseiller" (who was promising several extra mortars to the Yemeni chief), "Your generosity will be your undoing, my dear colleague." The counsellor flashed a smile at him before listening to my translation, as if to show that they no longer needed to conceal their true professions beneath diplomatic covers, or to feign ignorance of the language.

Next day a French helicopter from Djibouti took away the three released hostages (a couple of Germans and a Frenchwoman, a volunteer) and the body of the diplomat, who had died in the night. A slight distance away from this we witnessed the preparations. Waiting for takeoff, the rescued hostages exchanged addresses, invited one another to stay on vacation in France and Germany, then wanted at all costs to have a photo taken together with the crew of legionnaires. The body wrapped in a canvas sheet had already been loaded on board.

"Our whole life is no more than expectant medicine, wouldn't you say?"

The counsellor said it in French and fell silent, watching the passengers as they climbed into the helicopter uttering little admiring laughs. I examined his face turned in profile for a moment. No desire to impress could be read in it.

"So why all that charade about an interpreter?"

I deliberately adopted an emphatic, almost aggrieved tone.

"Well, to begin with, you weren't just the interpreter! And in bargaining of this type it's sometimes useful to plead an error in translation. . . . But, above all, think of this as a first step that could lead to other things, if you feel ready for a change in your life. You'll have time during the voyage to reflect on my proposal."

The helicopter took off, sweeping away the footprints on the powdery soil. We followed it with our eyes for a moment. As it moved away, what the machine seemed to be drawing across the sky was a heavy blanket of tawny cloud that was coming up rapidly from the direction of the ocean.

"One of the last of the Mohicans of the old school, that Bertrand Jansac," said the counsellor, turning away from the helicopter above the waters. "Or rather one of the last of the Mohicans, period . . . As for you and me, our boat will soon be leaving under full sail but, alas, without the protection of a . . . what did he call it? a 'navicert.' Am I right?"

Amid the torrent of actions and words of that last day a single phrase stuck in my mind and the temptation it presented gave a rhythm to all my thoughts: "If you feel ready for a change in your life . . ."

I was twenty-eight. My life, with all its weight of human flesh and death, could have been that of a much older man. And yet the child within me would still wince whenever someone asked, either idly, or with real curiosity, "So, where were you born? What do your parents do?" I had long since learned to respond with lies or evasion, or by turning a deaf ear. But this made no difference. The childish shudder slipped in, like a blade between loose-fitting plates of armor. All that had changed was that, as a boy, I was afraid people would discover the truth: to this fear and shame was now added the certainty that I had no means of making people understand the truth, and that I should never meet anyone to whom it could be confided.

I experienced this unease on finding myself in a cramped cabin on a ship that, while it was still secured, was already pitching under the first lashes of the storm. As we lay face to face on our narrow bunks our heads were so close that we could have whispered in one another's ears. At once my childish reflex was aroused: I pictured the counsellor questioning me about my early life. A moment later I called myself a fool, realizing that he knew everything. I faced a man who, although our situation lent itself to an exchange of confidences, would not seek to delve into my past. It was then that his proposal for "a change" in my life struck me as an offer that would liberate me. Indeed this thrilling liberation had already begun taking place with the speed of a blissful dream. Stepping aboard the ship I had been liberated from my name and the passport that documented it. In exchange, the counsellor had furnished me with another one: my first false papers, and a name that I was repeating inwardly in order to make it mine, along with a few notes on my new biography that I must learn by heart. I was perfectly well aware that the ease with which this metamorphosis was embarked on was simply a well established recruitment technique and that there was nothing improvised about his proposal to "change my life." At each fresh step in this direction the counsellor provided a kind of brief waiting time, to give me the opportunity to draw back—to refuse to exchange passports, not to embark with him on this dubious-looking little cargo ship, not to accept the pistol he handed me. I later came to understand that, for him, an approach of this kind and this change of identity was a sequence of almost automatic maneuvers, a routine he went through without paying any attention to my excitement. But at the time his actions appeared to me like the deft arrogance of a conjuror who, disdaining all acknowledged appearances, was liberating me by means of his shell game artist's legerdemain of the thing that weighed most heavily upon me: myself.

When he left the cabin for a few minutes I took out my new passport and spent a long time studying this face, my own, made unrecognizable by the information on the previous page. The man in the photograph seemed to be eyeing me with disdain. I felt passionately envious of his liberty.

When night came this jealousy consumed me with an animal fear, with a lust for survival that I would not have imagined myself capable of. In the darkness of the cabin I had the illusion that, battered by the waves, the ship itself was turning to liquid, melting like a block of ice. I could hear water everywhere—outside the hull, in the corridor, and suddenly, streaming across the floor of the cabin! I reached down with frenzied haste and patted a dry metal surface that vibrated beneath my fingers. My hand also brushed against my shoes, prudently lined up in absurd anticipation. I lay down again, hoping the counsellor had not guessed the reason for my restlessness. He remained silent in the darkness and appeared to be asleep. Without a porthole, our cabin felt to me like a steel coffin that had just become detached from the ship. I imagined it slowly descending into the glaucous depths of the waters. That pair of shoes neatly arranged beneath my bunk. The pistol that would rust in its case. It shifted slightly as the vessel pitched, and seemed to be caressing me under my arm, next to my heart. For me, all the treachery of life was concentrated into that caress: fully conscious, in possession of a new passport, with an identity that had finally set me free, I was going to die a slow death. The man in the photo, whose liberty I had so envied, was going to go to the bottom after a short existence full of promise.

I sat up on my bunk, clinging to the edge of it, as if I were perched on the brink of an abyss. And this brink tilted further and further, causing me to lose all notion of up and down. I uttered a plea and only afterward did I grasp the sense of what I had whispered: "They've got to do something. I don't want to die! Not now . . ."

I had no idea if the counsellor had heard me. But a minute later his voice seemed to ring out from the bottom of the abyss. He spoke in a monotonous tone, as if he were talking to himself and had already begun his story a moment earlier. Astonishingly, this litany contrived to hold its own through the fury of the waves and the wind's hysteria, like the straight and even wake of a torpedo in a turbulent sea. At first my own repeated entreaty ("I don't want to die. . . . Not now . . . please, not now . . ."), and especially my shame at having uttered it, had stopped me following the thread. But as what he was describing was totally remote from our own situation (he was talking about a desert), I finished by finding in the strangeness of his story the unique point on which my fevered mind could focus.

. . . A town, or rather a number of streets, had sprung up in the middle of a desert in Central Asia. Houses four stories high, all identical, with empty window frames and gaping doorways, as if the builders had abandoned their work just before completion. And yet the inhabitants could already be seen: sometimes you could glimpse a face in a window opening, sometimes when the sun flooded the inside of a room, a complete human figure. Outside, in enclosures protected from the sun by corrugated iron, there were animals asleep or scattered along the fence. A flock of sheep, some camels, horses, dogs. A single road led into the town, linking these three or four streets and then petering out in the sand. At the central crossroads there stood an enormous cube, formed from well-dovetailed planks, reminiscent of the casing around a statue that was being prepared for unveiling to the public at some forthcoming celebration.

The violence of the wave that crashed down onto the cargo ship was such that all sounds stopped for several seconds. It was impossible to tell whether the engines had suddenly cut out or terror had paralyzed all my senses. The ship was listing, hurtling faster and faster down a watery slope, and seemed no longer able to halt its flight. And it was in this silence, as if to break the spell and relaunch the functioning of the machinery, that the voice of the counsellor sounded again. He must have realized that his story was unintentionally maintaining a level of suspense that was not at all his purpose, and he brought it to an end in a few sentences that cleared up the mystery.

"The cube on the central square was our first atomic bomb. The townspeople were convicts condemned to death, being used as guinea pigs. The town had been especially constructed for this first test. We overflew it several times. The convicts waved to us. They didn't know what was due to happen the next night. No doubt some of them, even though they were in chains, hoped to see their sentences commuted. They were already beginning to like this town, where the windows had no bars. In the aircraft all the instruments that measured radioactivity were stuck at red. That night, at the moment of the explosion, we were more than nine miles away from the town. The order was to remain lying on the ground, not to turn around, not to open our eyes. For the first time in my experience I felt the earth leap into life. It moved beneath me. There was a shock wave that scattered the bodies of those who had tried to stand up. And also the howling of those who had turned around and been blinded. And the heavy shuddering of the earth beneath our bellies. The next day, on the way back to the convicts' town, I pictured the havoc, the ruined houses, the charred carcasses of animals. I had known cities bombed during the war . . . but this was beyond imagining. When the plane approached the place we saw a mirror. A vast mirror of vitrified sand. A smooth, concave surface that reflected the sun, the clouds, and even the cross of our plane. Nothing else. I was young enough to have an idiotic and arrogant thought: 'After this, nothing can ever trouble or frighten me again.'"

He broke off and I guessed he was silent so as to listen. He seemed to be evaluating the drumming of feet above our heads, linking this to the exchange of shouts outside the door, measuring these sounds against the fury of the storm. As his voice took up the tale again it seemed to lend a semblance of order to the pandemonium.

"Within less than a year there was none of that arrogance left. I was racing back and forth across the United States, a vast country where at that moment I felt like a rat being driven from one cage to the next with needles lodged in its brain. The Rosenbergs had just been arrested. The press accused them of having sold the American bomb to the Soviets, and the good citizenry awaited the verdict with a pretty carnivorous appetite. I had been working with the Rosenbergs for two years. In their apartment in New York there was a room converted into a photo laboratory where we prepared documents to send to the Center. It was in that room, by the way, that I had occasion to play chess with Julius. I knew the accusations leveled against them were absurd, out of all proportion, at any rate. They had no access to the secrets of the bomb. But public opinion needed a scapegoat. The Americans now knew that somewhere in the deserts of Central Asia we had exploded a bomb, copied from the one at Hiroshima, and thus ended their atomic supremacy. A real slap in the face. They must act ruthlessly. Some fanatic suggested the electric chair and this now seemed a real possibility. It was either a confession or the chair. I was convinced the Rosenbergs would talk. I had absolute faith in their friendship, but . . . How can I put it? One day I was coming out of the lab with Julius and caught sight of Ethel in the kitchen. She was sitting there, chopping vegetables on a little wooden board. The foolish notion struck me that she resembled a Russian woman. No, just a woman like the rest, a woman happy to be there, in the calm of that moment, chatting with her elder son as he stood there, leaning against the door frame, smiling at her. When I learned of their arrest I remembered that moment, that maternal look, and I said to myself, 'She'll talk. . . .' I left New York. I fled from city to city, the country was closing in on me. In a damage control exercise the Center shut down all the networks, stopped responding to calls. And I was pretty sure it was prepared to sacrifice some of us, as one amputates a gangrenous hand. In fact it was in Moscow that the consequences of their arrest were to be the most severe. When Stalin learned the news he ordered a complete purge of the intelligence service. Hundreds of people prepared for the worst. Even if I'd succeeded in getting back to Moscow, I should simply have been returning to be executed. I moved from place to place, then lay low for a month or two in the anthill of a big city. Every morning I bought the paper. 'The Rosenbergs talk!' 'The traitors confess all!' I was expecting a headline of this kind. I thought of Ethel getting the supper ready and chatting with her elder son as he smiled at her. They told nothing. Dozens of interrogations, confrontations, threats mentioning the electric chair, blackmail over the lives of their children. They even sent very persuasive rabbis into Julius's cell. Nothing. Julius was executed first. They made the same offer to Ethel: her life in exchange for a confession. She refused. I was able to go back to Moscow. No purges took place at the Center. And many things had changed during that period when the two of them were being hounded. Stalin had died. The Americans hadn't dropped their bomb on Korea or China, as they were preparing to do. We'd had time to catch up with them in the home stretch, as it were. Atomic war was becoming a double-edged sword. In a word, the Third World War hadn't taken place. Thanks to the silence of that woman who used to chop vegetables on a little wooden board while chatting with her son . . ."

The masses of water crashing against the cargo ship now seemed more rhythmical, as if resigned to the logic of the resistance offered them by this ludicrous vessel. I heard the counsellor get up and in the sudden flare of a match his face seemed to me aged, deeply etched. His voice had the slightly disappointed tone of someone who had been getting ready to spring a surprise but has missed the right moment to announce it: "Well, that's it. We're on the Red Sea. We won't be tossed about quite so much now." Perhaps it was slight irritation at having to break off his story to announce the news. He resumed it again but brought it to a swift conclusion.

"On account of our duels at chess Ethel nicknamed me 'Shakhmatov' or 'Shakh' for short. She knew Russian. There are only two or three people left who know this nickname. . . . Goodnight!"

In the years that followed he occasionally spoke of the Rosenbergs again. One day he told me why, at the moment of their arrest, he was sure they would confess. "Because if I'd had those two children, that's what I would have done," he said.

With the passage of time, I also came to realize how his storytelling had allowed me to forget my fear, that egotistical and humiliating fear of losing one's life just when things are promising to turn out well.

Last of all, that night taught me Shakh's nickname, which was known to very few people. You were one of them.

2

Everything expressed by their voices, their bodies and, no doubt, their thoughts that night seemed to me tinged with theatrical exaggeration. Their excessively enthusiastic judgments in front of this statue, before that picture. Their smiles, contorted with too much happiness. And, behind these rapt expressions, the all-too-evident lack of attention to what they were being shown. And the overly urbane and almost glee-ful hypocrisy with which they kept promising to meet for lunch one day. And the glances of the men, eyeing the women's figures quite bla-tantly, then immediately affecting icy indifference and poise.

At first I told myself that in an art gallery such an exaggeration of sentiments, either felt or simulated, must stem from the physical, and hence sensual, warmth of the works exhibited. A mistaken sup-position, for the pictures were all bloodlessly and coldly geometric and the sculptures—cubes superimposed on one another and trun-cated cylinders—looked hollow despite the weight of their bronze.

I then attributed these excessive reactions to the schizophrenia of this city cut in two, divided like two hemispheres of a brain, each with its own very personal vision of the world, its own customs and foibles. Berlin, where the streets ran headlong into the Wall, then reappeared on the other side, both similar and unrecognizable. In the western hemisphere of this war-disordered brain people felt them-selves to be charged with a special mission, none more so, I thought, as I made my way slowly through the crowd of them, than the guests at the very first exhibition in this new art center. In their eyes these great, brightly lit rooms were becoming an outpost of the Western World, confronting the alarming boundlessness of the barbaric lands that began beyond the Wall. Each of their gestures was projected onto the screen of the darkness that stretched away toward the east. Every word, every smile produced a reaction out there in that unpredictable blackness. Each truncated cylinder hurled defiance from its pedestal at the realistic paintings and sculptures of human forms that were being exhibited in the eastern hemisphere. The guests felt themselves to be observed by attentive eyes—jealous, hostile, or admiring. It was because of how they were seen from the other side of the Wall that they acted out these exaggerated emotions, going into ecstasies over a canvas, greeting a new acquaintance, sizing up a body or a face at a glance.

A waiter came and offered me champagne. I took the glass, thinking with a smile that what was almost a caricature of the Western World seemed like this because I was seeing it for the first time. I was still seeing it from beyond the Wall. It could not but be theatrical.

At the other end of the room, through the coming and going of the crowd, I caught sight of Shakh, dark suit, bow tie, his gray head inclined toward his interlocutor. I knew we should pretend not to know one another and that, just as he was leaving, someone would introduce us. This someone would be a woman whom I had never met but whom I should seem to have known for a long time. At the moment of this artificial introduction Shakh would be standing next to a dealer in rare stamps. In the most natural way I should make his acquaintance, so as to be able to meet one of his regular customers at his store a few days later, a specialist in arms sales and a passionate collector of stamps devoted to the world of flowers. Perhaps in the end it was our own playacting, woven into the worldly charade of that reception, that made me think of the theater. It was amusing to see the stamp dealer walking past within a few inches of me, not suspecting my existence. It was as if I were not merely hidden in the wings, but actually invisible on stage, among actors speaking their lines and playing their parts.

The feeling I had was a kind of highly lucid intoxication. I believed I could hear the intimate heartbeat of the Western life into which I must merge. This fusion had the discreet violence of carnal possession. I had to struggle mentally not to admit to being happy. This Berlin quintessence of the Western World was giving me back the aggressive lust for life I had thought was in terminal hibernation within me.

I had been aware of this reawakening already in Moscow, during the months of study and training, preparing me for my new work abroad. This preparation removed me further and further from the person I had been before. And it was not the fact of learning intelligence techniques or doing night parachute drops that confirmed this discontinuity. It was the pleasure of becoming a man with no past, of stripping myself down to this body trained for future action. Of being nothing but this future and, as for my past, to have only an invented life story, well rehearsed and learned by heart.

A couple stopped in front of a picture and I could hear the remarks of the woman, whose shoulder was almost brushing against mine. For her the pale spread of colors over the canvas was "You know, awfully strong, gutsy. And that red, you know, totally dominates the background." I turned my head slightly. Young, dark-haired, extremely elegant, her face truly transported by her contemplation. I admired her. All the Western World was there in this ecstatic hypocrisy in front of a feeble daub that had to be viewed as a work of genius. This shared lie was their unwritten constitution, the password to their social world, their genteel nonconformism. Their prosperity, the brilliance of this palace of the arts, and this woman's body, almost arrogant in its well-manicured beauty, were all underwritten by this unspoken agreement. As I looked at the woman, then at the picture, I experienced that mixture of fascination and disgust that the West had always aroused in the East. I was seized by a sudden impulse to squeeze the glass in my hand more and more tightly, to crush it, to see the couple turn around, to see the reflection of the blood in their eyes, to await their reaction with a smile.

At this moment I caught sight of you.

I saw a woman whose face was known to me thanks to the photos I had been shown during the final briefing for my mission. I knew her life, that borrowed life, as fictitious as my own life story, which she knew in her turn. She came in, not from the direction of the street, but through the vast bay window that opened onto a large garden. I had doubtless missed her first appearance in the room. And now she was returning after seeing the bulkiest of the sculptures exhibited in the open air.

My first impression left me perplexed: you resembled the woman who had just been showering praises on the picture. Dark-haired, like her, the same cut to your suit, the same complexion. At once I understood the reason for my mistake. You moved with the same assurance as she, responded to other people's greetings with as much ease, and your perfect mingling with the crowd of guests made you physically similar to the gushy woman. Now that you were coming to meet me I noticed the differences: your hair was darker, your eyes slightly slanting, your brow higher, your mouth. . . . No, you were nothing like her.

As you crossed the room, people stopped you two or three times and I had time to observe you through the looks others gave you, looks of exaggerated lust, appraising your body; possessing you. I pretended to catch sight of you, I began moving toward you, dodging between groups in conversation. It was at the moment when our eyes met that I saw passing across your brow what looked like the shadow, swiftly dissimulated, of very great weariness. I was vexed with you for thus, very briefly, puncturing the elation of the first day of my new life. But already you were talking to me like an old acquaintance and letting me kiss you on the cheek. We sauntered about, just like the others. Then, when we saw Shakh in the company of a man with a large, smooth, bald pate, we walked toward the garden bay, so as to be hailed in passing.

An unexpected scene brusquely interrupted this well-regulated playacting. A crowd gathered. A man who could not be seen over the heads of the throng gave a speech like a fairground barker's, in mangled German, reminiscent of that spoken by German soldiers in comic films about the war. We wormed our way into the throng and saw the man displaying a large spinning top to the crowd. His patter was already provoking laughter.

"The Soviets produce these in their arms factories. This means that first of all they can cover up the production of missiles and, secondly, they can give pleasure to children. Even though this machine weighs more than a shell and makes as much noise as a tank. Look!"

The man crouched and pressed down several times on the point of the top to activate the spring concealed inside its nickel-plated body. The toy hurtled into a waltzing rotation, with a tinny clatter, describing wider and wider circles, and forcing the spectators to retreat amid peals of laughter. Some of them, like one guest with patent leather shoes, tried to push the creature away with the tips of their toes. The owner of the top looked triumphant.

"I'm not mistaken, it's him, isn't it?" I asked you, as I moved out of the way of the people beating a retreat.

"Yes. He's aged amazingly, hasn't he?" you said to me, studying the man with the top.

He was a well-known dissident, expelled from Moscow, who lived in Munich. The toy made a last few turns and came to a standstill amid the applause of the guests.

We joined Shakh and the philatelist. This first contact took place as planned, down to the last word. But the vision of the top passed in front of my eyes from time to time.

Going out into the garden, we stopped for a few minutes among the large structures of bronze and concrete for which there had not been enough room inside the gallery. The trees were already turning yellow. "Under autumn leaves," you remarked to me with a smile, "all these masterpieces are much more bearable." And you added, in a voice that seemed to be hesitating over the need for these words, "I'm older than you. My childhood was in the first years after the war. Poverty that made us gnaw stones. I can remember the rare few days when we weren't hungry. Real treats. And worst of all, no toys. We didn't know what they were. And then one day someone brought us a box filled with treasures for the New Year: brand new tops that still smelled of paint. Exactly like that one just now. Later on, when they started making dolls and all the rest, we were already too old for toys. . . ."

I was on the brink of telling you that, despite those few years' difference between us, I too had known those great tops and that I loved their smell and even the clatter they made. I said nothing because then I should have had to talk about the child lost in the night in the Caucasus. And yet for the first time in my life that past now seemed to me admissible.

We never know where objects and gestures from the past will one day rise to the surface again, nor how, in the accumulation of years we have lived through. The spinning top in the Berlin art gallery came back to my mind three years later in the middle of that great war-torn African capital. The soldiers who had that day come to search the house where we were living went away carrying our few possessions with them. Two or three garments, a television set, some paper money you had purposely left out on the desk. As they left they were caught in the fire of a heavy machine gun that suddenly raked the fronts of the houses from the end of the street. The group scattered to recover their breath in a narrow alley. Only the last of them was hit as he ran. Caught on his side, he began turning around on the spot, his arms open wide and still laden with confiscated objects. Bullets of this caliber often transform the movements of a person running into a swift waltzing motion, like a top, I thought, and I saw the same memory reflected in your eyes.

During the search they had made me stand facing the wall, like a child being punished. As the mistress of the house you were from time to time asked to open a drawer, offer a glass of water. You performed these tasks without ever interrupting the swishing of an improvised fan: some of the revolutionary leaflets with which the streets were strewn and which had made their way into the houses through broken windows. Between these sheets of paper you had slipped the photos and coded messages that we had neither had time to send to the Center nor to burn. That would have been the one really dangerous discovery. Curiously enough, those leaflets in your hand wove a fragile protective zone around our lives that clearly made the soldiers uneasy. I sensed this tension, I understood it in these young armed men. They were struggling against the temptation to fire a short burst, which would have freed them from our watching eyes and restored the joyful savagery to their looting. But there were these slogans for revolutionary justice, freshly printed on the fan of leaflets. There was also the loudspeaker on a truck that had been showering the streets with appeals for calm and proclaiming the benefits of the new regime ever since the morning. Turning my head slightly, I could see hands stuffing into the bag a transistor, a jacket, and even the lamp clamped to the edge of the table, which you were helping to unfasten, while successfully avoiding giving an indication of the comic side of your involvement. You knew that the slightest change of mood might provoke the pent-up anger and the brief spitting of an automatic rifle. The soldier who removed the lamp also expropriated the banknotes left out on the desk. And, as this action looked more like simple theft than the others that had preceded it, he thought it politic to justify it by talking, in tones both menacing and moralistic, about corruption, imperialism, and the enemies of the revolution. These were the didactic and pompous tones of the loudspeaker. Ceaselessly repeated, such slogans ended up infiltrating even our thoughts and it was in this style that, in spite of myself, I formulated a silent observation, "The money that you have coveted is the end of your revolution. The serpent of cupidity has stolen into your new house."

When they had gone I turned around and saw you sitting there, still mechanically waving your fan of leaflets. The disorder in the room now matched the chaos outside, just as if this had been the purpose of their visit. Through the window we saw them quietly moving up the street, and a second later there came their flight under the crackle of bullets and the waltzing death of the soldier, revolving several times on the spot and scattering the confiscated objects all around him, those familiar fragments of our daily life. He collapsed, I glanced at you, guessing that you had the same memory: "That top . . ."

The evening of the private viewing in Berlin seemed infinitely remote. And yet scarcely three years had elapsed. I had a vision of the faces that were reflected then in the nickel-plated surface of the toy launched by that man with the forced laugh of a fairground barker. The dark-haired young woman swooning in front of a pallid canvas. Shakh speaking to the philatelist. And also the man who had succeeded in kicking away the top with the tip of his patent leather shoe. I had later chanced to pass the woman in a restaurant: in conversation with a friend, she was commenting on the menu and her descriptions were just as enthusiastic as the one she had earlier reserved for the picture. So she was less hypocritical than I had thought, I said to myself, just a little excessive in her praises. The philatelist continued to spend more than half his life in his shop piled high with stacks of stamped envelopes and albums, without having the least suspicion that he had entered our world of espionage for a few hours and left it again, unaware of what was happening to him. As for the man who had changed the trajectory of the spinning top by giving it a little kick, two years later he had lost his post as first secretary to a Western embassy in East Berlin, on account of an amorous liaison. It was Shakh who had told us of this misadventure. "He was not a novice, he knew that bed is the best trap for a diplomat. But it's a little like dying, it's something that only happens to other people." We thought the story would stop there: the tale of one of those stupid men in their fifties who swallow the amorous encounters set up for them hook, line, and sinker. But there was a detail that made Shakh continue. There was in his voice a chess player's fascination for an elegant series of moves. "The scenario was of a pathetic banality.

Even in intelligence schools I don't think they give such obvious examples any longer. On the other hand, as regards psychology, hats off to our East German colleagues. Here's how it was. The diplomat makes the acquaintance of a young Aryan beauty, falls for her, but remembers the need to be prudent. He hesitates. The young woman introduces him to one of her friends. Younger still and even more irresistible. The wretched diplomat doesn't resist. The first girl treats him to a terrible scene of jealousy and leaves him forever. Now he's completely reassured: have you ever seen a jealous female spy? Confident of his charm, he forges ahead. The sequel is an ultra classic case, even the subsequent reaction of his wife—and this scared him more than his own country's legal sanctions. . . ."

After the house search that day it was you who talked about the ghosts reflected in the brilliant spinning of a top. You knew that after all those hours, when our deaths could have been caused by one word too many or a gesture that might have annoyed the soldiers, what we needed was to move, to talk, to laugh about that diplomat who was ready to sell all the secrets in the world, provided his wife did not learn of his misconduct. As you talked you were putting our house back in order, filling the gaps that had been left by the objects carried away.

I listened to you distractedly, conscious that it was not the substance of these stories that mattered. In the gleaming top I could see a young man in a dark suit, a glass of champagne in his hand. This self of mine that looked like a brilliant caricature, with his lust for living, his feverish anticipation of the new life, his haste to immerse himself in the seductive complexity of the Western World, with a pistol in his armpit and an ice-cold glass in his burning hand.

Our life had rapidly erased that caricature, turning as it did into an exhausting hunt for men who manufactured death. Those who invented weapons in the sheltered comfort of laboratories, those at the highest levels who made decisions about their production and later their use, those who sold them and resold them, those who killed. From this human chain all we needed was to seize upon just one tiny link of information, an address, a name. And it was often in countries at war that the chain could be uncovered most easily. We would settle there under one identity or another (in that African city we were representatives of a geological prospecting company), we would endeavor to meet the person who was supplying arms to feed the imminent fighting. "Fighting that very likely wouldn't break out if there were not all these means of killing," I said to myself, two days before the start of the massacres, as I was talking to an arms salesman about to catch a plane to London. In the early days I used to think it would have been simpler to shoot down this Ron Scalper, him and his like, they were so palpably insignificant compared with the carnage that resulted from their trade. But this desire had been left behind among the fantasies of that young man with his glass of champagne in the middle of a Berlin gallery. In reality one had to cherish this salesman with all possible solicitude, for he was the first link that could uncover the whole chain. At the airport he had given me his London address—our next destination.

We went on joking, so as to forget the few hours we had lived through, when death was sickeningly promiscuous. You observed that a man who feels himself to be seductive becomes very nimble, like the diplomat with the patent leather shoes, slipping his foot between the legs of the other guests and deflecting the top with the adroitness of a soccer player. I told you about my impulse to kill the arms salesman I had accompanied to the airport two days earlier and my regret that such radical solutions are only effective in spy films. Picking up the books that the soldiers had flung to the ground during their search, I went over to the window and caught sight again of their ill-starred comrade lying in the road and of two furtive figures who emerged from a side street in the already encroaching dusk, went over to the corpse, picked up its booty scattered in the dust, and disappeared into their hole. You came and stood beside me, noticed a detail I had missed, and murmured with a smile, "Look, our album."

It was a big photograph album that the robbers of the dead man had left behind when they carried off the lamp and the clothes. An album in which the snapshots, cunningly contrived and carefully arranged in order, were designed to confirm the identity we were living under at that time: a couple of Canadian prospectors in charge of a geological search. Family photos, of a family that had never existed, with no other reality than that of these smiling faces of our purported nearest and dearest and of ourselves, in the settings of vacations or family reunions. This reconstruction had, of course, been made not for the benefit of looters in a hurry but for scrutiny by professionals, such as we had already had occasion to undergo during those three years. Tucked away in a dusty corner on a shelf, this album, with its cheerful aura of routine married life, was more convincing than the most carefully fabricated life story. Now it lay beside the soldier's body in this half-burned city, and what was strangest of all was to picture one of the townspeople leafing through it one day, believing it was a real family history, endearing at every stage, with all those sentiments that constantly recur, and the children growing up from one photo to the next.

Later on, during the night, I would sense that this past, photographed but never lived, aroused in you a memory of ourselves, of our actual life together, that we paid such little attention to under our borrowed identities. Our life had left behind no photos, no letters, had led to no exchange of confidences. Suddenly the counterfeit album reminded us that we had had these three years of routine complicity, an imperceptible closening of ties, an affection we avoided calling love. Far away there was our country, the weary empire whose physical mass we were ever aware of as the magnet that drew our thoughts, even through the African night. There were its scents and its winter smoke above the villages, the snows in its little towns, mute beneath the blizzards, its faces scarred by forgotten wars and exiles with no return, its history, in which the victorious din of sounding brass often gave way to weeping, to a silence cadenced by the tramp of a column of soldiers after a defeat in battle. And, buried deep in this snow and those muddy roads, there were the years of our child-hood and youth, inseparable from the pulse of joy and sorrow, from that living alloy that we call our native land.

Your words came like an echo of that distant presence: "It must be possible one day to tell the truth."

I felt caught in the act of having shared your train of thought. But above all I felt obliged to bear witness to the truth that had arisen behind the forged photos in a family album. What truth? Again I saw the corpse of the soldier stretched out on the ground, the young man who had just confiscated several banknotes from us in the name of revolutionary justice. I recalled that the previous day I had seen a burned-out armored vehicle and the arm with a leather bracelet on its wrist, an arm protruding from a chaotic jumble of metal and flesh. The wearer of the wristband was the enemy of the young revolution-ary. They were about the same age, had perhaps been born in two neighboring villages. Those who called themselves revolutionaries were supported by the Americans, those who had been defeated were, until the fall of the capital city, in receipt of arms from us and aid from our instructors. The two young soldiers were certainly not aware of the vastness of the forces opposing one another behind their backs.

Was that the truth you were referring to? I doubted it. For to be truthful one would also have to speak of the arms salesman, maybe at that very moment lying between the thighs of his young mistress, scrupulously attentive to his own hard-won pleasure. The two mes-sages you had slipped into your fan must be decoded: delayed and now useless information about the fighting already ended. Those two columns of figures that could have cost us our lives. And we should have died in the guise of a certain Canadian couple, whose existence would have been authenticated by the cheerful banality of a photograph album.

You got up. In the darkness I was aware that you seemed to be waiting for a response. I sat up as well, ready to admit my confusion: for this truth you had spoken of was constantly changing, giving rise to little murky, fleeting, sprawling truths. The tragedy of the massacres was sullied by my chatting with the arms salesman at the airport, by the vision of his chubby body, hard up against that of his naked mistress. Our arm-wrestling with the Americans was becoming mired in a political demagoguery revised so many times that we now found ourselves supporting a regime held to be conservative while they had their money on the victory of the revolutionaries. These labels no longer had any meaning, revolution meant access to oil wells. As for our own personal truth, all it amounted to was this score of faces, young and old, surrounding us on the pages of a photo album, these nearest and dearest whom we had never known.

I was about to say all that to you when, thanks to the glow from the fire that was petering out in the next street, I saw what you were doing, standing up in front of the window, your arms raised, repairing the torn mosquito netting. I guessed at how the tentative needle was working its way upward in the darkness, drawing together the panels of dusty fabric. With a newfound joy I sensed that this moment had no need of words. There you were, in the identity most faithful to yourself, in all the truth of the silence that followed a setback in our efforts to understand each other. And beneath the whole accumulation of masks, grimaces, and alibis that made up my life, there was just one day that seemed to match your truth.

Hesitantly, as if I had only just learned the words I was speaking, I began to tell you about the infant falling asleep in the depths of a forest in the Caucasus.

One day, in another city, in another war, I once more came upon you in silent contemplation. The windows onto the terrace had been shattered by an explosion and the table on which we often took our meals was strewn with shards. You were picking them up patiently, not saying a word, sometimes crouching, sometimes leaning with one hand on the back of a chair. You were wearing next to nothing, so suffocating was the heat of the Gulf at this moment of low tide. I saw your body and the mixture of fragility and strength that was apparent in your movements. The innocently carnal play of nakedness that does not know it is observed. A trunk with muscular curves, the firm outline of a leg, then suddenly, as if betrayed, this delicate collarbone, almost painful in its childish outlines.

Something rebelled in me. At its start this task of picking up the pieces always seems endless. But, above all, it was you, your life spared in the face of so many threats, over so many years, now being idiotically used up on this most rare evening of respite. A week before the fighting broke out we had finished piecing together a network of arms sales: nine intermediaries across Europe, buying and selling, so as to line their pockets on the way and, as always in this kind of traffic, to cover their tracks. To begin with the whole thing had looked seamless, impenetrable. Shakh had succeeded in obtaining a copy of the first of these contracts and had sent it to us in London. A banal transaction, even if, in reading the list of weapons supplied, we could

61

readily picture their harvest of death on the ground. Otherwise an arms sale like thousands of others. It was you who had detected the anomaly, the first link that was to enable us to work our way along the chain: nowhere in this contract was there any mention of technical assistance after delivery. As if the purchasers had no intention of using all these armored vehicles and rockets. You had mentioned resale via a third country. We tugged at the link and managed to gain access to this strangely unwarlike first purchaser. Then, another . . . Nine, until we reached the people in this ravaged city who were killing, and getting themselves killed, with the weapons listed in that contract. Commissions worth millions of dollars. And, among the beneficiaries, a fully operational Minister of Foreign Affairs.

Crouched by the window, you went on picking up the fragments of glass. Calm, resigned, unbearable in the tenderness of your silent presence, because of the madness of it, because of the injustice of fate that had assigned this house to you with its shattered windows, and this intimacy with death and the ghosts of those nine characters who had invaded your life.

My angry words remained unspoken. In our fragmented lives where the unforeseen was becoming the only logic, this table, wiped clean, that you were about to set, the way you did before the fighting began, this simple action made perfect sense. "I'll soon be finished," you said, standing up, and talked about the couple who were due to replace us. That, among other things, was our task: to prepare the ground for the colleagues who would take over the network after the end of the war. I noticed a slight cut on your left hand marked with blood. The sharp edge of a splinter, no doubt. Absurdly, amid all these deaths, this tiny wound pained me greatly.

That night I told you about the child who learned to walk around a block of granite stuck in the middle of the house built by his father.

★

The words I had held back when I saw you on the terrace welled up
a year later. We were in the house belonging to a couple of doctors
sent by a humanitarian organization, this being our identity at that
time. The villa next door was empty. Its owners had left as soon as the
first skirmishes in the streets had begun. And now from their garden
came the piercing cries of peacocks which the soldiers were amusing
themselves by torturing. One of the birds, its neck broken, was
writhing on the ground, the other lay there, spitted by an iron bar.
Glancing occasionally at this massacre, I was stirring papers and pho-
tographs in a bucket, where they were slowly being consumed by
smoky little flames. There was nothing left to steal in our house, it
had already been ransacked. But after a week of looting such activi-
ties were becoming more and more unmotivated, almost an art form,
like the torture inflicted on the peacocks. And I knew from experience that it was an unmotivated search that was often the most dangerous. The soldiers shot down the last of the birds, the most agile,
spraying it with bullets—a maelstrom of feathers and blood—then
made off toward the center of the city, guided by the bursts of gunfire. I crushed the ashes, mixed them up and threw them into the
middle of a parched flower bed. And set about waiting for you, that is
to say, rushing out regularly into the chaos of streets invaded by
yelling surges of people, who seemed to be simultaneously pursuing
one another and running away from those they were pursuing. I
encountered a road block, allowed myself to be searched, tried to
argue. And reflected that if they refrained from killing me it was
because the infernal din prevailing in the city was such that the soldiers could not hear me, otherwise my very first word would have
unleashed their fury. I returned home. I saw the empty house, with its
window overlooking the garden next door, in the middle of which a
peacock was pinned to the ground by a stake. You were somewhere
in this city. In distress, I guessed at your presence, perhaps in the

wealthy quarter, with its cluster of glass towers, two of which were currently surmounted by smoke, or else in the poor quarter, in the alleys near the canal encrusted with filth. I went out again, hurried toward each crowd gathering around a person who could be heard giving orders or whose execution was being prepared. In one court-yard, as if this square had been cut off from all the madness of the city, I came upon a seated woman leaning against a wall, who seemed far away, her eyes open wide, her cheek distorted by a ball of khat, which her tongue was slackly moving around. And in the street men were dragging a half-naked body along the ground, which passersby tried to trample on with roars of delight.

When you came home there was still enough daylight to see the fine tracery of cuts on your face. "The windshield . . ." you mur-mured, and you stood facing me for a few seconds, staring at me in silence. On your forehead the scratches you had wiped clean when you came in were once more filling with blood. I was silent, too, stunned by the words that had just come into my mind but could not be spoken, "In any event you wouldn't have died." Or rather, "Even if you'd died it would have changed nothing between us." I was particularly struck by the serenity, almost joy, that these strange, unspeakable, apparently cruel words had given me. I had tumbled into a dazzling light, far, far away from this city, somewhere beyond our life. I began speaking to you in harsh tones, harsher and harsher the more touching and vulnerable you became in your evening rou-tines: you undressed, went into the bathroom, asked me to help. I poured out a stream of water, drawing more from time to time from our reservoirs, the vessels that stood along the wall, and I continued talking, almost shouting, working up my indignation as if to con-vince myself that my luminous tumble had been simply an illusion brought on by tension.

"Do you know what our lives remind me of? Those samurais from World War Two who lay low in the jungle and remained at war fifteen years after the fighting had ended! No, it's worse than that. At least they laid down their weapons when they learned the truth. While we . . . It's true, we're about as much use as those madmen who ended up shooting at ghosts. We're chasing ghosts, too! We spent six months getting close to that idiot of a military attaché. Three months in Rome at the height of summer to arrange an informal ten-minute interview. I loathe that city! When I'm in that tourist bazaar I become a fool. We had to spend all those hours in that moth-eaten archive because our man was fanatical about uncial script or whatever that stupid stuff was. Then we had to locate him here—pure chance, of course. A chance about as broad as a shotgun cartridge in the magazine of a pistol. Of course our little strategists at the Center need their spectacular, instant results to earn their promotions. So now, quick as a wink, we have to recruit some guy the service has had its eye on for years. And to crown it all, he's just leaving. Did you hear his perfectly pleasant laugh? 'Oh, what excellent timing! The fighting's breaking out just when, as it happens, I was planning to take my leave.' And off he goes. Six months of work and several good chances of being bumped off in this filthy tropical climate. And all for nothing. No, sorry, I nearly forgot. We've obtained one piece of information of the first importance. The mines that are going to blow up the people here are of Italian manufacture. I guess you'll get a citation for that. Why are you laughing?"

I could see your smile reflected in the mirror in front of which you were drying your hair, tilting your head first one way, then the other. You did not answer me, gathering up your hair behind your head. The corners of your eyes stretched toward your temples and gave you the look of an Asian woman. I was silent, suddenly realizing that my sense of tumbling into the light had not been imaginary. That vision of clarity and space, taking us far away from the world, had come from your face, from your look, from that procession of days that lost itself in your half-closed eyes. "Even if you'd died it would have changed nothing between us." You came over to me and for a long moment laid your brow against my shoulder. And that night when I got up to take over the watch from you and let you sleep, you told me you were not sleepy. You began to talk about a day in winter, a house on the shores of a frozen lake. In this house there was a clock driven by weights, the chain had been tied in a knot by some wretched joker. This knot obliged your mother to raise the weights quite frequently. She had to watch out lest the knot should jam the machinery. And this vague domestic uneasiness contrasted in the child's head with the calm that prevailed around the lake, in the snow-covered forest.

I went out just before sunrise, after you had gone to sleep. I picked up the bodies of the peacocks, skirted the fence, and dragged them toward the ruins of a house. As I retraced my footsteps I frequently had to stoop to pick up the feathers that, in the gray light of dawn, punctuated the path with their dimmed iridescence.

Three days later it was already possible to cross the city again, negotiating here or there the right to pass through a tollgate consisting of two rusty barrels and a length of cable barring the route. The war was moving away from the capital, withdrawing into the interior of the country. At one crossroads, at a still furtive market, I was able to buy some vegetables and a wheaten pancake. When I returned I saw you from a long way off, beside the entrance that led to the garden. This was the one we used now, so as not to show ourselves in the street too much. You were seated on the threshold, your hands resting in your lap, your eyelids half closed. Close beside the door the water in the bucket you had just fetched shone violet, like the sunset sky. Seeing me at the end of the garden, you waved your hand slightly and I had this simultaneously clear and disconcerting thought: "There is the woman I love, waiting for me under a beautiful evening sky, at the door of this house, which we shall shortly be leaving forever, in this country where we nearly died." I repeated, "A woman I love," just to gauge how poor the word was. I longed to tell you what you were to me, what your silence and your patient calmness meant on the threshold of a house we should never see again.

You got up, went in, taking the water with you. I had a strong physical sense of how you were dreaming of days in a past totally foreign to this city, to this life. And even when, later in the night, it seemed that all there was of you was just your ardent body, the element of remoteness was still there. As we embraced, my hand squeezed your forearm and my fingers rediscovered those four notches cut in the flesh, scars from a burst of gunfire long ago. They were deep grooves that felt as if they had been incised by the claws of some large beast letting slip its prey.

We had to cross the country by car and leave it by sea. About sixty miles from the capital, on the far side of the uncertain line of the front, we drove off the road that was churned up by explosions. The mined area was ringed with bodies blown to smithereens, colorful piles of blankets and clothes and the carcasses of vehicles. The local who was escorting us spoke of "cunning" mines, that chose whom to kill. "Four women walked over it and nothing happened to them. Then a woman with a child came along and the mines woke up," he said, pointing to where the carnage happened.

We knew that, thanks to a pneumatic device, the detonators on these mines were activated only after several sets of pressure, so as to allow a whole column of vehicles to move onto the minefield. A column of vehicles, or a crowd of women and children escaping from their burned village. The celebrated Italian mines.

Perhaps it was on that day, on that road gutted by mines, that for the first time I thought about an end to the life we had been leading for several years. Resuming his seat in the vehicle, our guide confided in us, "The Russians deceived us. To begin with they promised paradise, all peoples are brothers and all that. Then we saw they didn't believe in it themselves. And now that they've gone forever we are killing one another for nothing."

I glanced at you to see whether, like me, you had picked up that "forever." But you seemed not to be listening, your gaze fixed on the blue radiance of the sea that appeared to our right at each upward turn of the road. At that moment I had the impression I was betraying you. Like a soldier who, on learning of imminent surrender and armistice, deserts his post without warning those who are still fighting.

This involuntary betrayal seemed to have no consequences. There continued to be cities that emptied at the sound of the first gunfire, as if at the drumming of the first spots of rain on a corrugated tin roof. (One day, as the westerners were hurrying off toward the aircraft in a rainstorm of great warm drops, their dread of the bullets beginning to reach the fringes of the airport was comically confused with their eagerness to protect themselves from the downpour.) There were ships maneuvering ponderously in bays that were too narrow and heading toward the open sea so slowly that we thought we could picture the rage of the passengers, glaring hard from the deck at the coastline already going up in flames, as if to push it away. We would stay. We knew that, after the fever of the fighting and the looting, the conquerors would be in need of diplomatic recognition, money, arms. At such times one could obtain results within a few weeks that in normal times would take years of work. The only difficulty was staying alive.

Nothing changed. Least of all the impression that dogged us in our rapid transits from Europe to Africa. Everything that in the North was words, discreet consultations, slow approaches to a key person, turned in the South into cries of pain, the whistling of bullets and bitter hand-to-hand fighting, as if a horrible, unbridled process of translation had become established between these two continents.

And yet it was in Africa that one day I again felt as if I were hiding from you what I could perceive more and more clearly: the end.

Two months after the conclusion of hostilities they arrived to take charge of the network following our departure. We were struck by their youth, like a reminder of ourselves several years previously, at the time of our first meeting in Berlin. What touched us as well was that they had cheerfully told us their actual first names, which had the comic assonance of the masculine and feminine variants: Yuri and Yulia. We were not used to confidences of this type, our own lives being confined to our borrowed identities. At the moment of going away you had a preoccupied air, like a mother anxious to forget nothing when she leaves the children on their own. They were to renew contact with us in Milan three months later. They did not come. We spent four days waiting for them. The Center spoke of a canceled mission. Shakh, whom I managed to contact in the United States, was perplexed, like a chess player robbed of a pawn and on the verge of discovering he has been cheated. He gave us the order to return to Africa. We found our old house without any trace of a forced departure or search. The tranquillity of the rooms had the sly alertness of a trap. The Center's response was as muddled as before. What this opacity signaled was no longer just a simple setback but a more wide-ranging collapse. An end. I decided to talk to you about this, then changed my mind. Out of cowardice, no doubt. Once again I felt I inhabited the skin of that soldier who, in the furthest outpost of an empire, is the first to learn the news of defeat and makes his escape without warning the last remaining fighters. Moreover, we knew what prison and torture could mean in countries like this in wartime. Especially for a woman. Yulia and Yuri . . .

The resumption of fighting dispelled these feelings of remorse in us. The city was bombed, we left the house and spent a long inconclusive day in one of the big hotels in the capital, abandoned by the westerners, looted, refurbished during the months of truce, and once more derelict. We were still hoping we could remain in the city. The bedroom had been made up a few days previously and it was eerie to see the bed with the sheets straightened and turned down by a professional hand, the little "do not disturb" card on the door and to know that the walls of the corridor were spattered with blood in several places and that in the foyer on the floor below prisoners had been tortured and raped. Now the hotel stood empty and through the window at the end of the corridor one could see the sea, dominated by the gray, asymmetrical shape of an American aircraft carrier. Its vast bulk—it looked as if it had been carved out of a monstrous bluish muscle—seemed to be blocking all movement of waves upon a flattened, slack sea.

One section of the troops defending the city had been driven back toward the coast, the soldiers took up a position on the first floor of the hotel, the impending victors surrounded the building, machine-gunning the windows in the expectation that the smoke would drive the besieged men out into a hail of bullets. We had time to cross the hotel garden, to skirt its little marina, and to reach the edge of the water. We knew that a boat would be evacuating the last of our military instructors. Out of breath, we stopped in the middle of the little beach where you could still see rows of white plastic beach chairs. And at that moment time was shattered, went into turmoil—a sequence of mad dashes and complete standstills. The sand ensnared our footsteps, as in a bad dream where running is impossible. The military vehicle that pulled out from beside the hotel building grew rapidly larger, bearing down on us, and already the first bullets were riddling the hulls of the dinghies upended on the sand. My shout was cut short and had no effect on you. You remained standing, your hand raised in a gesture of greeting that seemed to me absurd. The magazine slithered in my grasp like a piece of wet soap. As I fired I thought

I was aiming at the vehicle's scowling face—the evil grin of the radiator grille and the dull eyes of the headlights.

Dazed by my fear, I saw the shadow before I heard the noise. For a moment it blotted out the sun above my hiding place behind the boats. I raised my head. Its outline was very easy to recognize: an Mi-24, the combat helicopter used by the empire on all continents. I detected the movement of its two guns—and almost immediately, in the area of the vehicle that was now only a few dozen yards away, there was a ball of fire from the explosion. The machine landed, covering us with a whirlwind of sand and uprooting the straw parasols around the hotel swimming pool. Its steely ponderousness contrasted jarringly with this little tropical tourist paradise. As I climbed in, I saw on its fuselage the traces of direct hits, some hidden under a layer of gray-green paint, other, more recent ones showed a glint of bare metal. The blast from the takeoff flung the parasols around, likewise a blue sheet beside the pool, and outside the window the beach, the sea, the hotel building, which was already engulfed in smoke, were rapidly thrust back. I tried not to think about the people inside, surrounded and still fighting.

On the deck of the ship where we landed it was the red flag of the empire that caught our eye. And also the tired paint covering its contours of steel. In heading for clear water, the ship was obliged to cross the inner sea marked off from the boundless ocean by the presence of the American aircraft carrier. This vast yet closed-in expanse was defined by the escort frigates. We advanced slowly, as if feeling our way, although in brilliant light. On our left the aircraft carrier grew larger, dominated us, flattened us on the surface of the water. It seemed to be ignoring us. A plane took off, forcing us to cover our ears, another landed on the deck, mastering its terrible energy in a few seconds. Simply by their positioning the escort vessels indicated the fine dotted line of the course we were authorized to take.

"It's like being on the battleship Potemkin confronting the government squadron," you said, your eyes laughing in a face smudged with black.

That may have been the last time in our lives I saw you smile.

I saw Shakh a month later in a big German city where everything was ready for the Christmas holiday. He entrusted some documents to me that I was to pass on to a contact agent, made jokes about the change in climate that I must have noticed and about the very German seriousness of the holiday preparations. I guessed what a man of his age might feel in the midst of the festive animation in this city, in this country where, as a young man, he had fought in the war. He fell silent, sunk in that past, then returned to the memory that prevailed over all others and talked again about the Rosenbergs. I noticed now that the lines of his face had become more angular and that his shoulders remained slightly raised, as if by a self-imposed physical discipline. Listening to him, I did not say to myself, "He's rambling. . . ." but rather, "His is a totally different generation! One that can't see, or doesn't want to see, that we've moved into a new age." What was most surprising was that, in spite of myself, I saw you as belonging to the same generation, even though Shakh could have been your father. Age in years had nothing to do with it. Yours was the generation who . . . I suddenly grasped it with perfect clarity: a generation who did not believe it was the end. The end of the empire, the end of its history. And that this history and the men of this history would be forgotten.

"When they were executed," Shakh was saying, "I made a naive vow, I was naive, like all believers. Yes, I vowed to fight on until a monument had been erected to them, a real one, a big one at the very heart of New York City. But they haven't done it, not even in Moscow."

When he had gone I spent a long time roaming through the streets beneath a kind of snow, little gray stinging granules. Toward evening the weather became milder and real snowflakes fluttered down in the glow from the street lamps. Children congregated in front of shop windows in which mechanical Santa Clauses ceaselessly drew beribboned gifts out of their sacks. In the cathedral, in a more dignified and static replica of this, the three kings around the crib offered their presents, too. And the festive atmosphere was even in evidence in the street where there were near-naked young women smiling at the passersby from inside some of the wide bay windows on the first floor. Beside the chair on which each woman displayed herself, sometimes with open thighs, sometimes kneeling on the seat to show off curved buttocks, there was a little Christmas tree glittering with a string of flashing fairy lights. Before settling down in the bar where the agent was to find me, I plunged in among wooden booths, a noisy, festively decorated village that occupied the whole cathedral square. The warmth of the braziers was cut into by waves of cold, the voices, warmed with alcohol, lost their Germanic harshness, and for me a glass of mulled wine had the taste of an existence quite different from mine, yet very close at hand. At the bar, I reflected on this nearness as I became aware from a clock above the counter of the increasingly obvious lateness of the man I was to meet. A time came when the delay was such that, instead of the person expected, other individuals might well accost me, show me their cards, ask me to follow them. Such delays were generally the result of a series of setbacks. Mentally I pursued the series to its logical conclusion: the discovery of the two diskettes that Shakh had passed on to me, arrest, interrogation, a long prison sentence that I would have to serve somewhere in this country. It suddenly seemed to me so simple to get up, walk out into this brightly lit city, and lose myself in the evening crowd, in its wooden villages decorated with fir branches. My current identity, my papers, made me humdrum, invisible. I could have crossed the increasingly open frontiers of this new old Europe, settled down either here or elsewhere. The memory, already very remote, of my first day in the Western World came back to me:

Berlin, the private showing, and the stamp dealer who had for several hours, without knowing it, entered our games of espionage. Entered them and left them again forever. I should imitate him. Like him, I had a profession. I could close this parenthesis and return to it. Our lives, after all, are wholly made up of parentheses. The art is knowing how to close them at the right moment.

I glanced at the clock, ordered another drink. I recalled that, as I was strolling through the streets, I had encountered a scene that came back to me now with its whiff of bourgeois happiness: on the steps of a large private house a doctor in a white coat was bidding good-bye to an elderly patient who was accompanied by his aged wife. It was clear that the doctor was enjoying the coolness of a few snowflakes landing on his bare head and found it pleasant to step outside his office and make this show of courtesy, especially toward this particular patient, possibly his last before the holiday began.

Before we moved on again it was you who told me about the death of the man I had been vainly waiting for in that city with its fairy tale decorations. An anonymous hotel room, a body that no one claimed, his belongings painstakingly searched. No doubt they were looking for those two diskettes he had not had time to collect. So I had been waiting for a dead man. . . .

I would never find the courage to admit to you that while I was waiting for him I had felt envious of a respectable German doctor baring his head to the flurries of snow. And that I had placed you, alongside Shakh, in that blinkered generation who were living in another era.

When you told me about the agent's death you also spoke of Yulia and Yuri and I realized you had been trying to gather up at least those scraps of information that generally accompanied the disappearance of people like ourselves: a hotel room buzzing with police, a burned-out car on waste ground. "I should have warned them, well, explained to them that . . ." You looked at me, as if seeking help. "You should have explained to them," I thought, "that it was too late to have any illusions."

In the end I dared to say it to you. I yelled it in your ear, trying to overcome the noise filling that crazy airplane and the night sky around it, in darkness torn into blinding shreds by salvos from antiaircraft batteries.

The plane was evacuating the remnants of a war that the empire had lost beneath this southern sky. The bowels of the machine were piled high with the living, the wounded, and the dead, wrapped in long sheaths of black plastic. The mound of these cocoons stirred in the shadows, alongside the cases of ammunition and the tangle of weapons that looked like a huge metallic spider. The living, slumped down in the midst of this chaos, each resorted to their own stratagems for dealing with fear. Some tried to talk at the tops of their voices, drawing their neighbors' heads toward their mouths, others stopped their ears and, with their faces twisted into a grimace, huddled in upon themselves. Some slept and were confused with the dead. And when the plane began tipping over sharply on one wing and the wounds came back to life in this new position, the cries of the wounded redoubled and beyond the cocoons the grating of the metallic spider could be heard. I held you by your shoulders and my lips, enmeshed in your hair, burned your cheek and ear with these truths, carved into the stifling blackness of that flying cemetery. I was proclaiming the end, defeat, the pointlessness of the lives we had used up, the stupid blindness of Shakh, the misery of the peoples we had dragged into a suicidal enterprise. You seemed to be listening to me, then, when suddenly the aircraft went into a tight spiral and the howling of the wounded drowned out all other sounds, you broke away from me and, taking a flask from your knapsack, slipped in among bodies seated and lying there toward the front, where the flashlights of the nurses could be made out.

★

We arrived in Moscow after an absence of two and a half years and, as ever, spent little time there. Those years had coincided with the start of the great upheavals of '89 to '91. There was still a touch of grotesque comedy about recently acquired wealth, the new roles were not yet learned by heart, the new language remained hesitant. The actors made faux pas. Like the beggar trying to catch the warm gusts of air emanating from the door of a big store—a genuine war veteran, no doubt, but one who had attached all kinds of cheap insignia to his jacket to swell the numbers. These gilded disks eclipsed the tarnished silver of the medal "For Gallantry" that was hard won in the war. Or those two women waiting for clients outside a hotel for foreigners. Monumental in their fur coats, they seemed as immovable and unapproachable as statues of empresses. Their scenario consisted of pretending they had just emerged from the hotel, but the snow where they maintained their vigil had long since become pitted with little holes from their stiletto heels. "One day," I thought, "they, too, will have the right to a place in a heated window and even a little Christmas tree with a string of flashing lights."

It was a few blocks away from that hotel, beside the entrance to a restaurant, that we were caught up in the bibulous surge of a banquet that came streaming out onto the sidewalk. A score of men and women were roaring with laughter and congratulating one another on their great idea: to go and get themselves photographed between courses in front of the nearby Kremlin towers. "Get going, you guys!" yelled the ringleader. "Maybe they'll be putting up eagles instead of red stars tomorrow. This'll be a historic picture!" We stepped back to the edge of the sidewalk to let them pass. It was comic to see the clothes from fashion magazines on bodies that were too hefty or too square, all this stylish luxury combined with their broad, red, laughing faces. The women were rubbing their shoulders, shivering exaggeratedly with the cold, the men grabbed them by the waist, squeezed them, pawed them. One of them lifted his partner in the air and her dress rode up to reveal massive thighs, robustly and aggressively immodest. The ringleader banged with his fist on the door of a huge Mercedes and out jumped a sleepy man, his driver or his bodyguard, who handed him a camera. There was something undoubtedly legitimate and at the same time obscene about their merriment. I could not find a way to disentangle the two. I was waiting for your reaction but you walked along, saying nothing, occasionally raising your face toward the swirling of the snow.

"Behold, the new masters of the country!" I ventured at last, looking back toward the crowd of them as they returned to the restaurant. You said nothing. We were walking along an avenue beneath the walls of the citadel, beneath the towers surmounted by their mistily crystalline red stars. Faced with your silence, I wanted to provoke you, to compel you to reply, to drag you from your calm. "The masters change but the servants remain. How many years have we spent snuffling around like dogs in all those stinking little wars? And all for the greater glory of a dozen senile idiots barricaded in behind that wall! And now you're ready to do the same job all over again for that bunch of money-grubbers and their bimbos bursting out of their designer dresses!" I stopped, turned toward you, awaiting your response. But you went on walking, your gaze somewhat lowered toward the footprints ahead of us, which the snow was patiently obliterating. Soon there were a dozen paces between us, then a score, so that you looked to me as if you were all alone amid the trees with their snow-covered branches, very remote, and quite detached from the life I had been mocking. A moment before, stung by your absent air, I was on the point of turning my back and leaving you. Now that at every step you were becoming more and more of a stranger to me, I felt you within me with a violence that made my eyes swim. You were going away and I could feel the warmth of your breath in the night air, the coolness of your fingers inside your gloves, the beating of your heart beneath your coat. You turned. You were already so far away that I could no longer make out whether you were smiling or looking at me with sadness. I went toward you with a sense of finding you again after a protracted separation, at the end of an infinitely long walk.

By an absurd coincidence the merrymakers from the Moscow banquet caught up with us again in a restaurant in Paris. They were not the same people, of course, but their wealth came from the same source, they were pulling the same faces. We were looking for a quiet corner and this half-empty dining room was it. Thirty minutes later they made their appearance and settled at a long table that had been reserved. Trapped, we stayed to listen to them. There was no longer any need for me to talk to you about the "new masters," or about the years we had used up for nothing, or about the end. You understood what my thoughts might be, watching them giving vent to coarse guffaws with their mouths full, their monolithic backs, their fingers studded with rings. I could imagine what your answers might be. Later, in a little café where we went to escape them, you spoke quite calmly about the age we had seen come into being, which was now about to end.

"Ten years ago, or maybe more, I used to think just like you: all these wars to paper over the cracks of a shattered doctrine? All these efforts to please the doddering old fools in the Kremlin? One day, unable to bear it any longer, I said this to Shakh. Like you. For the glory of what cause? Toward what sunlit chasms? He listened to me and . . . began speaking about Sorge. I was simply furious. I said to myself, 'That's it, he's going to give me a propaganda lesson: "Richard Sorge, the hero of our time, the superman of our intelligence system, who passed on the date of Hitler's invasion, was betrayed by the bureaucrats of Moscow . . ." et cetera, et cetera. Ancient history.' But Shakh simply told me about Sorge's last moments. I only knew, like

everyone else, that the Japanese had executed him in forty-four after
three years of imprisonment. That's all. Well, at that final moment,
standing on the scaffold, Sorge called out in a strong, calm voice,
'Long live the Red Army! Long live the Communist International!
Long live the Communist Party of the Soviet Union!' Old-fashioned,
isn't it? Grotesque? I said as much to Shakh, in milder terms, it's true.
And he surprised me yet again. 'Do you think,' he said, 'Sorge didn't
know the true worth of Stalin and his clique? He certainly did, and
how! But it was by dying like that that he could show what those sons
of bitches were really worth!'"

I sensed that this man on the scaffold was your final argument. I
did not attempt to put in context his words as a condemned man. A
minute before death they had a right to stand unqualified. I was
watching you as you talked and sadly noticing all the signs that your
smile could no longer cover up: the strands of silver spreading
through your hair, the fine blue line of a vein imprinted on your
temple. You interrupted my look, which was no doubt too searching,
by taking a newspaper out of your bag. "Read that," you said.

It was a short column reporting the death of a certain Grinberg,
a critic of the Soviet government who had spent several years in the
camps, had been expelled to the West, and had run a dissident radio
station. The reporter noted that Grinberg had died in Munich in a
tiny flat, forgotten by everybody, with a jumble of papers on his bedside table: his writings that no longer interested anyone, bills that he
was unable to pay, letters.

"Can you guess who they're talking about?"

For a few seconds I delved into my memories both in Russia
and the West. Grinberg . . . No, the name meant nothing to me.

"The man who spun that top in the art gallery in Berlin, do
you remember? Almost . . . ten years ago. You see, he's lost his battle
as well."

We sat for a moment without speaking. Then you got up, leaving the newspaper on the next table, and murmured, "I'm not going

to play the gypsy and tell your fortune, but if you don't want to serve 'the new masters' it's time for you to go. Yes, go, withdraw from the game, get yourself forgotten, disappear. After all, it'll only be one more change of identity."

That night you tried to hold back your tears, so as not to wake me. I was not asleep but remained still, knowing that in your thoughts, and in these tears, I was already living under that new identity, in that distant life without you.

I had used up too many lives to consider the one I was embarking on without you in the West as a real wrench from the past. The Western World was, in truth, too familiar to us to deserve the harsh and weighty name of exile. You were right; to begin with, at least, it was no more than another identity. And I already knew that the best way to adopt a country, to adapt to it as quickly as possible, was to imitate. Basically, integration means no more than imitation. Some people are so successful at this that they end up expressing the character of a country better than its natives, very much in the manner of those professional impersonators who can take such and such a well-known personality and set alongside him a copy that is more authentic than the original, a distillation of all his physical mannerisms, a digest of all his tricks of speech. And yet it is at the moment when he has succeeded that a foreigner discovers the unspoken goal of this game of imitation: to make oneself similar in order to stay different. To live as they live here as a way of protecting your remote and distant self. To imitate to the point of splitting yourself in two and, by letting your double speak, gesticulate, and laugh for you, to escape back in your thoughts to those whom you should never have abandoned.

At first my conviction that I should see you again within a short space of time was only natural. By imitating daily life and material survival I was earning the right to this expectation, to journeys to European cities where meeting you seemed likely. I told myself it would not even be a case of rediscovering one another but quite simply of your quiet voice one evening on the telephone, or your figure emerging from the flood of faces and coats on a railroad platform. I cannot recall how many months it was before this confidence began to fade. At the same moment, perhaps, when I realized I had never stopped talking to you, rehearsing with you over and over, the years I had spent with you, justifying myself, in fact, in a desperate attempt at truth.

The idea then came to me of making a precise note of dates, places, recollecting names, signposting our shared past. It felt like finding oneself in the kingdom of the dead. Several countries, including our own, had meanwhile disappeared, their names and frontiers had changed. Among the people you and I had mixed with, fought against, or assisted, some were living under other identities, others were dead, still others had settled down into this modern era, in which I often felt like a phantom, a ghost from an increasingly archaic age. But, overwhelmingly, my striving after precise details was taking me away from what we had truly experienced. I tried to make a list of the political forces at work, the causes of conflicts, the notable heads of state. My notes resembled a strange reportage emanating from a nonexistent world, a void. I realized that in place of this inventory of facts, with its pretensions to historical objectivity, I should be describing the quite simple, often invisible, subterranean fabric of life. I recalled you sitting on the threshold of a house, your eyes lost in the light of the sunset. I again saw that young soldier's arm, that wrist with a leather bracelet, in the shell of a gutted armored car. The beauty of a child who, a few yards away from the fighting but a thousand leagues removed from all its madness, was building a little pyramid from still-warm cartridge cases. With tightly shut eyes, I traveled back to that house on the shores of a frozen lake, the drowsiness of that house you had sometimes told me about. More and more often I found myself admitting that what was essential was condensed into these glimpses of the past.

★

One day, answering the telephone, I thought I could hear your voice, almost inaudible in the susurration of a call that seemed to be coming from the other end of the world. I called out your name several times, mine too, the last ones we had been known by. After a dull crackling, a faultless connection was made, and I heard, too close to my ear now, a swift singsong delivery in an Asiatic language (Vietnamese or Chinese, perhaps), a very shrill and insistent woman's voice, giving continuous little giggles or sobs, it was impossible to tell which. For several days the sound of that brief, infinitely remote whispering stayed in my mind, that impossible double of your voice, swiftly obliterated by the screeching of the Asian woman.

The whispering, which I had thought I could recognize as your voice, reminded me of an evening in days gone by, in that city on fire outside our window with its torn mosquito netting. I remembered how the proximity of death and our complicity in the face of this death had given me the courage that night to tell you something I had never previously admitted to anyone: the story of the child and the woman hiding deep in the mountains, the words crooned in an unknown language.

I knew now that I was incapable of telling the truth of our age. I was neither an objective witness, nor a historian, and certainly not a wise moralist. All I could do was to continue that story, interrupted then by the coming of night, by the journeys that awaited us, by fresh wars.

I began to talk, seeking simply to preserve the tone of our conversation in the dark long ago, the bitter serenity of words spoken with death close at hand.

The words I silently addressed to you conjured up the white-haired woman and the child once more—but ten years after the night of their escape. A December evening, a little town lost in snow close to a switching yard, a few miles away the shadow of a big city, the city which its inhabitants, in their confusion, still call by the name that has been taken away from it, Stalin's. The woman and the child are sitting in a room that is low and meagerly furnished but clean and well-heated, on the top floor of a massive wooden house. The woman has changed little in ten years, the child has turned into an adolescent of twelve with a thin face, a shaven head, his hands and wrists red with cold.

The woman, her head bowed toward the lamp, is reading aloud. The adolescent stares at her face but does not listen. He has the look of one who knows a brutal and ugly truth, a look fully aware that the other person is in the process of camouflaging this truth beneath the innocent routine of a habitual pastime. His eyes focus on the woman's hands as they turn the page and he cannot help pulling a quick, dismissive face.

The boy knows that this room, with its reassuring coziness, is hidden away in a great dark *izba,* a log house swarming with lives, cries, arguments, sorrows, bouts of drunkenness. You can hear the long-suffering sobs of a woman in the room next door, the tapping of a cobbler's little hammer in the apartment opposite, the cry of a voice calling after clattering footsteps, amplified by the stairwell. And under the windows, in the winter dusk, the ponderous passing of trains, whose loads can be glimpsed—long tree trunks, blocks of concrete, machinery under tarpaulins.

The boy tells himself that this woman reading aloud is totally foreign to him. She's a foreigner! From a country that, to the inhabitants of that town, is more remote than the moon. A foreigner who has long since lost her original name and answers to the name of Sasha. The one trace that still links her to her improbable native land is this language, her mother tongue, which she is teaching the boy on Saturday evenings, when he obtains permission to leave the orphanage and come to this great black *izba*. He stares at her face, her lips, as they emit strange sounds, which, nevertheless, he understands.

Who is she in reality? He remembers old stories she used to tell him, now overlaid by the new experiences of his childhood. It seems she was the friend of his grandparents, Nikolai and Anna. One day she took the boy's father, Pavel, into her house. She is the woman who crossed a suspension bridge, holding onto the worn ropes and carrying the child by his shirt gripped in her teeth.

These shadowy figures, who are the boy's only family, seem insubstantial to him. He listens to what the woman is reading: through the canopy of foliage a young knight catches sight of a castle keep. The boy's face sharpens, his lips tighten into a defiant grin. He is getting ready to tell this woman the truth that he now knows, the brutal, bald truth she is trying to cover up with her "canopies," "keeps," and other fancy, old-fashioned rubbish.

It is a truth that burst forth that morning at the orphanage when a little gang leader, surrounded by his henchmen, yelled these words at him, half words, half spittle, "Look. Everyone knows about your father. The firing squad shot him like a dog!"

All the truth in the world was concentrated in this spat-out remark. It was the very stuff of life. His assailant certainly could not tell how the boy's father had died, but he knew that's all there was in their orphanage: children of parents fallen from grace, often former heroes, who had died in prison, executed so as not to tarnish the country's image. The children invented fathers for themselves who were polar explorers trapped by ice, pilots who were missing in the war. Now this spittle-word has deprived him forever of a tacitly agreed fiction.

The woman breaks off from her reading. She must have sensed his inattention. She gets up, goes to the wardrobe, takes out a hanger. The boy gives a little cough, preparing a harsh tone of voice in which to interrogate, accuse, mock. Especially to mock these Saturday evenings, once a paradise to him, as she read aloud amid the clatter from the railroad and the drunken sobs, there at the heart of that great snow-covered, grudgingly inhabited void which is their country. He turns to the woman, but what she says anticipates by a second the words he already feels burning in his throat.

"Look, I've made this for you," she says, unfolding a shirt of coarse gray-green cotton. "A real soldier's tunic, wouldn't you say? You could wear it on Monday."

The boy takes the gift and remains dumb. With a mechanical gesture he strokes the fabric, notices the lines of stitching, absolutely regular although done by hand. By hand . . . with sudden pain he thinks of her right hand, the hand wounded by shrapnel, those numb fingers that must have been forced to master the to-and-fro of the needle. He understands that all the truth in the world is nothing if you omit this hand streaked with a long scar. That the world would make no sense if one forgot the life of this woman, come from abroad, who has unflinchingly shared the destiny of that great white void, with its wars, its cruelty, its beauty, its suffering.

He sinks his head lower and lower so as not to show his tears. The woman sits down, ready to begin reading again. Just before her first sentence he blurts out in a halting whisper, "Why did the firing squad kill him?"

The woman's reply does not come straight away. From one Saturday to the next, it will take several months. She will speak of a family in which, little by little, the boy comes to recognize people who had previously only existed in the misty legends of his childhood. Her recital will reach its conclusion one summer's evening after the sun has set, in the still warm and fluid air that bathes the steppes.

It was this light that I had in my mind's eye as I told my silent story, relating to you what Sasha had told me.

3

The horse turned its head slightly, its eye violet, reflecting the brilliance of the sunset, the sky clear and cold. Nikolai slipped his hand beneath its mane, gently patted its warm neck, heard a brief, plaintive sigh in reply. They were walking along the edge of a forest which, at nightfall, seemed endless and gave off the scent of the last sheets of ice lurking in the thickets. Nikolai knew that at any moment the horse would repeat the maneuver, a look turned toward its rider, an imperceptible slowing down of its pace. He would then have to chide it gently, in a soft voice, "For shame, lazybones! He wants to turn in already. Very well, if that's how it is, I'll have to sell you to the bandits. See how you like that." At these words the horse lowered its head, with an air at once resigned and sulky. After their two years at war together it even understood its rider's jokes.

These hours of dusk were the best time to avoid meeting anyone. You could still see where the horse was putting its feet but in the open camps scattered across the plain the soldiers were already lighting fires and it was easier to skirt around them. He had to avoid the Reds, whose troops he had just quit. To avoid the Whites, for whom he was still a Red. To steer clear of armed bands, who varied their color to suit their looting. And the forest in spring, with the leaves still in bud, offered poor protection.

He had already been riding for more than a week, first traveling up the course of the Don, then turning off toward the east. The steppe, up till then monotonous and flat, was now broken up by forests and valleys. There were more villages. During the first days he took his direction from the river and from the sun. Everywhere it was the same limitless Russian soil. But the closer he came to his own village the more his perception seemed to sharpen. As if the lands he was crossing had changed in scale, so that places came into focus with more and more detail. The day before, still dimly, he thought he had recognized the white steeple of the district capital. That morning a bend in a river, with the bank all trodden down at the approach to a ford, reminded him of a journey he had made before the civil war. Now he was almost sure he could travel clear of the forest before nightfall and link up with a road they used to take to go to the fair in the town. Yes, the corner of the forest, then a sandy slope, then, off to the right, this road. Half a day's trot from home.

During his long journey Nikolai had seen fields strewn with the bodies of men and horses left behind after a battle, villages populated by corpses hanging in front of doorways, and also that face he had at first taken for his own reflection when he peered into a well, before realizing . . . Dead people, fire, ruined houses no longer surprised him as long as he was a part of that immense ragged army, marching toward the south, driving the Whites before it. Killing and destruction was what war was all about. But now in the silence and emptiness of sunny days in May, and, above all, in the radiance of the evenings, the battlefields and deserted villages he skirted around were detached from the war, from its logic, from its causes, which a week earlier had seemed to justify everything. No more logic now. A field abandoned, as if capriciously. No sod turned, no seed sown for two springs. And there, on a slope running down to a little stream, the blackened, swollen carcass of a horse. And the cawing that rent the silence as the horseman approached.

Yet at the start of the war, it was the capriciousness of it that had carried him away. The commissars' talk was all of the new world, and the first novelty was that you could give up plowing. Just like that, on a whim. He was twenty-four at the time and not easily imposed on, but the freedom they offered him was too tempting: to do no plowing! It was intoxicating. They also said the bloodsuckers must be killed. Nikolai remembered Dolshansky, the landowner to whom their village had once belonged. Dolshanka, it was called. And he tried to picture this ancient nobleman as a bloodsucker. It was not easy. Among the peasants only the oldest had experienced serfdom. The village was rich. Dolshansky, long since ruined, lived in more poverty than some of the peasants, and had only one obsession: he spent his time carving the wood for his own coffin. No, it was better to picture the bloodsuckers in general, then one's anger mounted and slashing, shooting, and killing became simpler.

The horse lowered his head. His pace slowed and Nikolai felt a slight jolt: the filly walking behind, attached to a rope, was moving sleepily along and each time they slowed down it bumped its head against his horse's hindquarters. Nikolai smiled and thought he could hear something like a stifled laugh in the horse's brief snort. He did not scold him, simply whispered, "Come along, Fox, we've not far to go. Once we're past the forest we can rest!"

It was not his red coat but his cunning that had earned the horse this name. To begin with Nikolai had thought he was simply stubborn. In one of the first battles Fox had refused to launch into the attack with the others. Some fifty cavalrymen were due to come surging out of a copse and bear down on the soldiers preparing to ford a river with a convoy of wagons. The commanding officer had given the sign, the cavalry hurtled forward, accompanied by a whirlwind of broken branches. But Nikolai's horse reared up, pranced about on the spot, wheeled around, and would not go. He had beaten him savagely, kicking his sides with his heels, whipped him furiously, smacked his muzzle. The worst of it was that the success of the attack seemed a foregone conclusion. On the riverbank the soldiers, taken by surprise, did not even have time to pick up their rifles. And he, meanwhile, was still struggling with that damned horse. The cavalry were a hundred yards from the enemy, they were already crowing with delight when two machine guns, in a terrible flank assault, began to mow them down with the precision of an aim calculated in advance. The cavalrymen were falling before they realized it was a trap. Those who succeeded in turning around were pursued by a squadron that emerged from the scrub covering the bank. It was with only a handful of survivors that Nikolai returned to the camp. He still believed the business with his horse was pure coincidence and that he would have to get used to its peevish temperament. Later the coincidence repeated itself. Once, then twice, then three times. His horse would come to him, recognizing his whistle above the din of a camp of a thousand men and thousands of animals. Would lie down, obeying his word of command, would stop or break into a gallop, as if reading his mind. It was then that Nikolai began to call him "Fox" and to have that grim affection for him that arises in war, amid the mud and the gore, when in the first minutes after a battle each becomes violently aware that the other is still alive, silently close at hand, something even more astonishing than his own survival.

Along the trails of war Fox had seen horses drowning, horses ripped apart by shells, a stallion with its front legs torn off attempting to stand up again in a monstrous leap, and a team abandoned in the peaty depths of a bog: the horses sinking deeper and deeper, the prisoners of a useless gun they were hauling. And a White officer, a rope around his neck, being dragged along the ground by a horse gathering speed under the blows of a whip and the bawling of the soldiers. Fox must have understood in his own way that everything happening around him had long since eluded the grasp of these men, as they killed one another, beat their horses, made speeches. He also understood that his master was not fooled.

Nikolai did not seek to judge. Greatly aged over these two years, he was content to reach this very simple conclusion: it was certainly possible to give up plowing and sowing, but then the fields became covered in corpses.

The sleepy filly gently bumped into Fox's hindquarters with her muzzle again, for he had once more imperceptibly slowed his pace. There seemed to be a reassuring aura of happiness about the trust shown by this drowsy young animal. Nikolai inhaled deeply, recognizing the subtle sharpness of the snows hidden in the ravines and the dry scent of the meadows as they gave off the warmth of the day. Night had not yet fallen, to the west the sky was still a translucent purple, but, most important, close in front of them the density of the forest was already lightening, heralding the freedom of the plain and the road that led to Dolshanka. Nikolai coughed and began whispering to himself the questions and answers he was preparing, just to be on the safe side, afraid he might be interrogated about his sudden appearance by some local revolutionary tribunal or, more simply, by curious neighbors.

The story he had composed during his ride passed over one crucial fact in silence. He had fled his regiment because of a machine. An apparatus placed on the big black desk in the building occupied by staff headquarters for the front. Nikolai arrived in this town as a dispatch-rider, with a letter from the commanding officer of their regiment. In the courtyard he had noticed a score of civilians, old men and women with children, guarded by several soldiers. He had been told to wait in the corridor. The door to the office was half open and he could listen to the argument between the commissars. They had to decide whether or not to execute the hostages, the civilians in the courtyard, by way of reprisals. One of the commissars was shouting, "Not till we receive instructions from Moscow." Then suddenly an object sprang into life on the big black wooden desk. It was that strange apparatus around which they were all gathered. Nikolai, his curiosity getting the better of him, peered around the door. The machine was vomiting forth a long strip of paper that the commissars pulled out and read like a newspaper. "There! It's clear now," an invisible voice behind the door had proclaimed. "Read it! 'Shoot them as enemies of the revolution. Display notices in public places. . . .' "

Nikolai had handed over his letter, leaped onto his horse and, as he left the courtyard, had seen the "enemies of the revolution" being led behind the building. He no longer knew how many executions of this type he had already seen during those two years of war. But that white snake coming out of the machine constricted his throat with an anger and a grief that were of a quite different order. He was choking, tugging at the collar of his jacket, then suddenly brought his horse to a halt in the middle of the road and said aloud, "No, Fox, wait. Let's cut off across the fields instead."

To banish this memory, which constantly returned to him, Nikolai reached with his left hand behind his back, to feel the handles of the two new pails fastened to the saddle. Along with several sets of shirts and pants of coarse cotton they were his only spoils. He shook the buckets softly, the zinc made a reassuring, domestic clatter. It was his dream to come back from the war with two buckets, something really useful, and he never wearied of picturing them being carried on a yoke by a young woman, his future wife. There had already been one in his kit, which he had abandoned when he deserted. Going to sleep amid soldiers wandering about in the darkness and horses passing between sleeping bodies, he used to put his head in the pail to protect himself from being kicked by a hoof, which happened from time to time in these nocturnal caravans. And also to ensure it was not stolen. Leaving it behind was his greatest regret at the moment of flight. However, lose one, find ten. Passing through a burned-out village he had found these two new buckets discarded beside the well, at the bottom of which, seeing the swollen face of the drowned man, he had thought he was glimpsing his own reflection. And as he was leaving that place of death he had caught sight of a filly fastened to a tree. She could scarcely remain upright. The grass around the trunk was eaten down to the ground and for as high as she could reach the tree had no bark left. She must have been there for several days.

They would soon be out of the forest. The plain could already be sensed in the last red glow of the sunset through the latticework of the branches. Suddenly Fox repeated his ploy: his head tilted, his eye seeking the rider's gaze. Nikolai scolded him, threatened to sell him at the fair. The horse moved forward, but as if unwillingly. The sandy slope that ought to be opening out onto the intersection of the roads was slow to appear. On the contrary, by the last of the forest trees the road plunged downward, and the horse's hooves made a sucking sound, like cupping glasses. A little farther on old bundles of brushwood crackled underfoot. You could sense the damp of a river close at hand. They must go back up toward the forest and prepare for the night. As he went in among the trees, Nikolai made out a long glade beyond the bushes, whose budding leaves appeared blue in the deceptive transparency of the dusk.

He sensed the danger even before Fox halted. A swift shudder passed across the horse's hide. Fox came to a stop then began backing away in a nervous dance, pushing against the sleepy filly. "Wolves," thought Nikolai and he grasped the butt of the rifle behind his back. The horse continued stamping and snorted jerkily, as if driving flies away. The shadows in among the trees were already too deep, the eye could no longer make out shapes. And the moon, very low, baffled the vision with its milky shimmering. The tree trunks acquired doubles with pallid highlights. As yet invisible, someone or something was watching them.

Fox shied suddenly, dragging the filly along behind him. A black smudge, a scrap of bristling fur, sprang up almost at their feet and disappeared into the underbrush. It was in following the animal's flight that Nikolai lowered his eyes and saw them. At the corner of the glade, in the murky gloaming, these heads emerging from the earth

ANDREÏ MAKINE

and, closer to the bushes, the shambles of several bodies stretched out on the ground.

Nikolai's first impulse was to turn back, ready to move away, almost reassured by his discovery, less dangerous than an encounter with the living. But, a moment later he thought it would make sense to examine the method of execution and thus to see what he ran the risk of encountering on the road next morning. He leaped to the ground, left Fox, who was still trembling, approached on foot.

Ordering prisoners to dig their own graves and burying them alive was not uncommon during that war, he knew. What perplexed him, rather, was the anarchic manner in which the killers had acted in this glade. Some of those buried had had their faces slashed with a saber blow, one of them had been decapitated, as if his torment did not suffice. Then Nikolai reflected that the buried men must have begun cursing their enemies as they prepared to leave and thus provoked the massacre. They must also have yelled so as to be finished off, to avoid having to witness the sly circling of wolves around their defenseless heads when evening came. Nikolai imagined their shouts, the return of the soldiers, the coup de grâce, the silence. There were also men shot down with bullets, in haste no doubt, or in a gesture of idleness.

Nikolai went back to Fox, fondled his cheek and told himself the two of them had both been more frightened by the leaping of the little dark carnivore gnawing at the corpses than by the heads sticking out of the earth. As he was remounting he heard the filly groaning softly. He recalled that Fox had jostled her when he backed off and might have pulled the knot in the halter too tight. He dismounted again, slackened the rope, ruffled the young animal's mane. Suddenly the groan was repeated, but it came from the glade.

"Whatever happens, he'll die," thought Nikolai, placing his foot on the stirrup. It was no longer a groan but a long sigh of pain hissing in the darkness. Nikolai hesitated. He pictured the glade at night, the buried man seeing the wolves approaching or feeling the teeth of a rodent. He seized his rifle and walked toward the dead.

Among the wounded men who had to be finished off in wartime he knew two types: the first knew their wound was fatal and thanked their executioner with their eyes, the second, much more numerous, clung to the half day of suffering that was left to them to live. He strode across the glade that was still once more. Some of the heads were bowed toward the earth, others, rigid, seemed as if they had fallen silent at his approach. One of them was grinning in a grimace of pain. "So it's him," thought Nikolai and he lowered the barrel of the rifle toward the back of the man's neck. He had no time to squeeze the trigger. From the other side of the clearing the lamentation started again, more distinct and as if conscious that he was there examining the slain.

He found him at some distance from the others. A very young soldier whose shaven head rose up from a dark mound. Nikolai leaned over, touched the buried man's neck, found no wound on it. The soldier opened his eyes and groaned at length with a rhythmical sound, as if to prove that he was indeed a human being. Nikolai walked toward Fox ("I'm leaving now! Let them all go to hell!" a voice whispered inside him), hesitated, took out a flask, went back toward the head. The soldier drank, choked, his cough sounded almost alive. Nikolai began to dig, first with his hands to free the neck, then, when he reached the shoulders, with an ax blade. He liberated the back and, as he had expected, found the arms forced behind him and bound together with wire. Going down deeper, he noted with satisfaction that the soldier had not been buried standing up, but kneeling, to save time, no doubt.

Now he must lift him out. Nikolai placed himself behind the still-inert body, found a good purchase for his feet, took hold of the soldier under his arms. And at once let him go. In gripping the buried person, his fingers had just pressed against a woman's breasts.

He took hold of one of the freed hands, turned it toward the moon to examine it. The hand was frozen, bruised, black with earth. But it was a woman's hand all right, he could not be mistaken.

With a man everything would have been easier. He would have tipped him onto his back and then heaved him out of his hole. But with her . . . Muttering oaths that he was not even aware of, Nikolai dug at the front of the body. His fingers touched the remnants of a coarse wool garment and bare skin came through where it was torn. Further down the earth was warm, heated by the living energy spreading outward before being extinguished.

The woman said nothing, her half-closed eyes did not seem to see the man digging her out. Lying in front of her, Nikolai thrust aside the earth in broad armfuls, like a swimmer. It was when he arrived at the middle of the body and disengaged her belly that, all of a sudden, he raised himself up on his knees and shook his head, as if to rid himself of a mirage. Then he leaned forward and, already with a grown man's authority, felt the torso stained with earth, the round belly, heavy with a life.

She remained motionless, crouching close to the great fire he had lit in a recess in the steep riverbank. Two buckets filled with water were heating, suspended above the flames. Nikolai worked as he would have done in building a house or at a blacksmith's forge. Precise, confident actions. The thoughts colliding with one another in his head had no connection with what he was doing. "What are you going to do with her? What if she dies tomorrow morning? What about the child?" He also told himself that generally in these killings they opened the bellies of pregnant women and trampled on the infants. And that the killers in this glade were probably drunk or in too much of a hurry. And that they had already killed so many people during the war they were becoming lazy. He did not listen to himself. His hands broke sticks, drew charred wood out of the fire, spread it out on the clay of the riverbank. When the earth was sufficiently hot he trampled the embers, covered them with young branches, one armful, then another, and laid out the woman's unresponsive body on this warm couch. The water in the buckets was already boiling hot. He mixed it with the river water. Then he undressed the woman, threw her rags into the fire and began to bathe the body smeared with mud and blood. He coated it gently with still-warm ashes, turned it over, washed it, drew water from the stream, put it on again to heat. At each new rinsing the bitter stench of defilement and earth was dissipated a little more, carried away by a blackish trickle that lost itself in the river. It was the scent of young foliage steeped in hot water that now emanated from this woman's body. Returning to life, the woman for the first time looked up and focused on Nikolai, a look that finally expressed comprehension. She sat with her arms folded across her breast in the middle of a little lake that steamed in the night. He wanted to question her but changed his mind, drew a new shirt from his pack and began rubbing the body, which was unresisting, like a child's body. He dressed her in two other shirts, helped her to put on some pants, laid her down beside the fire, wrapped in his long cavalryman's coat. During the night he went to sleep for a few minutes, then got up to stoke the fire. He moved away in search of wood and turned, saw their fire and a shifting circle of light, surrounded by darkness, defined by the dancing of the flames. And this sleeping body, an incredibly foreign, unknown being, which seemed to him, he could not say why, very close.

Feeling his way, he gathered up dead branches, then turned to see the fire. Sometimes a scarlet flash glittered in the darkness. It was Fox lifting his head and seeking him with his eye by the light of the flames. The silence was such that Nikolai could hear the horse's breathing from a long way off, little sighs, now sharp, now reassured. And when he came back toward the fire he had the strange feeling that he was returning home.

★

In the morning they crossed the place where the rutted road was piled high with bundles of brushwood, advanced up a valley still white with mist, and finally found the meeting of the ways he had vainly sought the previous evening. Several times Nikolai tried to talk to the young woman, whom he had mounted on Fox's back, deciding to go on foot himself. She did not reply, sometimes smiling, but her smile resembled the tensing of a face on the brink of tears. Finally, toward noon, when they needed to make a halt to eat something, he lost his temper somewhat, irritated by her refusal to speak, "Listen, what's the matter with you? Why don't you say anything? It's finished. We're far away. They won't harm you any more. At least tell me your name."

The young woman's face twisted into a grimace, she tilted her head back slightly and forced open her lips. Between her teeth, in the place of a tongue, Nikolai saw a broad, oblique gash.

When he had recovered his wits, he realized that she had been mutilated so that she could no longer tell what she had seen. But tell it to whom? Everyone saw the same thing during these years of war. Moreover, how could one describe those heads in the clearing, those eyes being extinguished one by one? While the birds built their nests on the branches above them.

Dolshanka, half depopulated during the war, did not notice his return. The village had been scoured by so many waves of armed men, Reds, Whites, anarchists, bandits pure and simple, and then Reds again, by so many lootings, fires, and deaths, that the villagers were no longer surprised at anything. There was just one old woman who asked him as he was passing in the street, "Tell me, soldier, is it true the Bolsheviks have abolished death?" Nikolai nodded.

Over several weeks, before the child was born, he had time to teach the young woman to read and write. It was perhaps the greatest pride of his life: he never boasted about rescuing her from the tomb but he enjoyed talking about the lessons he gave her in the evenings, after the wearisome labor of plowing. Thanks to his teaching she could tell him her first name, writing it out in capital letters: Anna. And choose a name for the child: Pavel. And sign the papers on the occasion of their marriage. A girlhood friend of Anna's, who came to see them at Dolshanka from time to time, quickly got used to these words, thoughts, questions or answers, traced on a sheet of paper or in the dust on a road. Her friend spoke with a slight accent. From the south, Nikolai reckoned. He told himself that his wife must have had the same lilting voice as this Sasha.

For his part, he did not need the angular letters to understand her. The work on the land, the silence of their house, the lives of the animals, none of this had any need of words. He and Anna would look at one another for a long time and smile. During the daytime, catching sight of one another from afar, they would wave, without seeing the expressions on one another's faces but picturing the tiniest detail.

The world around them was becoming more and more talkative. People held forth about work instead of working. They made decrees for the happiness of the people and let an old woman starve to death in her *izba* with its collapsed roof. Above all there was the one who talked about the workers, that young, scabby little muzhik they called Goldfish, on account of his red hair, who had never plowed a furrow in his life. And those who promised happiness, like that man, ageless, faceless, expressionless, you might have said, so pale and evasive were his eyes, that unfrocked monk, who chose to be called Comrade Krassny. This champion of happiness never smiled, included the word "kill" in every sentence, and displayed particular ruthlessness toward anything even remotely connected with the Church. When it came to it, the one Nikolai preferred to these two was the former sailor, Batum, an emissary of the town soviet who at least did not conceal his true nature. He robbed home distillers and drank himself, lived openly with two mistresses and, when the peasants challenged him, chorussing, "You have no right . . ." would drown their complaints with his merry croak, "Here's my right!" roaring with laughter and patting the enormous holster of the automatic pistol at his thigh. There were many more besides. They all called themselves "activists." They talked endlessly, made everyone listen to them, and would not let anyone else utter a word. Nikolai tried once, arguing with a speech by Comrade Krassny. Goldfish exploded, his eyes contracted with anger, "We'll have to shorten your tongue, like your good wife's!" Nikolai lunged at him but came up against the barrel of the automatic pistol. Batum was drunk. He could well have fired it without even feeling the trigger beneath his finger. Nikolai walked out of the House of the Soviet. It had once been Count Dolshansky's home.

Sometimes, as the plow jolted slowly and ponderously along, Nikolai told himself that this whole new order of things was only a transient clouding of people's minds, comparable to the posturing of a drunkard. Yes, it was a kind of hangover that would one day come to an end of its own accord. How could they change essential things, all these prattlers in leather jackets? This Krassny, whose principal achievement was mobilizing activists to tear down the domes of churches in the vicinity of Dolshanka. Or Batum, whose repertoire of gestures, when he did not have a bottle in his hand, was limited to two: unbuttoning his fly and reaching for his revolver. Nikolai shook his head, smiled, leaned heavily on the handles of the plow. No, they were powerless against the course of this plowshare polished by the earth, against this earth, open in the expectation of seed, against this wind that still had a snowy chill but was already mingling with the warm exhalation of the plowed lands.

At other moments when he talked with the villagers, who grew increasingly wary of speaking about such things, or learned that yet another committee had been created (Committee of the Poor, Committee of the Godless, Committee of the Horseless—it seemed to him as if the activists invented a new one every day), Nikolai no longer felt this confidence in the solidity of things. He stopped at the end of the field to let Fox catch his breath and ran his eyes over the plain that sloped gently up toward the houses of Dolshanka, pictured all those people who, a few years before, during the war, had passed through these places, killing, dying, burning houses, raping women, torturing men, burying them alive in fields reverted to wilderness. Then he said to himself that this seed, nourished with so much blood, was bound to produce a good crop. And that perhaps the noisy efforts of the activists had a hidden force, whose meaning for the moment eluded him.

This force made itself manifest in the spring of 1928 in the same field amid the morning warmth of the same plowing. Without interrupting his slow progress behind the horse, out of the corner of his eye Nikolai observed the approach of four figures from the village: Goldfish, Krassny, Batum, and a stranger dressed in a long leather coat, no doubt an inspector eager to monitor the first steps taken toward collectivization. A group of activists, men and women, followed them some paces behind. Nikolai knew why they were coming. For several months now the talk in Dolshanka had been of nothing else. The posters pasted on the door of the soviet announced it clearly: the organization of a kolkhoz, a collective farm. The only obscure point in Krassny's declarations concerned sewing needles. The peasants had not fully understood if these had to be handed in to the kolkhoz, along with their animals and their tools. Some people, afraid of being suspected of opposing the Party's policies, had even brought their crockery to the soviet. Others were biding their time in the hope that this excess of madness would abate. Nikolai was of their number.

He finished the furrow and, when he reached the headland, stopped the horse and waited. Following the activists' progress across the field, he felt a choking rage that reminded him of a day long ago: disconsolate hostages gathered in a courtyard and that slim paper snake slithering out of the telegraphic apparatus to proclaim death. He had not slept a wink the night before, wrestling with thoughts that led nowhere. "Run away, taking the family with him? Burn the house down so as to leave nothing for those parasites? But run away where? In neighboring villages it's even worse, they're putting people in prison who own two horses. Into the forest? But how could we live there, with a child of eight, when the nights are still cold?" Picturing this escape, he saw the whole country peopled with activists, entangled in coils of ticker tape.

They were drawing close. Nikolai bent down, removed a tuft of dry grass that had become wrapped around the plowshare and, with his other hand, checked his secret store: in the rounded rut by the headland his fingers brushed against the handle of an ax. Now he felt free. No more reflection, no more hesitation. They would surround him, he would lean over, as if to change the angle of the plowshare, would seize the ax, would bring it down on Batum, then on the inspector. Goldfish, the most cowardly, would try to escape. Krassny, incapable of action, would start yelling. He felt as if his head were enveloped in icy, liquid glass. With hallucinatory precision he saw the gleam of a turned furrow, a black beetle scurrying along, climbing onto his boot. The wind stirred for a moment and he could hear the words, still indistinct, of the people coming toward him.

He looked at them, then lifted his eyes higher, toward the slope rising up from the plain, where the first *izba*s of Dolshanka could be seen. And, as he did from time to time when plowing, saw the figure of Anna. She was standing there, motionless, the two pails placed at her feet. At this distance he was unable to discern the expression in her eyes and he knew that she could not but maintain her silence. But, more than any voice, more than the trembling of her eyelids that he could sense, it was the very air of that morning that suddenly diverted him from the moment he had lived through. The air was gray, light. The wind bore with it the humid sharpness of branches scarcely touched by greenery and the last resistance of the remaining snowdrifts hidden in the woods. Nikolai felt that the woman over there, his wife, Anna, and he at the other end of the plain, were linked by this air, by its pale light, the mark of a spring day, one of the springtimes in their lives.

The four men slowed down before accosting him, as if they were surrounding a wild beast ready to spring. For a second he thought he had forgotten their names and the purpose of their expedition. He was still far away, lost amid the suddenly awakened memory of all the springtimes, of all the snows, of all the dawns and all the nights he had lived through and seen with Anna. Especially that night on the banks of a river, beside a wood fire, on the road back from death.

He greeted the delegation of the activists with a tilt of his head. And made an effort to restrain a smile. Their extremely grave and worthy expressions contrasted with their boots, transformed into veritable elephants' feet by the clods of clay stuck to them. In place of the anger of the past months, Nikolai experienced only the irritation provoked by the stupidity of children at a difficult age, stupidity that is dangerous and impossible to avoid until "they get over it." Goldfish took a pace forward, looked behind him, to make sure that Batum was there, and launched into a carefully prepared tirade.

"So, bourgeois landowner, you don't read the newspapers, you treat the decisions of the soviet with contempt."

Here Krassny intervened, but in tones which formulated the condemnation rather better: ". . . and you continue to make use of property that belongs to the people. And you are not prepared to hand it over!"

Nikolai pretended to listen with an attentive and respectful air. And he spoke without abandoning this expression, even adding to it the look of an obtuse but well-meaning peasant.

"Hand it over to the soviet? But how could I hand it over? It would be the worst kind of fraud!" he exclaimed, with an air of offended honor.

The activists exchanged glances, disconcerted.

"Fraud, how's that? Now what do you mean by that?" the inspector exclaimed in amazement, his voice becoming increasingly loud and rasping.

"Well, take a look at this, Comrade Inspector!"

And profiting from the confusion, Nikolai grasped him by the elbow and led him toward the horse.

"Now, just take a look. Do you think it'd be honest to hand over to the kolkhoz a horse in a state like this? Have you seen these hooves? But how to get it shod? The last blacksmith we had was arrested by Comrade Batum two weeks ago. Yes, the blacksmith, Ivan Gutov. And look at that. That's not a plow, any more. It's scrap metal. And why? Because the screw for adjusting the plowshare's broken. But as the forge is closed . . . I tell you, hand on heart, giving this to the kolkhoz would be worse than fraud. It'd be . . ." (Nikolai lowered his voice) "It'd be sabotage!"

It was the key word of the age, the conclusion of so many verdicts published in all the newspapers, the word Krassny was so fond of in his speeches. This time the three activists avoided the inspector's gaze. Batum, shifting his feet, was removing the mud from one boot with the other. Krassny cleared his throat. Goldfish licked his lips. Nikolai sighed and, without giving them time to react, announced in resigned tones, "But, after all, if Comrade Krassny decides it's better like that, there's nothing I can do. I'll bring the horse and the plow right away. Why delay? I'll come with you. And the secretary will give me a paper to say the kolkhoz accepts broken implements."

He leaned on the plow, lifting the plowshare, and urged the horse on. Goldfish nervously seized one of the reins.

"No, wait, you can go on plowing. Today . . ." he stammered and turned to seek the inspector's approval. Nikolai pretended to be outraged.

"How can I go on plowing? With a horse that's no longer mine? Do you take me for a thief? No, if it's decided, it's decided. I'll take it to the kolkhoz, I'll hand over the plow. Handed over, received, signed. This afternoon I'll bring the cart as well. Here, take the ax, for a start!"

Nikolai knew that the yard in front of the House of the Soviet was piled high with confiscated farm carts, furniture, piles of crockery. The rooms inside resembled the store for a great village bazaar. Goldfish stretched out his hand to take the ax, but withdrew it at once, as if to avoid a trap. The inspector had come to Dolshanka to see how, without losing face, they could calm down this mania for expropriation. It was he who resolved matters.

"Here's what we're going to do. I see, comrade, that you take the welfare of the kolkhoz to heart. A good deal more than some others" (he gave Goldfish a stern look). "I'm going to propose your candidature for the post of head of the collective stable. As for the blacksmith, I have a couple of words to say to Comrade Batum."

Nikolai resumed his work, plowing a furrow over the footsteps of the retreating activists. Goldfish and Batum were trying to convince the inspector, waving their arms and beating their chests.

Nikolai looked up toward the rim of the plain and saw Anna. She was walking slowly away beside the trees in the main street.

Next day, with the blacksmith released, they shod the horse. The peasants were returning from the House of the Soviet, their arms piled high with recovered crockery and tools. That night a long convoy, coming from neighboring villages, passed under their windows: a long spluttering of weary sobs, punctuated by the rumble of wheels and the clatter of horses. Whole families who would never be seen again.

Watching his son living and growing, Nikolai lost the habit of going back in his mind to the earlier world. For Pavel was happy. He marched along in the middle of a troop of children his age, sang songs in celebration of the brave revolutionaries, and even came home from school one day with a photo: his class, two rows standing and one sitting down, with the bugler and drummer on one knee in front of them, all proud to be wearing the red scarves of the pioneers, and behind them, on a broad strip of calico, these words painted in white letters: "Thank you, Comrade Stalin, for our happy childhood!" Talking to his son, Nikolai realized that there was some truth in this stupid inscription. The boy really believed that the Red Army was the finest and strongest in the world, that the workers of all countries aspired only to live like the people of Dolshanka, and that somewhere in Moscow there existed that mysterious Kremlin, surmounted with red stars, where the being dwelt who spent his days and nights thinking about every inhabitant of their immense country, who always made wise and just decisions, and unmasked enemies. Pavel also knew that his father was a hero, for he had fought against the Whites, those same Whites who had mutilated his mother. He detested the kulaks and, echoing the stories from his manuals, called them "bloodsuckers." One day, when leafing through his son's history book, Nikolai came upon the portrait of an army leader whom he had encountered during the civil war. The soldier's face had been carefully crossed out in ink. He had just been declared an "enemy of the people." Across the whole country, Nikolai reflected, in thousands and thousands of schools, millions of pupils were picking up their pens and, after a brief explanation from the teacher, blotting out these eyes, that brow, that mustache with waxed ends.

At such moments he longed to talk to his son about that earlier world, of his own youth before the war, before the revolution. All you had to do, he thought, was to make a subtraction, yes, subtract the present from the past and tell the difference in happiness, in liberty, in the lack of worries that the past contained. The arithmetic seemed so easy, but each time he tried to relive the old days the difference became blurred. For before the revolution there had also been a war, that of 1914 (and the bolsheviks had had no hand in that), carts piled high with the wounded and he a mere youth, on a field covered in corpses, weeping with pain, his horse killed and he unable to withdraw his leg, crushed beneath it. And at Dolshanka, long before the Bolsheviks arrived, the days were as rough and long as plowing, as tough as thick tree trunks beneath the saw, and tasted of hard-earned bread. So all that was left of the happiness of times gone by was just a few dawns, that cool wellspring in the hollow of a little valley on a day of harvesting in the blazing heat of summer, that road in the last snowstorm. As now. As always.

Not knowing whether to rejoice or to be desolate that these moments of happiness, though recurring, were so rare, Nikolai recalled that night beside a river, already long ago, Anna sleeping by the fire, the unique joy with which that instant was filled. In what time could he locate that night? The war, his escape, the country whose name and borders were still provisional, himself the enemy of both Reds and Whites, a woman whose name and life history were unknown to him. She, barely surviving death, the night scattering its stars over the river, the fire, the silence. All his happiness derived from that alone.

One day he tried to explain the earlier life to his son. And even thought he had found the words he needed. He spoke of the czar, of old Count Dolshansky, of the revolution. It was a warm, still October day. The fields were already bare, the riverbank where they sat was carpeted with long, yellowing grasses. Noticing the flight of wild geese in the sky, Nikolai realized that for several minutes now the boy had not been listening to him. The birds were reflected in the river's smooth flow and Pavel was following their reflection, which seemed to be traveling upstream, amid long willow boughs and some stranded boats. Nikolai fell silent, looked where his son was looking and smiled: this limpid gliding of the wings over the water was more beautiful than the flight itself.

After the famous spring of the confiscated needles there were two years of famine, a hundred dead in Dolshanka, several arrests. The disgust Nikolai had experienced that day at the sight of the telegraph machine became so familiar that he no longer noticed it. Everyone knew that the famine had been organized. But in order not to lose your reason, to survive in the midst of this madness, it was best not to think about it, it was better to concentrate on the straightness and depth of the furrow.

Besides, even during those years, they could still wake up in the middle of a beautiful October day with a flight of birds above the river. Or again on that day of great frost: coming home, Nikolai saw Anna beside the window, one hand on the cradle of their second child and the other holding a book. He went up to her, sat beside her, quite numb from the icy wind, glanced at the pages. It was a foreign book, Anna was looking only at the pictures, of men and women in ample old-fashioned clothes, of unknown cities. In the houses in the village one still came across these volumes from the scattered library of Count Dolshansky, and since people could not read them they used them for stoking up the fire or rolling a cigarette. "Now that, even if you asked me, I couldn't teach you!" he said, laughing, running his finger along the enigmatic letters. Anna smiled, but in a slightly distant way, as if she were trying to call to mind a forgotten word. There was infinite calm in their *izba* at that moment. The child was asleep, the fire hissed softly in the stove, the window, all covered in ice, blazed with the thousand scarlet granules of a sinking sun. This brilliance, this silence were enough for life. Everything else was a bad dream. Speeches, hate-filled voices talking about happiness. Fear of not being hard enough, not showing yourself to be happy enough, hate-filled enough toward all the enemies, fear, fear, fear. While all life needed was these minutes of a winter sunset, in a room protected by this woman's silence as she leaned over the sleeping child.

As in a bad dream, changes came, hard on one another's heels, contradicting one another, defying comprehension. One summer night Batum died in a hayloft at the center of a blaze started by his cigarette butt. His mistress escaped. He, being too drunk, was enmeshed in the bundles of hay. How could you comprehend that? This man, who had driven so many people to their deaths, had perished in the manner of a simple village drunk such as almost inspired pity. It was beyond the kolkhozniks' comprehension. Goldfish got married in the district capital and remained there with his wife, a woman with an enormous bosom who stood a whole head taller than her husband. This mass of flesh seemed to have engulfed the red-haired revolutionary, along with his volatile temper and all his grudges. You could see them together: he looked like a placid little official carrying crackers and a bottle of milk in a shopping bag. The inhabitants of Dolshanka shrugged their shoulders. Comrade Krassny's career within the Party apparatus was meteoric. His name, preceded by his latest title, appeared in the town newspaper on several occasions—and on the last of these without a title but with a qualifying phrase that had become current: "Unmasked traitor, lickspittle of the bourgeoisie, spy in the pay of the imperialists." Those who had known him at Dolshanka wondered why it had taken more than ten years to "unmask" him. But there was already a whole younger generation in the village to whom in this year of 1936, the names of those activists from the twenties meant nothing.

Thinking about these young people, Nikolai took note of the solidity of the new world. Little by little the revolution was casting aside the revolutionaries and life was reverting to essentials, land and bread. Gutov, the blacksmith, passed on his anvil to his son and was elected president of the kolkhoz. He was already a member of the Party and had drawn Nikolai into it, saying, "You need to join, neighbor, otherwise they're going to dredge up another Goldfish for us." For a long time now the portrait of Stalin in every house had become almost invisible in its conspicuousness, as familiar as an icon used to be in the old days. Nikolai had great faith in the endurance of the snows, the rains, the winds, in the constancy of the fields, in the blissful routine of days that would set everything to rights. And when the heads began to roll again in Moscow he thought of the vast stretch of plains, forests, snows that lay between them and the capital. With the hope of a weary man, he was eager to convince himself at any price.

In spring when the work was at its height, the president of the kolkhoz was arrested. They spent several nights without going to bed, watching at the window: Nikolai, Anna, Pavel (who had come home from the town for a week's holiday), and Sasha. Above all, they did not want to be surprised when they were asleep and find themselves in the black car only half-dressed, like so many people taken for questioning. No one spoke and Nikolai was glad he had not succeeded in explaining to his son the difference between their current lives and life in the old days. Now the young man could judge for himself.

The car arrived very early in the morning. Anna woke Nikolai who had fallen asleep sitting on a chair. They took him immediately. He just had time, as if gulping a rapid mouthful, to take note of what he was leaving behind: their faces, the hesitant wave of a hand, the light of a lamp on the table.

At the town, even before the start of the interrogation the examining magistrate declared that the president of the kolkhoz had told them "everything, absolutely everything," that their conspiracy had been "unmasked," and that it was in his own interest for him to confess the facts. The questions came hurtling at him but during the first few minutes Nikolai heard them as if through a wall: the former blacksmith's treachery had hit a raw nerve in him, found a vulnerable spot he had not been aware of. Then he thought about the tortures that could extract all kinds of calumny, grew calmer, and resolved to defend himself right to the end.

Listening to the magistrate, he realized that this man knew nothing about him, had not even the vaguest conception of where Dolshanka was or how its inhabitants lived and, in fact, had no file on him of any kind, just a dozen sheets of paper that needed to be substantiated by the accused's replies, so as to make a guilty man of him as quickly as possible. That night, in the cell, where two-thirds of the prisoners remained upright for lack of benches, Nikolai talked to an old man, who from time to time gave up to him his place by the wall, against which everyone was eager to lean. The old man was due to return to the camp for the second time, having already spent six years there. It was he who explained to Nikolai that the number of people found guilty was subject to planning, just like the tons of the harvest. And as the forecasts in the plan always had to be surpassed . . . They talked until morning. Before being taken for interrogation Nikolai learned that the old man was three years younger than himself. An old man of thirty-nine.

The judge was counting on settling the matter in an hour. After several questions, he announced the main charge, which the evidence given by the president of the kolkhoz made irrefutable: Nikolai had written scurrilous satires that his wife read out to the members of the kolkhoz, thus disseminating counter-revolutionary propaganda.

Nikolai managed not to betray his feelings. Calmly he explained why what was imputed to his wife was impossible. In the magistrate's eyes he thought he could see flitting past all the variations that would have made it possible to circumvent this line of reasoning. You could accuse Anna of an attempt on Stalin's life, of wanting to set fire to the Kremlin or poison the Volga. But you could not accuse her of speaking. "I shall send the doctor tomorrow for an expert opinion," barked the magistrate and he called the guard.

The doctor spent scarcely a minute in their house. When he took his leave he apologized, heaving a sigh and raising his eyes to heaven. It was Sasha who described the scene to him when Nikolai was finally freed.

Returning home after a week's absence, he paused beside the locked door of the smithy. Thanks to nights spent among prisoners packed close together, he could imagine what a man like Gutov must have experienced who had spent several months in those overflowing cells. He made an effort not to imagine the torture. And the nights following the torture, with his mouth filled with blood, his nails torn off. Gutov must have lived through that and in the course of one night, through the suffocating mists of pain, invented this accusation which would save those he denounced: Anna talked to the kolkhozniks. Continuing on his way, Nikolai noticed that beside the *izba* of the smithy the first grasses and flowers were already thrusting up in bright fresh tufts, as happened every spring.

With superstitious confidence, he allowed himself to believe that life had finally triumphed. And that Gutov's death, especially such a death, was a sufficient sacrifice. And that he and Anna had now paid their dues to the unexpected guest. All the books Anna had gradually accumulated in their house were in agreement about this ultimate justice: well-earned happiness, paid for by trials and suffering.

When, less than a year later, he found himself at the bedside where Anna lay dying, he had a momentary belief that he could understand everything, right to the end: life was no more complicated than the simpleton he had one day encountered in the neighboring village. A woman seated at the crossroads with her legs wide apart, very pale eyes that looked through you without seeing you, lips that babbled happily of "planting three sabers under every window of every *izba*," and hands that ceaselessly shuffled a little pile of fragments of glass, pebbles, tiny worn coins in the folds of her dress.

He shook himself, so as not to let himself be carried away toward this grinning folly. And saw Anna's gesture. She was offering him a little gray envelope. He took it, guessed he should not open it until the time came, and, hearing a noise, went to greet the doctor. In the doorway he passed Sasha coming in with a flask of water. Everything was repeating itself, as some months before, but in a different order: the doctor, silence, the proximity of death. Like the little fragments of glass juggled in the simpleton's blind hand.

Three days previously Anna had been returning from the district capital, walking along beside the river on ground that vibrated, awakened by the break-up of the ice, by the sounds of the thaw. The sunlight, the creaking collisions of ice floes, and the wild chill of the liberated waters were mingled together in a joyful giddiness. The people Anna passed had dazed looks, confused smiles, as if they had been caught drunk in broad daylight. When she went up to the old wooden bridge at the end of the village she thought for a second she must be drunk herself: the bridge no longer straddled the river but reared up, turned in the direction of the current. It must only just have been torn loose, for the children running between its handrails had not yet noticed anything, fascinated by the frenzied whirling of the ice blocks, and their crashing against the pillars. If she had been able to call to them she could have stopped them going to the end of the bridge. But all she could do was hasten her step, then run, then make her way down the frozen slope of the riverbank. Like beads on a broken necklace the children had slipped down into a gulf of black water. The rescue should have been a noisy one, attracting lots of people, but on the deserted riverbank in the sunshine there was just the sound of a little whimpering and the crunching of broken ice. Anna dove into the water, feeling with her hands for the little bodies that had just disappeared. She struggled against each second of cold, first pushed the children up onto the riverbank, then dragged them toward the nearest *izba*, undressed them, rubbed them down. Her own body was ice and, an hour later, fire.

It was only a month after the funeral that Nikolai found the forgotten envelope almost by chance. Elegant handwriting that he did not recognize and which had no connection with the capital letters he had taught Anna stared up at him. And yet it was indeed a letter from his wife. She told him her real name, the name of her father, the great landowner whose estate used to border on the lands belonging to Dolshansky, a distant relative of their family. She did not want to take the lie to the grave with her. She thanked him for having saved her life, for having taught her life. Nikolai spent several days getting used, not to Anna's absence, but to her new presence in the years they had lived together and in the years before. He had to picture Anna as a young girl who had lived in St. Petersburg, went on long journeys abroad, and whom nothing had prepared for meeting him and living in an *izba* at Dolshanka. Sasha had told him what the letter had not time to tell.

One night he woke up, struck by the vividness of what he had just dreamed. The light in this dream was the same pale light before the dawn as outside the window. He was walking toward a forest so tall that, even with his head tilted back, he could not see the tops of the trees. He was moving forward, guided by singing that drew him ever closer: its resonance embraced all the beauty of this forest still swathed in night mist, all the expanse of the sky as it began to grow pale, and even the delicate shapes of the leaves he brushed aside on his way. At the surface of his dream there fizzled a doubt: "She can't sing. . . . She's . . ." But he went on walking, recognizing the voice better and better.

He recounted this dream to Sasha, who still came to see them in Dolshanka, as in the old days.

A year and a half later, one fine morning in June, Nikolai was returning from the town on horseback. The sun was not yet risen and the forest beside which the road ran had the resonance of a vast, empty cathedral nave. The calls of the birds still had a muted, nocturnal sound. Before making his way up a sandy slope he turned aside, and went into the forest, searching for the place known only to himself. But more than twenty years later the glade of long ago was disappearing under a whole copse of aspen. He was about to rejoin the road when suddenly a thunder of hoofbeats arose. The noise was growing louder so rapidly that it could only be a horse ridden at full gallop. Nikolai tugged at the reins a little, and stationed himself behind a tree. A horseman appeared on the road. A soldier crouched over the mane of his horse, welded to it as if into a single dark arrow, streaking past the trunks of the birch trees. His face was frozen in a grimace, baring his teeth. "A madman," Nikolai said to himself, tossing his head. The dust swirled gently around the marks left by the flurry of hooves.

Passing through the village adjacent to Dolshanka, he noticed the simpleton sitting on a stack of felled pine trees. Several of the trunks had already been squared off, trickles of resin gleamed on their pink flesh, like drops of honey. The sight of this pale wood, ready to be erected into the wall of an *izba,* promised happiness. The simpleton was asleep, her mouth half open, as if she had some news to tell. Her hand, as she slept, continued to shuffle her glass treasures, scattered over the worn fabric of her dress.

On arrival at Dolshanka close to noon Nikolai saw a big crowd in front of the village soviet. The women were weeping, the men frowning, the children laughing and being cuffed. A voice repeated several times, mechanically, "Hitler, Hitler . . ." Others were saying, "The Germans." The war had just begun.

It seemed to him that there was no disruption in the sequence of days. Quite simply the normal routine of work in the fields now found correspondence in the parallel advance of the front line. The names of the fallen cities left him incredulous, these were already in the depths of Russia, where the presence of the Germans seemed like an optical illusion, a cartographical error. He remembered the films of the past few years: the enemy was always defeated close to the frontier. The songs he found himself humming promised, "Like Stalin, we'll confront the foe!"

Vitebsk, Chernigov, Smolensk . . .

One day even this bizarre topography disappeared. Cities were on the move, as if on a crumpled map. Routed Soviet soldiers fled through Dolshanka: the Germans had encircled several divisions. The village, surrounded, found itself on a strange territory located within the enemy army. The circle tightened, driving the villagers into the forest, then beyond the river all riddled with bullets, onto a charred wheatfield, and finally into the main street of the district capital, where there was still fighting. People stumbled about on this map that was being ripped apart under their feet, crumpled by tank tracks, pitted with explosions. With a rifle picked up close by a dead soldier Nikolai hid behind a fence observing the Germans' progress. They seemed not to notice the tremors of the map, advanced calmly, with precise and economical movements: a burst of gunfire, a house burned with a flamethrower, a tank clearing the street ahead of them.

He left his hiding place, the smoke from the blaze burned his eyes. A number of civilians ran across the road with a determined air. They must know the way out of the encircled town. He followed them as far as the long trains on the railroad sidings, near the station. One by one they dove under one train, then under another. When Nikolai climbed up from beneath the last train he just had time to catch sight of the German soldiers stationed at the bottom of the embankment, precisely where people were coming out. He did not feel the pain but had time to think of his son, already mobilized. "I must tell Pavel these people are machines." The soldiers kept firing, reloading, firing. If fugitives had continued to emerge from beneath the train these nine soldiers would have spent the rest of their lives killing them.

4

Pavel believed those minutes would continue ripping his sleep apart for long nights to come: the din of the caterpillar tracks a few inches above his head, the collapse of the trench he had fallen into when trying to get away ahead of the tanks. If he had not stumbled he would have continued running amid the breathless stampede and panic of the other soldiers. But he had slipped on a lump of clay, hurtled into a trench that was half dug and therefore quite shallow, had not had time to get up again. The roaring bulk had covered him with its shadow, the steel links of one track were hacking at the earth just above his face. For a moment he had felt as if he were being sucked into the entrails of the machine. The acid smell of the metal and the glaucous trail of the exhaust had filled his lungs. From beyond the trench cries and the crunch of bodies under the tank tracks could be heard through the throbbing of the engines.

That night, slumped down in a fir copse among some survivors from his company, he lay in wait for the return of those seconds spent under the tank. He fell asleep but the dream went off on a tangent, pushed open a secret door, translated everything into its own language, at the same time precise and oblique. Instead of tanks, a gigantic brand new machine tool with nickel-plated screws and levers covered in oil and grease. Its bowels vibrate with a rhythmic sound and disgorge punched disks at regular intervals. You have to slip your hand very nimbly into the coming and going of the mechanism and insert the steel plate into the press underneath the punch. And each time his hand goes in a little bit further, his body stretches up a little bit higher inside the machine, trying to avoid the rotation of the great cogwheels, the driving belts. Moreover the timing of the huge machine is not very well regulated. It is as if it senses the reaching out of the hand, the contortions of the body within its bowels. The fingers grasp a square of metal, the hand goes forward, the shoulder penetrates into the machine, the body worms its way in, edging between dozens of gears, crankshafts, cylinders. He manages to put the metal in place, withdraws his hand just before the punch comes down, and seeks to extricate himself. But all around him the machine is shuddering, without wasting a second, without the smallest opening via which he might reemerge. And through its noisy workings, he recognizes a room, light, and objects that come from his childhood.

The dream did not return on the nights that followed, for there were no nights. Always a flight toward the east, then an abandoned village that, during the brief hours of darkness, they attempted to transform into an entrenched camp. And in the morning, after disorderly resistance, a fresh retreat before the steady advance of the tanks and the German soldiers who smiled as they fired. The grinning of these men as they killed made a deeper impression on him than the tanks.

During those first weeks of the war he had to forget all he had learned during his military service. He still recalled the sergeant wetting his forefinger with saliva, raising it in the air to check the direction of the wind and explaining to them how much they needed to aim off. If anybody had spat on his finger to test the direction of the wind during these painful rearguard actions he would have been taken for a madman. The Germans fired their submachine guns and smiled. They responded with jerky small-arms fire from bolt-action rifles, often their only weapon at the start of the war. And they retreated, without being able to retrieve their wounded, without remembering the names of the villages surrendered. It seemed to him that he and his comrades in arms were fighting in a battle from one of his father's stories; their old-fashioned rifles, their troops of cavalry. On the opposing side quite a different war was being waged—a rapid sweep of armored vehicles across land turned upside down by aerial bombardment. Perhaps the Germans smiled when they saw the sabers flashing above the horses, as one smiles at the passing of an automobile several decades old, one that quaintly recalls a bygone age.

During these murderous days of the collapse there were, too, irrelevant little vignettes that sometimes made it hard to concentrate, to think only of the gray-green figure in one's sights. A dog, wounded by shrapnel, groaning and writhing on the spot, which looked their way with tears in its eyes. They had abandoned several comrades in fleeing from that burned-out hamlet, but it was the sight of the dog, that rust-colored ball with its broken back, that kept coming to mind. And in another place there was a sweet tangle of plants filled with the lazy buzzing of insects, the vegetation of a glorious summer that continued as if nothing were happening, just next door to *izba*s in flames, where people trapped inside were screaming. The soldiers of his detachment were hiding in a ravine, their rifles thrown to the ground, not a cartridge between them. The warm air, heady with the scent of flowers, was already growing heavy with the acrid emanations coming from the village. Later, a child's face glimpsed in a packed railroad car. Eyes that happily still understood nothing, that reflected a world from which death was still absent. The train set off. Together with other soldiers Pavel was in position around the station, hoping to keep the Germans at bay for the time it took the train to leave the town.

On his way out of a ruined village at the start of the autumn he picked up a page from a torn newspaper, an issue from the previous week. Reading it, you might have believed the enemy had only just crossed the frontier and was about to be driven back any day now. That night there was fighting some sixty miles from Moscow.

He had known for some time now why the Germans smiled when they fired. It was a grin that had nothing to do with joy, but was the unconscious grimace of a man whose hands are absorbing the recoil from a long burst of fire. Like most of his comrades in arms, Pavel was currently equipped with a German submachine gun, recovered in battle. And now they smiled like the Germans. And they no longer ran away in front of tanks, but dove into a trench, pretended to be dead, then got up and threw hand grenades. On awakening they would pry the panels of their greatcoats up from the frozen earth and turn their faces toward the birth of the light, hoping for sunshine. Moscow, which grew ever closer, lay somewhere within this chill vapor, they sensed it, like the swelling of bare veins, throbbing beneath the wind on that icy plain.

He found himself saying that he had seen all that could be seen of death, that no massacred, broken, dismembered body could any longer surprise him with the capriciousness of its mutilations. And yet death remained astonishing. As on that morning by the bright light of the sun, which rose in the direction of Moscow. A soldier whose eyes had been burned in an explosion ran toward the tanks, blind, guided by the sound of the engines and his own agony, and rolled under the tracks, setting off a grenade. Or yet again that young German without a helmet, half lying beside an overturned field gun, his bloody hands pressed against his shattered sides, crying out in the whimpering voice of a child, weeping in a language that, until then, Pavel had only heard barked out and had believed to be made only for barking.

And then, for an infinite second, there was the vision of his own body, lying there, inert among the snow-covered ruts. The explosion of a shell blotted out all sounds and it was in this silence of a vanished world that he saw himself as if from outside and very far away ("as if from the sky," he would later reflect): the body of a soldier in his mud-spattered greatcoat, his arms outstretched, his face flung back, looking up toward a glorious winter sun that would have shone with the same splendid indifference if no one had been left alive on this December morning. He was certain he had lived through those few moments of detached and painless contemplation, certain of having observed the fragile lacework of hoarfrost that surrounded the head of that unmoving soldier. His own head. When he regained consciousness at the hospital and could hear once more, he learned that they had almost abandoned him for dead on that field where there was no one else alive. Mainly to satisfy her conscience, a nurse had approached this corpse with its head trapped in a frozen puddle, had crouched down and held a little mirror to the soldier's lips. The glass had misted over slightly.

On his return to the front at the end of the winter of 1942 he noticed that the world had changed during his absence. In the mornings now, as they resumed their military duties, they had the sun at their backs. And in the evening, during the last miles before they halted, the most wearisome ones, when their boots weighted down with mud seemed to be taking root in the earth, the sun was shining ahead of them to the west, in the direction of Germany. As if in the frozen fields near Moscow the points of the compass had been switched.

There was a comforting logic to this turnaround by the sun. It was the only one in the war's capricious chaos. If he had had the time to reflect on it he would have noticed yet another piece of logic: there were fewer and fewer men in the ranks born, like him, at the very start of the twenties, men who had been fighting since the first day of the war. It was only years later that survivors of his generation might have the leisure to study a population census diagram arranged by age, a triangle with indented sides, like a pointed fir tree, widening toward the base. Moving down from the top to the level of 1920, 1921, and 1922 it would be deeply cut away, as if a mysterious epidemic had exterminated the men born in those years. Only one or two percent of them would be left. Branches pruned almost back to the trunk.

In the fierce thrust of troops toward the west, Pavel had discovered that survival most often depended not on logic but on being aware of chaos's little tricks, its unpredictable whims that defied common sense. A victory could be more murderous than a defeat. The last bullet would kill someone exclaiming in relief at the end of the battle, the first man to light a cigarette. And, whatever happened, you could never say whether it was life-saving or lethal.

It was as he walked through a town that had barely been retaken from the Germans that this notion had struck him of a victory cutting down more men than a lost battle. The streets, now empty, still had an uncertain, disquieting appearance, distorted by eyes that had bored into them when taking aim to fire; by breathless running from the corner of one house to the next. The dead looked as if they were searching for something they had lost in the dust of the courtyards, amid the rubble of gutted buildings. A few minutes before, the length of the silence, longer than a simple pause between bursts of fire, had proclaimed the end and the soldier crouching next to Pavel behind a section of wall had stood up, given a satisfied yawn, as he inhaled the damp air of that May evening. And sat down again immediately, then crumpled over on his side, a pinch of snuff still held between his thumb and forefinger. At the corner of one eyebrow, there was a hollow rapidly filling with blood. Pavel threw himself to the ground, thinking there was a hidden sniper. But, on examining the wound, he recognized the work of a stray piece of shrapnel, one of those bits of metal that came from heaven knows where at the end of a battle, unheralded by the sound of an explosion. Moreover, in the storm-darkened sky the thunder was imitating explosions with muffled rumbling at the other end of the town. Pavel got up and called to the medical orderlies who were running across the street with two bodies loaded on a stretcher.

In the company of other soldiers he walked past houses pitted by shells, then, hearing the sound of running, turned the corner into a less damaged sidestreet and began checking the buildings, one after the other. In the last but one he found himself alone. Corridors, classroom doors, and, in the classrooms, blackboards with pieces of chalk in the grooves beneath them. Some of the windows were broken and in the half-light of a stormy evening he felt he recognized that very particular moment in May when the last lessons of the school year were dissolving in the joy of heavy showers of rain and wet clusters of lilac outside the open window, all in a stormy darkness that suddenly invaded the classroom and created a subtle, dreamy complicity between them and the teacher. On the blackboard in one of the rooms he saw this inscription, written up with scholarly application: "The capital of our country is Berlin." Teaching was being done in accordance with German programs drawn up for the "Eastern territories." Moscow was deemed to have sunk without trace to the bottom of an artificial sea. He emerged from the classroom and heard shooting in the corridor on the ground floor. Some German soldiers were still hiding in the building and it was not easy to track them down in these dozens of rooms, where all the time the eye was being distracted by the chalk handwriting on the blackboard, or the pages of some abandoned textbook.

Pavel was not surprised that the memory of these empty classrooms was more tenacious than that of the battle itself, although he received a medal for it and the date of it was marked by victorious gun salutes in Moscow. He knew only too well the unpredictable caprices of war and what the memory retained of it. And it was also by a caprice of ill humor that the commanding officer refused him a week's leave, time to go to Dolshanka, which was less than sixty miles from the reconquered town. It was now the third year of the war, a year made up, like the previous one, of a thousand troop movements, painful advances and chaotic withdrawals. Amid this tangle of trajectories there was one fixed point, unchanged since he had left: his family house, the plantain leaves around the wooden front steps, the familiar creaking of the door. Despite all the towns burned to a cinder, despite all the deaths, the calm of this house seemed to be intact, down to the smile of his parents on the photo in the dining room: his father with his head turned slightly toward his mother, as if waiting for her to say something. In this town, so close to Dolshanka, a town half flattened by shelling, he had been seized by doubt. He just wanted to reassure himself that the photo was still smiling on the wall. His commanding officer's refusal struck him as a bad omen, which was confirmed several days later. They walked onto a mine-field like a troop of blind men, into a fountain of shrapnel, into the pain, but, before the pain, the sight of a body cut in half and still crawling: the soldier with whom he had been discussing different fishing tactics an hour earlier. At the hospital he brooded on his grudge against the commanding officer. On the day he was allowed to get up and go out into the corridor he learned that their whole division had meanwhile been wiped out by the German artillery in an ill-conceived offensive. He experienced neither joy at having escaped nor remorse. War made everything one could say or think about it simultaneously true and false, and there was too much evil and too much good mixed up in every moment for one to be able to judge. One could only hold one's peace and watch. Beside the window a young soldier was learning how to light a cigarette, clasping it between the remaining stumps of his hands.

Then came a day in March 1944 when, despite all the murderous caprices of chaos, Pavel thought he could discern a purpose, a great goal that could no longer be doubted. Some yards from their camp, in the middle of a gray plain, with no landmarks and no limits, some soldiers were digging in the ground and sticking a newly squared-off post into the hole. The smells of the freshly turned earth and the bark added a strange note to the inscription on a narrow horizontal panel that they nailed to the top of the post: "U.S.S.R." It was difficult to imagine that there, beneath their great muddy boots, between the stems of the dry plants, lay the frontier, that invisible dotted line he had seen only on maps at school. They had taken almost three years to get there from Moscow. Some of the soldiers were walking back and forth, amused at being able to travel abroad by taking a single step. That night the political commissar spoke to them about their country being "cleansed of Nazi defilement," and the "liberating mission" that was entrusted to them in enslaved Europe. Listening to him Pavel said to himself that the marker on the frontier was more eloquent than all the speeches in the world.

He did not understand why crossing the frontier aroused a fear of dying in him. Perhaps because, for the first time in long months, the end of the war and a return home were no longer unthinkable. And, like a gambler who has won a lot and is afraid of losing it all during the last minutes of the game, he became aware of his winnings, of this life, preserved up until now amid so many deaths, which, with every day of fighting, became more precious and more threatened. In an inadmissible thought, he recognized that, so as not to die, he would have been ready to employ cunning, to drag his feet during an assault, to hide behind someone else's back, to pretend to fall. But he knew the laws of death, which often targeted such sly foxes and spared the daredevils.

The hope that he might return home served only to sharpen his fear. He pictured himself marching down the street in Dolshanka, his chest covered with medals, and could imagine nothing more beautiful than that one moment. During hours of respite he found himself polishing his medals and the buckle on his belt while privately rehearsing a hundred times the same scene he dreamed of: the main street of his native village, the admiring looks of the villagers, himself making his way with blissful stateliness toward the house, whose silent, vibrant expectation he could imagine. During these preparations for his return, made between battles, he had the sensation of transporting a part of himself into the future, thus enabling it to escape from the war, to be living in the post-war era already.

That day the clay he had found on a riverbank was dissolving like soap. The tarnished silver of his two "For Gallantry" medals grew bright, the silhouette of the infantryman in the middle of the red star shone like a layer of mica. He put the decorations away, cleaned his fingers with a handful of sand. The water on that April evening seemed almost warm. And in the stillness of the dusk a bird hidden in the willow groves was repeating two notes with joyful insistence.

As he stood up he heard a brief guffaw. Soldiers from the company, he thought, taking advantage of the halt to bathe or wash their clothes. The guffaw rang out again but was too abrupt for it to be true laughter. Pavel made his way around the willow thicket, stepped over a thick, half-submerged tree trunk, pushed aside a cascade of branches, and saw them. A woman on her back on the beach by the river, her head toward the water, a man with his two hands clamped around her head to stop her crying out, another holding the woman's wrists, the third writhing on top of her.

He had taken rapists by surprise before and had fired shots in the air to make them run away. And been cursed as a stupid motherfucker by the woman who was doing it for two tins of food. This time he must act quickly. The guffaws were those of a half-suffocated mouth. The woman managed to free her head, to gasp a mouthful of air and at once her face was smothered by a broad palm. Pavel beat a path through the branches, overturned the man who was twisting the woman's hands, knocked down the one who was crushing her mouth. And just had time, in a fraction of a second, to catch sight of the woman's face and recognize it. That is to say not to recognize it but to tell himself that he had certainly seen it before, or dreamed it, or imagined it. The first soldier hurled himself at him. Pavel dodged him and grasped the tunic collar of the one who was still lying there, made him topple over to one side and, before he could make out his face in the gloom, recognized the voice cursing. It was one of the company's officers.

Afterward he came to understand that it was the close proximity of death that precipitated things. Had the rape been acknowledged the three men would have been court-martialed and shot. Had he not intervened the woman would have suffocated. The soldiers were drunk, they would have noticed nothing. Had they not been drunk they would in any case have killed her to silence her. Each one in his own way hurled back death, as in close combat you hurl back a hand grenade, a few seconds before it explodes, in a frenzied game of hot potato.

Later he thought about this game, this deadly counting-out rhyme in which the last word had fallen on him. It was weeks later, for at the time everything had happened too quickly. He was arrested, his stripes were torn off, his decorations (those medals burnished with clay) were confiscated. A truck picked him up with a load of men whose uniforms bore no distinctive insignia. He knew he had joined a penal company and this meant death in the very near future.

From the very first battle the distance that lay between him and death could be measured in the numbers killed. Two hundred soldiers from his company advanced directly toward the German positions, without any artillery support, without tanks, on a bare plain. One submachine gun to five men. He knew that behind them a barrage section was ready to shoot down anyone who tried to retreat. Caught between two fires, they could only advance toward death or retreat toward it.

He jumped into a trench behind a dead man, a soldier whose chest was cut to pieces by a burst of fire. For a second this body distracted the attention of two Germans as it fell, they moved aside to avoid the corpse. That second allowed time for a sideways knife thrust, the snatching of a submachine gun from one of the Germans, a shot that was just ahead of the other soldier's move. Pavel always ran, flung himself to the ground, fired a little ahead of the others. Now everything seemed slow to him: the knife plunging slowly in below the German's ear, the fall of the body, flailing and spattering him with blood, the look from the other soldier, hampered by the narrowness of the trench, struggling with his weapon jammed between his belly and the earth wall, who just had time to realize that he was too slow. An instant after the fighting had finished, the moments when Pavel had succeeded in staying ahead unfolded in his mind's eye with delayed action. He emerged from the trench and walked along beside it, moving toward the small group of survivors gathering around the commanding officer. They looked at one another as if seeing one another for the first time.

With the remnants of other penal companies a new one was formed: two hundred men with no name, no rank, and—the late comers—no weapons. They were thrown in wherever men could only die, as in that long valley, pitted with crevasses of marshland, which Pavel crossed during the third battle. The Germans hidden in the copse fired at them and gave away their own positions. Now a real offensive could be launched. The men of the penal company were simply bait.

As a new company was brought together the commissar repeated that they must "wash away" with their blood the wrongs done to their country. He had no fear of repeating himself to the company for the contingent was renewed at almost every battle. "A month, or at best two," thought Pavel, when calculating the life expectancy of these men, on the basis of the number of survivors.

This life expectancy found expression in a mathematical formula thanks to the prisoners from the gulag, who were numerous in these so-called kamikaze companies. One of them (like all the others, he had no name, simply a tattoo on the back of his hand: an anchor) was a man whose eyes were unaccustomed to the sun, his face burned by the cold of the far north. He showed Pavel his meticulous counting of the days, five notches on the handle of his knife: for a month of service in the penal companies, he explained, their sentence was reduced by five years, two months wiped out seven years in the camps, three months was worth ten. There was no better equation to express the times they were living through. Anchor was killed after eight years of war (i.e. two months and a few days). Pavel retrieved his knife, its handle notched with hope.

He found himself remembering the face of the violated woman. Not to pity her or to feel self-pity and regret his action. It was the similarity of her face and features to those of another, seen somewhere before, that haunted him. He thought of his sister, his mother, and also of Sasha. Of other women's faces. At times they had had in their eyes the same aura of pain and beauty. One day in a Polish town, passing in front of a church half-destroyed by shelling, he solved the riddle. The memory of the church at Dolshanka came to mind. Likewise demolished, in this case with stubborn vindictiveness: the cupola torn down, the roof burned, a section of wall blown up with dynamite, the work of Comrade Krassny. The interior, open to the sky, had been colonized by nettles and young maple saplings. Obscenities erupted across the wall, scrawled on it with a fragment of brick. Alone, in the corner, at a height beyond the reach of human hands, a face leaned down toward anyone who entered through the gaping door. The eyes of a woman, large and sorrowful, a gaze that came from a fresco blackened by fire.

As they were almost certain they would not meet again the next day, men in the penal companies talked to one another differently from ordinary soldiers. Very simple statements, a tone of voice that was not concerned to be understood, to convince, or to impress. Words you use when talking to yourself or addressing ghosts. Before a battle they knew in advance that a few hours later nine voices out of ten would have fallen silent forever on this earth. This made their voices calm, detached, indifferent to what the ghosts of tomorrow would think. Sometimes the narrative would break off and one could sense it continuing underground among silent memories.

"So as not to crush it, this egg," Anchor was relating two days before he died, "I tied my wrist to my thigh when I was asleep. The egg always kept warm in my armpit. Everyone in our hut helped me to hatch it. During searches we passed it from one to another. We hid it from the guards, like it was a bomb or a gold ingot. What do you expect? There's not much to do in a camp. A tractor had knocked it out of its nest. All the other eggs were smashed but this one hadn't broken. We really wanted to know what kind of bird would come out of it."

What did come out was a tiny bundle of life, a little pulsating thing, covered in down, with a gaping yellow beak that the prisoners fed with a chewed-up mess of bread and saliva. In the end the guards got to know about it but did not interfere. They understood that no one in the camp would have batted an eye if they had doubled the quotas of work, or deprived them of food, or increased the punishments. But had they laid a finger on that little creature, already learning to fly in the stifling air of the barrack huts, there would have been a revolt.

Anchor was killed and Pavel never heard the end of the story. He simply pictured a young bird, under the transfixed gaze of the prisoners, flying out over the lines of barbed wire.

When he was telling his story Anchor sometimes called himself "the brood cock." This nickname amused another prisoner, who had joined the company at the same time as him and who, unlike the rest, made a point of preserving his real name amid the anonymity of the other soldiers. If he spoke to anyone, however briefly, he would tell them his name, Zurin, happy to take possession of it again after being a mere serial number for so long. It was this desire to assert his own identity that gave him the urge to tell his story.

Wounded in the battle of Brest Litovsk, he had been captured by the Germans, had spent a month behind barbed wire, had managed to escape and rejoin our troops and then, in a reverse process, had been arrested, judged to be a traitor, and sent to a Soviet camp.

Pavel had already heard the stories of such escapees who had, without realizing it, fled from one death to another. He knew the meaning of Stalin's words when he declared, "None of my soldiers will be taken prisoner by the enemy." This meant they must never give themselves up alive.

It was not Zurin's fate that struck him but one episode in particular that the soldier related clumsily, stumbling, as if he felt at fault in admitting to his capture.

It was, he told them, the final day of the battle for the citadel of Brest Litovsk. The Germans had just dislodged the last of the defenders putting up resistance in the underground bunkers. Some of them perished when the vaults caved in, others were burned by

flamethrowers, asphyxiated by smoke. They lined up the survivors on
the central square of the citadel in front of the German troops, who
observed them with mocking curiosity. The fighters blinked in the
sunlight, too harsh after long weeks spent in the dark in bunkers.
Their uniforms had been transformed into crusts of hardened mud.
Bandages stained with earth and blood, solid hair plastered over their
brows, lips raw with thirst. They looked like beasts that had just been
hauled out of their lair. Beasts who had lost count of the days and,
moreover, did not know that the frontier fortress they were defending had long since been abandoned by the rest of the army in its
retreat toward Moscow.

Exactly as if they were dragging forth a captured animal, two
Germans dragged out another of the fighters on a makeshift stretcher
and set him down at the feet of the rest. His face touching the stone,
he looked as if he were listening to a distant noise. A fragment of
bone, very white amid the dirty fabric of his tunic, poked out from
his shoulder. He remained motionless, lying between the Germans
and the row of prisoners. One of the officers rapped out a brief
command. A soldier ran off, came back with a bucket of water, and
emptied it over the recumbent man. The latter turned his head. It
could be seen that half his face was charred—the same black surface
as the walls and the bricks vitrified by the flamethrowers. Painfully, he
raised himself onto one elbow. In this face made up of burned skin
and mud an eye glittered, conscious and still full of the darkness of
the underground chambers.

The officer leaned forward to meet this one-eyed gaze. In the
scorched face the lips moved. In place of spittle, a clot of brown blood
hurtled from this mouth and flattened itself against the officer's boots.

" 'Now we've had it,' we said to ourselves," Zurin related. " 'The
Kraut will finish him off with a pistol. Then they'll give all of us hell
just to pay for that gob of spit.' "

The officer stood up and a fresh command snapped out. The
line of soldiers quivered and with a fierce clicking of heels came

rigidly to attention, their eyes fixed on the officer. He stared hard at them and barked out several words that rang across the square. Zurin understood German, the enemy's language they had learned at school, reading Heine. "This is a true soldier," said the officer. "You should fight like him!"

For a long moment the square remained silent. A line of German soldiers at attention and this man dying, stretched out on the pavement, his brow against the stone.

In the new company, made up of the remnants of the previous ones, Pavel spoke to nobody. He had already grown accustomed to the futility of forming a tie with anyone, knowing the most you might be left with from such a friendship, formed on the brink of death, was either a knife with the handle notched for days of survival or an unfinished story. And if he now embarked on a conversation one night it was because the offense attributed to this new recruit seemed too improbable. They said that on attacks this man had refused to shout Stalin's name.

The two were on guard duty and spoke in whispers, unable to see one another in the darkness. The German positions were very close, you could not even light a cigarette. The soldier's responses left Pavel perplexed. "He's pulling my leg, this guy," he said to himself from time to time, and in the gray light of the June night he tried to make out the features of his strange interlocutor. But the reflected moonlight showed only quick flashes from his spectacles and the pale patch of his forehead.

"Is it true you swap your vodka for bread?" asked Pavel, seeing this refusal to drink the statutory hundred grams before an attack as a bizarre piece of bravado: those few burning mouthfuls gave you the courage to tear yourself up from the earth when the bullets and shrapnel came whistling past. "Don't you like drinking or what?"

"I do, but I'm always hungry. You see, I was a rich kid. My parents force-fed me like a turkey when I was little."

Such honesty was disconcerting. Pavel told himself that, questioned in that way, he would have invented a rather more heroic reason for his refusal. He would have said he did not drink because he was afraid of nothing. He would certainly never have admitted to a past as a spoiled child.

"And is it true they put you in a penal company because of Stalin? You really refused to shout?"

"Look, there was a political commissar who hated my guts. There was nothing I could do about it. He never left me alone. One day he got me out in front of the troop and ordered me to shout: 'For our country! For Stalin!' I refused. I said we weren't attacking."

"But on an attack you shouted?"

"Sure, like everyone else. When you shout you don't feel so scared. You know that yourself."

That night Pavel learned that the soldier had gone as a volunteer to the front at the age of seventeen, lying about his age like so many others. He came from Leningrad and had not received a single letter since the start of the siege, even after the blockade was lifted. When their guard duty was relieved the soldier remained stock still for a moment, with the dazed irresolution of someone who is suddenly overtaken by a wave of sleep, until then held at bay. As Pavel was moving away, he turned back and saw him thus: a figure all alone, in the expanse of the fields at night, beneath a sky already filling with the first light.

He caught up with him again next day during a halt. Now that the company had been slimmed down to half its size by an unsuccessful attack it was easier to locate faces. The soldier greeted him, held out his hand. "He's Jewish," thought Pavel and experienced a mixture of disappointment and distrust, derived from a source he himself was unaware of. He often heard it said at the front that all the Jews stayed behind the lines or were in cushy jobs in supply. Yet they had all of them come across many Jews in the front line or severely wounded in the hospital, as well as in the rushed interludes that came

between the trivial actions before a battle (a tongue wetting a cigarette paper, a joke, a hand brushing aside a bee) and the first steps
taken afterward, on a strip of earth covered with silent or howling
bodies. And yet he continued to hear that refrain about cushy jobs
and crafty little bastards in supply. Now he realized that among the
men of the penal companies these remarks were no longer heard.
The extreme proximity of death swept away the tawdry trappings of
names and origins.

"I'm called Marelst. That's my first name."

Pavel stared at him and could not suppress a smile: he was tall,
very thin, with the narrow, bony shoulders of an adolescent and
glasses that had a diagonal crack across one of the lenses. His physique
corresponded very little to the forename derived from the contrac-
tion of Marx-Engels-Lenin-Stalin. One of those revolutionary relics
from the twenties. On his tunic, above his heart, you could still see
the tear marks left by his confiscated medals.

"Did you have a Red Star?" asked Pavel, noticing an angular
patch, darker than the rest, on the fabric bleached by the sun.

"Yes, and a 'For Gallantry,'" replied Marelst, and corrected himself at once, so as to eradicate the note of juvenile pride that had
crept into his voice. "Yes, I had them. But, when it comes down to it,
I tell myself there's no way I'd have got anything else, short of capturing Hitler in person."

As they marched in a column that extended along a road over
the plain, he noticed Marelst three files away from him carrying
the steel base for the mortar, the most cumbersome burden, for one
never knew how to balance it on one's back. Pavel eyed the slightly
bent back, the swerves in Marelst's step necessitated by the rocking of
the base. A back like any other, Pavel thought, distractedly, a soldier
dragging his weary feet in the dust of a road in wartime. He recalled
his distrust and vexation on learning that this man was a Jew. Unwillingly he noted that this vexation seemed to him inexplicably justified
by, and even inseparable from, the fact of being Russian. He would

have liked to find the reason for it. But from his childhood days the possibility of being a Jew had remained purely theoretical, for no one had ever seen one in Dolshanka, where even the people from the other end of the village were regarded as foreigners. Later, away at school, there were a few old sayings of folk wisdom about Jews "raking in the money with both hands." This wise saw was curiously contradicted by their history teacher, a veteran soldier and a Jew who had lost one arm, and whom it was difficult to picture as a raker-in of money.

The next day (after they had been hurled, as usual without artillery support, into the stone maze of a little Polish town), he observed Marelst yet again, while trying to comprehend it all. There were many wounded because of the bullets rebounding in the narrow streets. Pavel was carrying a soldier whose tunic was swollen with blood, like a strange wineskin. As he came around a corner in the street he caught sight of the figure of Marelst, he, too, with a human burden. For a moment they walked together in silence, both of them sunk in that torpor at the end of a battle, when, finding your body still alive, you resume possession of it, as of your thoughts of a few hours ago that now seem several years old. From time to time Marelst gave way at the knees and straightened himself up with an effort, as he adjusted the position of the wounded man on his back. The lenses of his glasses were spattered with mud; one of the broken earpieces had been replaced by a length of wire. Pavel stared at these glasses, this face, saying nothing, struck by the disproportion: the broad bruise on his chin, a banal bruise, just like one you might receive in a mere fist fight, a mere bruise left by a battle that had just killed so many men. There was a curious irony about this flick of the wrist, with which death seemed to hurl back a man whose hour had not yet come.

Marelst must have noticed this look, or had he guessed that his origins did not find favor? That evening, seated by their campfire, he spoke in that level, dull voice the men in penal companies used to probe the depths of their past lives in whispers, lives which, from one day of reprieve to the next, seemed more and more foreign to them, as if lived by someone else. Somewhere halfway through his story, anxious no doubt to avoid the tones of a confession, he stopped and announced with uncompromising irony, "As a matter of fact, I've decided not to die. So nothing I'm telling you is final. Life continues, as the hanged man said when he saw the first carrion crows arriving. No, you'll see. We'll come through. We'll drink our hundred grams in Berlin. A hundred grams, what am I saying? A barrel." Later, when recalling that story told at nightfall, Pavel could not quite pinpoint the moment at which this gleeful outburst had occurred. As he remembered them, Marelst's words had had a grave, intense rhythm, into which it would have been impossible to introduce the merest scrap of humor.

In this story there was Marelst's father, a young clockmaker in Vitebsk, who one day walked out of his shop and hurled a heavy clock onto the sidewalk, together with its mahogany case, then began to trample on the fragments of glass as he wept. They thought he was mad. In a certain sense he had become mad, on learning that the house of his brother, who lived in Moldavia, had been pillaged and that the looting had degenerated into killing and they were driving nails into the skulls of newborn babies. He felt as if he could hear the crunch of the metal points piercing these heads scarcely covered with hair and could see the children's wide-open eyes. This noise and this vision pursued him relentlessly, so that he could no longer hear the watches ticking or respond to the smiles of his nearest and dearest. What tortured him as well was knowing that for the most part the looters were workers with three days' hunger in their bellies, jealous of the down quilt possessed by his brother. He felt that he had the strength, born of desperation, to seize the terrestrial globe and shake all the evil out of it. He would soon need this strength at the time of arrests, during the years of secrecy, in exile. In the revolution he became the all-powerful governor in his native town, and was then called to Moscow by Lenin himself. The goal seemed to him clearer than ever: not a single person must be left in this country, in the whole world, whom hunger transformed into a killer. To this end, some people must be given food. And, among the others, a few must be killed. During the civil war he understood that more than just a few must be killed. A few thousand, he began by thinking. Then a few tens of thousands, a few million . . . At a certain moment he caught himself having forgotten why they were killing people. It was the day his secretary had laid on his desk a fresh bundle of denunciations: in one of them he found a form of words that reminded him of the convolutions of a snake: "Citizen N. must be arrested, as he is suspected of being a suspect." It suddenly seemed as if his secretary was waiting for his reaction through the half-open door. That same year he learned that one of his old comrades from the time of secrecy had committed suicide. He tried to think calmly. The choice was becoming limited: he should either follow this friend or forget, once and for all, why they were killing people. He had three children. The youngest, Marelst, was born the day tears had been seen in Stalin's eyes as he stood beside Lenin's coffin. "I have a family," Marelst's father argued with himself. "And besides, you can't make a revolution in kid gloves." A big apartment right opposite the Kremlin, a chauffeur-driven car, a new secretary, even younger and more amenable than the previous one—when she left his office straightening her skirt he experienced a long moment of pleasant torpor, which no questions could any longer disturb. When he learned of the famine organized in the Ukraine and the millions dead he told himself that what was needed, so as not to lose your reason, was to extend this torpor over the entire duration of days. Marelst was ten in that summer of 1934 when they went to the Crimea. The excitement of the long train journey with his parents, his brother, and his sister kept him awake. He saw what he should not have seen. In one station, in a night blinded by floodlights, a crowd of women and children being driven toward cattle cars by soldiers brandishing their rifle butts. "Who are those people?" asked Marelst from his bunk. "Kulaks and saboteurs," his father quickly replied and went down onto the platform to threaten the stationmaster, who had dared to hold up their train in this ideologically dubious situation. His mother put her hand over Marelst's eyes. And he experienced a complex pleasure, comparable to the taste of the cake they had eaten on his sister's birthday: the white cream that lingered on your palate, fine chocolate chips, tiny flakes of crystallized fruit. In the same way he relished both in his mouth and through all his other senses the calm of their compartment, moving gently as it slid along beside the platform, the delicious swaying of his bunk, the smell of the cold tea on the little shelf below the window and, above all, in a foretaste of happiness to come, the Crimean pebbles that you had to pour from one hand to the other, searching for the mysterious chalcedony his father had told him about. The existence of the kulaks, who were being loaded into those hideous cattle cars, only served to add spice to his contentment. He was just about to go to sleep with this taste of patisserie on his lips when suddenly it was as if an icy gust of wind whirled around in the darkness of their compartment. The child was gripped by fear, an irrational fear and an idea that passed his understanding: one day he would be punished for this sugary taste of happiness in his mouth, for his joy at knowing the others were being crammed into freight cars without windows. He would learn how to formulate this fear some years later. For the moment there was only the fleeting draft of cold air and the vision of a woman trying to protect her child in the cut and thrust of rifle butts. He understood this fear during the winter of 1938. In the space of two months his parents grew old and now only spoke in whispers, feeling their way from one word to the next. All conversations carefully avoided the secret, betrayed precisely by this effort not to mention it: the imminent arrest of his father, the disappearance of what it came to them so naturally to call their life, their family. His father succeeded in forestalling the nocturnal ring at their door. In the government building where he was the minister in charge the staircases soared up in a broad, majestic curve and the space between the handrails was at least a yard across. His father threw himself into it from the top story and the employees going up and down had time to see this body as it streaked past the floors and several times struck the ironwork of the banisters. Someone tried to catch the open panels of his jacket in flight but all he was left with was a rapid burning beneath his nails. Thanks to this death, his father did not become an "enemy of the people" and their family, although dislodged from the prestigious apartment building, was not deported. They went to live with friends in Leningrad. The memory of the night when he saw the cattle cars as a child—the memory of his happiness—came back to him every day, together with that burning under the fingernails, which he imagined thanks to the employee's description. But the first battles had wiped out both the memory of this shame and the need to exonerate himself. There were too many deaths, too many bodies sunk in the mud of the fields, too many regrets encroaching on one another: the day when an abandoned wounded man reached out to him with his bloodied hand and he didn't stop, the next day, when an officer, standing up to go into the attack a second before him, was mown down by a burst of gunfire and Marelst had to climb over him. All that remained of his former life was a notebook filled with poems from his youth. A notebook now being dismembered, page by page, and used for cigarette papers. At first he saw this as a brutal lesson from life, as it reduced these sheets of paper, with their labored and melancholy sonnets, to ashes. But very quickly the taste of the coarse tobacco that drove away the smell of blood and rotting flesh gave the notebook a new significance—the silence of soldiers after a battle, rolling a cigarette with part of a poem. From now on there seemed to him to be infinitely more truth in the calm of such moments than in anything that might have been said about life or death in those rhyming verses.

★

As he talked, Marelst raised his head from time to time and the lenses of his glasses caught the light of the fire, making his eyes disappear, as if beneath a spurt of blood. Pavel told himself that in peacetime they would never have met and even if they had met would never have understood one another. "A man from Leningrad," Pavel would have thought with suspicion, "the son of a minister." It occurred to him now that the war had simplified everything. There was this fire, drying the slabs of mud on their boots and causing it to flake, the darkness over this plain, lost somewhere between Poland and Germany, this scrap of land in the night, just snatched back from the enemy. And this man, sitting close to the fire, a man talking very quietly, as if in his sleep, who was quite complete in what he was saying. Pavel suddenly understood that there was nothing else: darkness, a man, a voice. Everything else was a peacetime invention. Man was simply this naked voice beneath the sky.

The next day, as they set out on the road again, he thought that after the battle he would tell Marelst what he had always kept to himself: the story of that woman buried alive, with her child in her belly, a woman with no voice but whom he could always understand.

In the next battle they were due to liberate a concentration camp. Transformed into a fortified base, it was holding up the offensive of an entire division. It was not known if there were any prisoners left in the huts: all that could be seen was some thirty captives tied to posts around the camp as a shield. They would have to attack without firing a single shell, without hand grenades. "With our bare hands?" exclaimed a newcomer in amazement. No one answered him. Three penal companies were thrown into the assault, six hundred men. After the first attack, which was driven back, Pavel saw that the rolls of barbed wire had half disappeared under inert bodies. Further off, all along the fence, the bound prisoners watched in silence the ebb and flow of soldiers letting themselves be killed without being able to respond.

At the fifth or sixth wave, when only a quarter of the three companies remained, Pavel, by now deaf and with the taste of burned blood in his throat, withdrew in a group of a dozen soldiers toward a broad ditch to the rear of the camp. Someone leaned down to take a drink but straightened up again immediately: his hands had drawn up a viscous, yellowish pulp. It was a narrow, dead river, blocked with ashes. They shuffled for several seconds, without mustering the resolve to pass through this stagnant liquid, where several corpses floated. Marelst came up at this moment and Pavel saw his figure moving forward, wading in up to his knees, up to his belt, up to his chest. His arms held his submachine gun high above his head. When he reappeared on the far bank, coated with a thick crust of scum, the soldiers raced after him and time went into turmoil, as if to make up for the delay. On one watchtower the barrel of a machine gun aimed at them frenetically. The scum came to life, seethed with bullets. The machine gunner twisted about at the top of the watchtower, struggling against the dead angle. An attack from that direction had doubtless not been foreseen. The soldiers rushed toward the barbed wire. And, as always in combat, everything disintegrated into a series of increasingly rapid and random flashes. A beam of the watchtower blows up. The machine gunner with his brow torn open by a burst of fire. He falls and reappears, his face is intact—it's another German. The bullets lash the scum, rake the bank. One soldier stops, sits down, as if to take a rest. Pavel swerves around him as he runs, hurls an oath at him, then realizes . . . In the distance a mass of gray-green uniforms pours out between the huts—the German reinforcements. To the left, tied to a post, one of the prisoners seems to be smiling; no doubt he's already dead. The first line of barbed wire. The soldier running in front of Pavel leaps and suddenly straightens up, fingers his throat. The lower part of his face has been blown away by a fragment from a hand grenade. His body falls, a bridge across the jagged wire. They climb over his back. Someone else falls. The bridge grows longer. The sky is turned upside down by an explosion. The earth shakes his body and hurls it into the blue. What he sees: an encounter between a clod of earth and a cloud. The sky is beneath his body, which is drowning in the blue. A torn-off arm, as if someone had abandoned it behind a roll of barbed wire. A German's eyes, his mouth open, and the smoothness, almost tenderness, with which the bayonet plunges into his belly. Another explosion. The skewered body protects him from the shrapnel. The gaping door of a barrack hut. The pile of skeletons in striped garments. A German lying in wait behind this heap. A grenade scattering the dead. A section of the wall crumbles—the violence of the sunlight. The German writhes amid the striped bodies. A hut burns. A half-naked being crawls to safety out of the flames. The deafness is total. Explosions are heard by the stomach, the lungs, and pressure on the temples. Silence also comes from inside, from the belly. The eyes, still feverish, ricochet from one wall to another, from a shadow to a door that suddenly bangs, blown by a blast of wind. Then the body no longer hears anything. Gradually the ears start hearing again in their turn. Silence. The chirping of a cricket in the grass between two lines of barbed wire. And, crumpled up against the wall of a hut, a soldier with a broad trail of blood across his chest. And his cry ("water") which for the others is no more than the proof that their hearing has returned and their own lives are intact.

The soldiers walked back and forth across the camp, like runners after a race, strolling about to let the fever of the effort die down. They checked all the huts, they freed the bound prisoners (most of whom collapsed beside their stakes). The commanding officer counted. About forty of the wraiths clad in striped garments showed signs of life, some of them by opening their eyes, some by attempting to get up. Out of the six hundred members of the three penal companies twenty-seven soldiers remained.

Pavel found it difficult to disengage Marelst's body. He had to lift the other bodies, draw out the barbed wire. Most notably, the soldier's fingers seemed to be clinging to the earth. In his comrade's knapsack Pavel found two letters sent from Leningrad before the siege. He kept them.

Despite the fighting that started again the next day and the infinite diversity of the mutilated bodies, he could not forget Marelst's gesture: the hand that had found the time to feel for the lower part of his face, ripped away by shrapnel. He had often thought about his own death, about the last second before dying, about the possibility or impossibility of knowing how to die. This gesture became an answer.

The assault on the camp earned the survivors an amnesty and posting to ordinary units. They heard the news without showing any joy, as if this change did not concern them.

The war had grown younger. Pavel noticed this as he observed the latest conscripts, their indifference to being killed or their fear of dying, their awkwardness in suffering, their youthful receptiveness to all that war offered. He had forgotten how he, too, in the old days, would address amateurish prayers to death, polish his medals, dream of returning home, wait for letters.

On the opposing side this youthfulness was also visible. In the German ranks the bullets easily eroded the soft stratum of very young men, adolescents recruited from the *Hitlerjugend*. Once this layer was torn away, the core seemed almost mineral in its toughness: soldiers who had survived Stalingrad, Kursk, Königsberg. Soldiers who knew that their native cities, or the cities from which they received their letters, had been transformed into charred ruins by aerial bombardment. For a long time the war had become their only country. And the soldier who knows that no one anywhere awaits his return is much to be feared.

Pavel encountered just such a soldier late in the day in the suburbs of Berlin, where their company was floundering about among little pockets of resistance. The red flag was already flying over the Reichstag, the victory had been announced, but there, behind a church with a dome shattered by shelling, there were still several concealed snipers who refused to give themselves up. There was one in particular, his face blackened by smoke, who was riddling the street from a hiding place behind a pillar eroded by bullets. He seemed invulnerable. After each burst of gunfire, as the dust cleared, you could see his stiff profile visible behind the column and the shooting started again. The young soldiers, perplexed, shrugged their shoulders, took careful aim, or, on the contrary, began spraying the whole façade, their faces contorted with rage. They finally took him out with a grenade launcher. Drawing closer, Pavel grasped their mistake at the same time as the others did, and whistled in astonishment. In a niche between two pillars stood a bronze statue crammed with their bullets. The German's hiding place had been close by, lower down. He lay there, dead, his face turned toward them. His left hand, covered in blood, was made fast to the butt of the machine gun by a length of wire. This had taken the place of smashed ligaments, so that he could continue firing. Browned with the soot of fires and the dust, his face closely resembled the metal of the statue. His features were expressionless.

This shooting had taken place while around the Reichstag victory was being celebrated. They arrived too late and Pavel did not even have time to write his name on the mutilated walls. The order to board the trucks had already been given and he had failed to find a piece of plaster on the ground strewn with cartridges and shrapnel. His greatest regret was not having written Marelst's name there, as he had for so long promised himself he would.

He felt there was something incomplete about those days of victory. The inscription not written . . . No, much more than that. The war was over, he thought, and the very idea seemed strange. From one day to the next all that tide of faces, dead or alive, of bodies unscathed or massacred, of cries, of tears, of dying breaths, all that was located in the past now, relegated to the past by the joy of the May sunshine in Berlin. Without being able to say as much, Pavel was waiting for a sign, a change in the color of the sky, in the smell of the air. But the weeks flowed by, confident of their newly established routine rhythm. The trucks arrived at the station. The trains filled with soldiers and traveled slowly back toward the east.

One day at dawn, already in Russia, while the train was stopped beside a village, Pavel saw a young woman rinsing bed linen, squatting at the edge of a stream. The strangeness of that calm morning bordered on madness. In Pavel's understanding, without his being able to put it into words, it was impossible, after all that had happened in the war, for anyone to be kneeling there calmly on the bank at this time, making those pieces of white cloth undulate in the water. It was impossible to have those legs, those thighs. That body made for love ought not to exist. She should have arisen, looked at him and shouted for joy, or wept and fallen back to earth. He shook his head, got a grip on himself. The soldiers around him were asleep. He sensed his face trembling in a grimace of jealousy. The girl stood up, grasped the handle of the pail filled with the laundry she had just wrung out. He followed her movements, desired her, and, despite the violent joy that filled him, felt as if he were betraying someone.

They crossed Moscow at nightfall in trucks, from one station to another. Pavel did not know the city and was unconsciously expecting that the street speeding past the open back of the van would teach him about the mystery of this life without war. As they waited for a red light at a crossroads he saw the open window of a restaurant, the kitchen end. It was a heavy July evening. Painstakingly, a cook was carrying a vast saucepan, his body leaning backward, his mouth tensed with the effort. It was strange to think of a life in which this great cooking pot and its contents were important. At the far end of the kitchen a door opened and, as the truck carried them away, Pavel had time to see, moving past him, the dining room of the restaurant, the cluster of lights on the chandelier, a woman leaning over her plate, a man shaking his hand to extinguish a match. "They're having dinner," thought Pavel, and this activity seemed quite disconcertingly strange. At the station, while awaiting the departure of the long train composed of freight cars on which they were to be made to embark, he overheard the parting words of a couple saying their good-byes beside a suburban train, "Tomorrow, then, about seven." He made a face and shook his head, as if to rid himself of a fit of giddiness. This rendezvous at seven o'clock was located in a time, in a life, in a world that he could never enter.

★

He was still living in the days when after a battle the soldiers would pace numbly up and down among the dead, getting used to being alive. It was from those days that he had his knife with the notches on it, left by a soldier from a penal company. Back in those days there was the soldier who, before crumpling up, had fingered the emptiness in the place where his jaw had been torn off. That night a cry woke him. "The tanks! Over there on the right!" yelled his neighbor, wrestling with a nightmare. There were several sniggers, several sighs in the darkness, then once again silence and the drumming of the rails.

He was sure, now, that in Dolshanka he would find a new life, even one in which he could forget. In the district capital, before setting out on the road, he saw a woman gathering raspberries behind her garden fence. The house opposite had had the roof blown off by an explosion and seemed uninhabited. He observed the woman's hands, strangely delicate and white, her fingers stained with purple juice. Her forearms were full, unbearable to look at. He gave a little cough, approached with a hesitant step, leaned on the fence with aggressive casualness and asked the way to Dolshanka. "What's that you say, Dolshanka?" said the woman, amazed, and shrugged her shoulders. In her tone of voice there was both flattered curiosity at speaking to a soldier and a desire to flaunt her pride. Pavel walked away, then turned back, thinking: "What a cow! Why not grab her, snatch her basket, rape her?" But one part of him, a very gentle part, was already crumbling, melting warmly and touching his heart, including in the happiness of that morning both the woman with her red-stained fingers and the old wooden fence as it began to grow warm under the still-pale rays of the sun.

As he walked along he thought about his return to Dolshanka, a return so often pictured that now the desire seized him to steal in quietly, passing through kitchen gardens, to avoid people's stares, their greetings. Unconsciously, he was transporting to Dolshanka all the people he had encountered on the return journey, in Moscow, in the district capital. He pictured the village filled with this war-free vitality, a happiness that was already routine, confident of its rights. There would be the bustle of young people in the main street, the long-drawn-out strains, at once merry and plaintive, of the accordion, crowds gathering, questions, a multitude of unknown children. And in order to be able to bear this agonizing gaiety he would need to down a good glass of vodka, then another.

Not to go back at all? The idea suddenly struck him as plausible and it was at that very moment he noticed that the road, a road of which he knew every twist and turn, had changed. It was not the line of burned-out trucks outside the district capital, nor the shell craters that gave this impression. Quite simply, the earth road was disappearing here and there under the advance of the forest. Young wild cherry trees were growing in the middle of it, grass filled the ruts. He found himself catching his boot against the cap of a fly agaric fungus, walking around an anthill. But the major landmarks were still there: the oak grove that plunged down into a ravine, a large chalky mound surrounded by fir trees. Pavel bent down, touched the layer of sand and pine needles. It was formed into a solid crust, all interwoven with stems and roots. Continuing on his way he unconsciously accelerated his pace.

Before going into Dolshanka the road made a sharp bend, hugging the winding course of the river. If you looked back you could see the place you had just passed, as you see the last coaches of a train on a curve in the track. Pavel turned his head and by the red light of the sunset, shining low over the earth, he saw the swaying dust from his footsteps as it lingered in the still, warm air on the far side of the loop in the road. He saw more than this trace. He almost pictured himself there, exactly as he had been a moment ago: a soldier who had just dusted his boots, straightened up his tunic, and washed his face, scooping up warm water from among the reeds. And for a few seconds he felt very remote from this happy double who was so thrilled to be going home. He walked past the copse at the entrance to the village, gave the bottom of his tunic one more tug, suddenly stopped, then ran, then stopped again.

What he saw did not frighten him, so deep was the stillness. The greenery from the orchards that had run wild covered the charred remains of the *izba*s almost completely. The trees had grown unchecked across the street, breaking the straight line of it. Dolshanka no longer existed. But its ruins did not have the violence of recent destruction. The rains had long since washed away the blackness of the burned walls, wild grasses hid the foundation stones. Only the stoves with their chimneys still reared up, showing where the houses had stood. Pavel crouched down, drew open the little cast iron door to an oven—the creaking of the hinges was the only sound evocative of a human presence in this silence of plants.

Walking slowly along the main street, he spoke out loud. Even spilling out at random, his words lent a semblance of logic to these moments. He recognized the forge, brown with rust, the horns of the anvil sticking out among the nettles. Still talking, he made this very simple calculation: the village had been burned during the German offensive in the autumn of 1941, so for four years, the snow, the trees . . . He stopped in front of a building whose walls remained almost intact, remembered it as the House of the Soviet. Above the door lengths of rope bleached in the sun hung from great nails. And on the ground skeletons covered in shreds of clothing were sitting or lying stretched out, with sharp stems and leaves growing through them, surrounded by large creamy umbels with the scent of mulled wine.

He spent the night in the square of blackened tree trunks that still marked the site of their vanished house amid the underbrush. He no longer felt any pain. From his first steps around the site of this blaze of long ago (beneath the debris of beams reduced to pieces of charcoal he had caught sight of an iron bed, all black, and had recognized it), from the first crunching of glass underfoot, his grief had crossed the threshold of what was bearable and had numbed him. There were just a few absurd little details it still hurt him to see. In the evening it was the garlands of white flowers growing around the chimney: near to the ground the flowers were already closed but high up, where the sun was still shining, their bell-shaped trumpets stood out. He had gone up to them, tugged forcibly at the garland. And now, in the night, there was this shadow. Something nosing about swiftly behind the ruins of the house (a stray dog? a wolf?)—and the fear, and the humiliation of feeling fear. Here. At this moment. But the real torture was the sky, with the stars, slightly hazy from the heat, which beguiled the eye with the geometry of their constellations, learned at school and since then stubbornly unchanged. There was in their soft light a kind of mild deception, a promise eroded by millions and millions of prayers never granted. Even when he closed his eyes he did not escape these timeless patterns. He sat down and suddenly imagined himself to be very old, yes, an old man watching beside his ruined house. And in this imagined old body, the body of a dying man, without memories, without desires, he felt unspeakably happy. But he was twenty-five and it was summer 1945. The interval of time that lay between him and that old man now seemed of inhuman duration. He took out his pack, his hand felt the butt of the automatic pistol, wrapped in a scrap of cloth.

He left the village before first light. As he walked along he sensed his own gaze pursuing him. A scornful gaze. He knew that if his courage had failed him it was because of the woman with her hands stained by raspberry juice.

To begin with he managed to find pretexts for his wanderings. He made fruitless attempts to find his sister and spent several months in the area traveling from one town to the next. Then he went to

Leningrad—so as to meet Marelst's family, or so he persuaded himself—as if there were still any hope of finding someone alive after several years' silence. An official whom he asked for information about Dolshanka, a very perspicacious official, sensed this nomadic mania in him and reprimanded him, saying, "It's time to roll up your sleeves, comrade, and play your part in the reconstruction of the country!" Indeed, if everyone had embarked on searching for the survivors of all the burned villages . . . He found no one in Leningrad. Nevertheless, very conscientiously, he rang the bell on all the floors of a great, damp, sinister apartment building, constructed around an enclosed courtyard that could give no life to a tall tree with pale leaves. His zeal produced a result he had not intended. An old woman emerged from a cavernous apartment, regarded him almost joyfully, and suddenly began talking louder and louder, recounting the story of the siege, the frozen corpses in the streets, the apartments inhabited by dead people whose bodies were no longer even collected. He backed away onto the landing, stammered a word of farewell, began his descent. He knew all these stories. The woman sensed that he was escaping her and shouted out with demented glee, "And in our building people ate their own dogs! And the ones who didn't eat their dogs died. And the dogs tore their corpses to bits." As Pavel hurtled down the staircase the voice, amplified by the echo, pursued him as far as the exit, then through the streets, and, later still, on the train, in his sleep.

Once he had been staying in the same place for several weeks, he believed, he would begin to forget. Forgetfulness, in these post-war days was, more than ever before, the secret of happiness. Those who had no desire to forget drank, took their own lives, or traveled around from place to place, like him, in an endless semblance of returning home.

One day happiness snapped him up. The woman looked like the raspberry picker and was even closer to what a man starved of flesh longs for: a weighty plenitude in her body that gave her breasts, her buttocks, her belly, a life of their own. Returning home after one or two days' absence (he was with a team installing electric cables along the roads), he would lose himself in this body, in the sickly sweet steam of boiled potatoes, and rejoice that one could live without anything other than the heavy flesh of these breasts and the pungent smell of this *izba* on the outskirts of a district capital.

Twice only he had doubts about this happiness. One evening he was watching his companion stirring the contents of a broad frying pan, from which arose the bluish aura of bacon rashers in burned fat. "She looks as if she were mixing it up for pigs," he thought unmaliciously, numbed both by his day's work in the rain and the happiness. "But one could very well turn into a pig if things go on like this," he said to himself, aware of the faint tremor of an awakening, a rush of memories. And he hastened to plunge back into the agreeable torpor of the evening.

The second time (their team had returned earlier than expected on account of frosts, he removed his muddy boots in the hall and went noiselessly upstairs) this happiness almost turned him into a killer. The bedroom door was ajar and already from the kitchen he could see his companion naked, and, glued to her, a very thin man, who seemed, as he huffed and puffed, to be trying to push her out of bed. He looked for the ax in the entrance hall and could not see where it had gone. The few seconds of searching for it calmed him. "What? End up in jail for the sake of that lump of pork and that worm with a wrinkled ass? I'm not crazy." He put on his boots and hurried to leave, knowing it would have been enough for him to see the woman's face, or hear her voice, to kill. He spent the night with a friend and did not sleep, at one minute almost indifferent, at the next planning revenge. In a moment of weariness he believed he had understood what kind of woman she was, whose life he had shared for a year. He had never thought about it before. The war was a time of women without men and men without women, but also one of women who, more from the chance of a town being near the front than from lewdness, had made love recklessly, accustomed to men who went back to the war and whom death made irremediably faithful to their mistress of one night. "Filthy whore!" he muttered in the darkness of the kitchen where his friend had made up a bed for him, but in reality this curse was a way of trying to silence a covert pardon. His concubine reminded him, through her very infidelity, of the days of war. She was still living in those days. "Like me!" he thought.

In the morning the desire for vengeance got the better of him. He went back to the *izba* and found it already empty. The woman had gone to work, leaving him a saucepan of potatoes. He withdrew the cartridges from his automatic pistol, determined to put them in the stove, picturing with malicious glee the fireworks that evening. Then he changed his mind, went up to the bedroom, drew his knife. He stabbed at the down quilt halfheartedly, as if to satisfy his conscience, and stopped. A few feathers fluttered around the bed. The room already looked unrecognizable to him, as if he had never lived there. He stroked the notches on the handle of the knife, then gathered up several things that belonged to him and left. In the hall he noticed the ax, propped in a corner behind the door.

Once again he lived nowhere for several months, still playing at the soldier's return, cunningly avoiding the new life the others were embarking on, so he could stay in the company of those who were no more. Thinking about them one day, he remembered his mother's friend, the foreign woman, Sasha, who was so very Russian and who often came to see them at Dolshanka. He caught up with her in the little town where she lived, near Stalingrad, allowed himself to be persuaded to stay at her house, and began to work at a railroad depot.

The third anniversary of the victory was approaching, the town was being covered in red and gold panels with triumphal slogans, and the radiant faces of heroic soldiers. Pavel had the strange impression that the people around him were talking about a different war and coming more and more to believe in the war that was being invented for them in the newspapers, on billboards, on the radio. He talked about his own war, the penal companies, about attacks made with their bare hands. The head of the workshop rebuked him, they grappled with each other. Pavel let go when he saw a long scar on the chief's arm, crudely sutured the way they used to do it at the front. When their quarrel had abated and they were alone the man took him outside behind a pile of old ties and warned him, "It's all true, what you say. But if they take you away tomorrow for your truth I want you to know I had nothing to do with it. There are spies in the workshop." Pavel told Sasha about it. She gave him bread and all the money she had in the house and advised him to spend the night with an old friend who lived in Stalingrad. She was right. They came looking for him at three in the morning.

He no longer needed to find a pretext for his wanderings. He simply needed to move farther and farther away from Stalingrad, make himself invisible, merge into the new life he had so far been running away from. He left the Volga region heading west, then through one chance or another began descending southward, thinking of the sea, the ports, the teeming, colorful south, in which his dubious air of a vagabond soldier would pass unnoticed. For a long time now stations and trains had become his true home. The weeks spent at the depot had given him the self-confidence of a professional. More than once he detected the presence of a military patrol. He would change, put on his blue overalls, and pass as a railroad worker. Then he became a soldier again: engineers rarely refused to help a "defender of the nation."

That day Pavel was in uniform. The train he had spotted that morning was already unloaded and was due to start at any minute. Its destination suited him. He still had to negotiate with the engineer or, if he were refused, leap into a freight car after the train had started. It was while he was keeping watch between two warehouse storage buildings that he heard their voices: two men's voices, backing one another up—with menacing jocularity—and that of a woman, whose strongly oriental accent he noticed straight away. Curious, he turned the corner and saw them. The men (one of them leaning on a broom, the other, switching his lamp on and off, teasingly, for it was still light) were preventing the woman from leaving, blocking her path, pushing her against the warehouse wall. They were doing it without violence but their movements had the authority of a cat playing with an already damaged bird.

"No, my beauty, first tell us where you're going and what train you're catching, then tell us your name," repeated the man with the broom, moving his shoulder forward to check the young woman.

"And then we'd like to have a look at your papers," chimed in the railroad worker, shining his lamp in the woman's face.

She took a more vigorous step to free herself, in her voice a weary cord snapped, "Let me alone!" The man with the lamp thrust his hand against her chest, as if to ward off an attack. "Now you be nice to us, honey, that's all we ask. Otherwise the militia are going to want to know about you."

The woman, dazed, her eyes half closed as if to avoid seeing what was happening to her, could no longer repulse the four hands that were pulling at her dress, squeezing her waist, pushing her toward the gaping warehouse door.

In an effort to forestall the warnings to be prudent sounding in his head Pavel moved up to them with one bound. It was not an urge to come to the rescue that decided him but an irrational vision: the violent contrast between the beauty of the woman, the chiseled delicacy of her face, and the quagmire of words, physiognomies, and actions that held her fast.

His sudden appearance and his uniform made an impression on them, even frightened them. At the sound of his harsh voice the railroad worker turned, stepped away from the young woman, bent down to pick up the lamp he had put on the ground. He stammered, "No, look, it's like this, Sergeant. . . . She's a thief. When we saw her she was lifting stuff from the warehouse."

He began justifying himself, invoking the sweeper as a witness. But gradually, as he got the better of his fear, he realized that the sergeant had a bizarre look about him: his cheeks covered with a four-day beard, a tunic coarsely patched here and there and with no collar, his top boots battered and swollen by wear. Appalled by his mistake, he changed his tone.

"And what about you? What are you doing here? Did you want to visit the stores, too? So she was with you, this thief? You're two of a kind."

Pavel, scenting danger, tried to silence him. "Right, shut your trap, you! Leave the woman and go tap some wheels! Get going! And not another sound from your whistle."

But the other man, on whom it was dawning more and more clearly that this soldier who had given him such a fright was on shaky ground himself, exploded, "What's that? Wheels? Just who do you think you are? You wait. We're going to find out what regiment you've deserted from! Hold him, Vassilich! I'm going to call the patrol! They're here, somewhere, near the station."

Pavel threw off the sweeper as he tried to seize him, turned and saw the man was not lying: an officer and two soldiers were making their way along the track. He struck out to stop the two men shouting. One fist impacted against a clammy, slippery mouth, the other hand hit a chin. But the yelling continued, only in shriller tones. And the fingers twisted, clutching at his tunic. He struck again. The lamp fell, rolled along the ground, lit up by itself, and its beam cut across the wheels of a train that was just moving off. In the distance the two soldiers of the patrol began to run, the officer quickened his pace.

It was the young woman who dragged him away from this fruitless brawl. Rooted to the spot close to the wall, she suddenly seemed to come to her senses and sped like an arrow toward the train that was moving forward with somnambulistic slowness. Pavel grabbed his pack and followed her, wiping his bloodstained hand on his trousers.

They climbed onto the platform of a freight car, jumped down onto the track on the other side, rolled under another train, and seeing that the soldiers had run around it right at the far end, dove under again, ran the length of the train and crawled between the wheels once more. The whistle blasts of the patrol guided them, now far off, now deafening, separated from them by a single line of freight cars. And their eyes had time to take in the calm of a workman, quietly smoking, sitting on a pile of ties, and the enamel plaque (with an improbable destination) on an old freight car on a siding, and even the inside of the compartments (children, tea, a woman making up the bed) in a passenger train that came hurtling past at high speed and saved them, separating them from their pursuers. They raced forward, drawn along by the draft of its passing, and found themselves once more between the express train and a freight train that was hardly moving at all, as if it could not make up its mind to leave. They saw the opening of a sliding door, for the first time exchanged a look of complicity, and climbed in. Pavel closed the door, found the young woman's arm in the darkness. They remained there without moving, listening behind the thin wooden partition to the coming and going of footsteps, shouts, whistle blasts. Footfalls came closer, walking beside the train, which was still sliding along with agonizing slowness, and a voice addressing someone on the other side of the track shouted, "Hey, they must be somewhere. I saw them! Tell him to bring his dog!" Their eyes were already accustomed to the darkness. They stared at one another fixedly, both sensing that each one's danger, so unique, so linked to each one's past, was now merged with the danger the other was escaping. That their lives were merging. In the distance an angry voice rang out, an order, then there was some barking. And it was at that moment that a shudder ran through the train and Pavel sensed in his own body, at the same moment as in the woman's, an involuntary straining of every muscle in the infantile desire to help the train move off. Its speed accelerated very little but after a dozen clanks of the wheels the noise changed, became more resonant, more vibrant. The train began crossing a bridge and moved faster and faster.

Very early in the morning Pavel got up, quite numbed by a night of watching, his head filled with fleeting visions of the day before. He slid open the heavy door of the freight car and suddenly stepped back a pace, alarmed, dazzled. Against a still-dark sky, beyond heavily wooded valleys, there gleamed the snowy peaks of the Caucasus, almost menacing in their beauty. Their faintly bluish bulk seemed to be growing closer with every second, towering over the train. And, thanks to their height, the whole space reared up vertically. It was impossible for someone who had always lived on the plain to imagine life at the foot of this silent grandeur.

The young woman came to the door as well and looked out, tossing aside her long hair which the wind blew in her face. Through the clattering of the wheels Pavel cried out in admiration. She nodded her head but expressed neither surprise nor fear. She seemed not to be interested in the snowy peaks on the horizon but was studying the wooded hills and the rare villages, still slumbering.

Pavel wanted to get off at the first opportunity, attracted by a large town the train stopped in for a few minutes. This vertical country seemed too foreign to him. The woman held him back.

They jumped from the car when the train slowed down on a bend as it emerged from a long tunnel in the middle of the mountains.

The woman walked quickly, climbing down the slope covered in trees and shrubs that were unfamiliar to Pavel. He followed her with difficulty, getting caught up in brambles that she knew how to avoid, slipping on little screes concealed beneath the heather. With no pathway the forest seemed virgin. Emerging onto the bank of a stream, the woman stopped. Catching up with her ("Does she want to shake me off or what?" he had said to himself a few moments earlier), and without being able to conceal his anxiety beneath a tone of bravado, Pavel asked, "So, are we going to climb up Kazbek mountain, while we're at it? Where are you taking me?" The woman smiled and it was at that moment he noticed how tired she was. Without replying she walked out over the pebbles and into the stream, plunged into it fully clothed, and remained still, letting the water wash her body, her face, and her dress with its frayed sleeves. Pavel wanted to call out to her, then changed his mind. He smiled and walked off toward the rocks that led into the river a little downstream. Everything suddenly seemed simple to him, as if foreseen by an unusual order of things that he had yet to fathom. He undressed behind the rocks and slipped into the water. The sun was already at its height and roasted their skin. Their clothes dried in a few minutes.

During this halt on the bank he learned what he had already guessed. The woman was a Balkar. One of those Caucasian people deported in 1944. Some of them had tried to return secretly, but were caught well before they had seen the snow of the mountain peaks.

She showed him her village in the distance: a deserted street, orchards with branches bowed down to the ground under a vain abundance of fruit, and in the yard of one house, hanging on a line, a row of washing in tatters.

For reasons of prudence they settled several miles from there. From time to time Pavel went down into the empty village where he found a few carpenter's tools, a box of nails, an old tinder box. One day he saw wheel marks imprinted in the thick dust of the road. He identified them as a military four-wheel-drive. The months passed, the vehicle did not reappear. He said nothing to the woman. "My wife," he often thought now.

The shelter they had built in the rocky fold of a valley was a day's walk from a little town with a railroad station. It was from this town that Pavel sent a letter to Sasha. She was the only one to know of their secret life. The only one to come and see them once or twice a year.

She came, too, for the birth of their child and stayed longer that time. One evening Pavel was returning from the beehives set up on the other side of the valley at the edge of a chestnut forest. He crossed the stream, carrying a pail filled with fresh honey on his shoulder, and stopped to catch his breath at the foot of the little slope that led up to their house. Through the half-open door he saw the figures of the two women. Sasha was standing, a candle in her hand, his wife was sitting down, her face bent over the child. He heard not the words but just the music, slow and even, of their hushed conversation. He thought of Sasha with the wistful gratitude inspired by a person who expects no word of thanks, who never even thinks of such a thing, and who gives much too much for it ever to be possible to repay her. "If she were Russian she would never have dared to come here," he said to himself, realizing that this was a very imperfect manner of expressing the woman's nature. A foreigner, she took greater liberties with the weighty laws and customs governing the country: she did not consider them to be absolute, so they ceased to be absolute.

From the place where Pavel had stopped he heard the rippling of the stream, the supple and resonant murmur that filled their house at night, merging with the sounds of the forest, the crackling of the fire. Below the rock, facing their house, the water was smooth and very black. The sky tossed into it the reflection of a constellation that swayed gently, changing its shape. He was amazed to think that man needed so little in order to live in happiness. And that in the world they had fled, this little got lost in innumerable stupidities, in lies, in wars, in the desire to snatch this little away from others, in the fear of having only this little.

He lifted the pail and began climbing toward the house. His wife was standing on the threshold with their son in her arms. The child had waked up but was not crying. The stars cast a weak light on his tiny brow. They remained there for a moment in that night, without moving, without saying a word.

She who was telling me the story of Pavel's life broke off the narrative at this nocturnal moment. I thought it was simply a pause between two words, between two sentences, and that the past would once more come alive in her voice. But little by little her silence merged with the immensity of the steppe surrounding us, with the silence of the sky that had the dense luminosity of the first moments after the sunset. She was seated in the middle of an endless expanse of undulating grass, her head tilted slightly upward, her eyes half closed, gazing into the distance. And it was when I realized there was nothing more to come, that I suddenly understood: the end of the story was already known to me. I already knew what would happen to the soldier, his wife, their child. The tale had been confided to me more than a year before, one winter's evening in the great dark *izba,* the day when the words a youth yelled at me had almost been the death of me. "The firing squad gunned your father down like a dog." After that, from one Saturday evening to the next, the story had continued, giving me what I had missed most at the orphanage—the certainty that I had been preceded on this earth by people who loved me.

As I looked at this white-haired woman seated a few yards away from me, it was becoming clearer to me all the time that the real ending to her story was this silence, this tide of light hovering over the steppe and the two of us, bonded together by the lives and deaths of beings who now survived only in ourselves. In her words and henceforth in my memory. She did not speak but now I could picture her shade: in the depths of the house hidden in a narrow valley in the Caucasus. There she was, a woman holding a candle, smiling at a young mother as she walked in, carrying a child in her arms, at a man who was setting down on a bench a heavy pail covered with a cotton cloth.

Mentally I spoke her name, Sasha, as if to ensure that the woman sitting on the grass of the steppe beside me was one and the same as that other who had so discreetly, so constantly, threaded her way through the life of my family. At that moment she made an effort to get up, no doubt noticing that the night was drawing in. Clumsily, I hurried to come to her aid, to offer her my arm, sensing for the first time the frailty of her body, the frailty of age, which at fourteen one finds hard to imagine. In this hasty gesture my fingers grasped her injured hand. I felt an instinctive trembling, that decorous reflex certain disabled people have when they do not want to cause alarm or elicit sympathy. She smiled at me and spoke in a voice that had rediscovered its serene and precise tones.

After walking for several minutes I realized that I had left behind the book we used to take with us during those long days spent on the steppe beside the river. I told Sasha, ran back, and when I turned, saw her in the distance, all alone amid the limitless expanse filled with the translucency of the evening. I walked slowly, catching my breath, and watched her waiting for me in that absolute solitude, with the detachment that made her presence like a mirage. I was not thinking about the history of my family, of which she had just given me the last memories. I was thinking about her, herself, this woman who in a most discreet manner, almost accidentally, I might have believed, had taught me her language, and in that language had taught me about the land of her birth, the land that had never left her during her long life in Russia.

From afar I recognized her smile, the gesture of her hand. And with all the ardor of my youth I made a silent oath to give back to her one day her true name and her native country, just as she had dreamed of it in the endlessness of this steppe.

5

"No, listen, let's face it, politically speaking the country's a corpse. Or rather a phantom. A phantom that would still like to frighten people but simply makes them laugh instead."

They were talking about Russia. I did not intervene. If I occasionally found myself at very Parisian gatherings of this type, it was never to join in the conversation. I accepted invitations because I knew that, in this highly composite world, there was always a chance I might encounter a guest who, learning where I came from, would exclaim, "Well I never! Only yesterday I met a compatriot of yours in Lisbon, at So-and-so's place. Now, what was her name?" In this way, at any rate, I imagined that, by questioning this providential guest, I could locate a trace of you, hold onto it, narrow down its whereabouts to a continent, a country, a city. For more than two years I had been patiently revisiting the places where your presence seemed to me likely, cities where, even briefly, we had once lived together. From now on, instead of this questing (I had often told myself that, logically, those must be precisely the cities you would avoid), I took to listening for some clue that might slip out amid the cocktail party chatter, between a couple of pronouncements on the subject of political corpses or similar pieces of conventional wisdom.

That day Russia-as-phantom scored a bull's-eye. The conversation took off.

"A black hole that swallows up everything thrown into it," someone added.

"They're allergic to democracy," affirmed the first.

A woman reaching out with her cigarette toward an ashtray said, "I've read somewhere that they now have a shorter life expectancy than in some African countries."

"That, darling, is probably because they smoke too much," declared her husband, playfully spiriting away her pack of cigarettes.

Everyone laughed. They changed the subject. On the pretext of going for another drink, I moved away, eyeing their little group among other circles that were forming and breaking up on the whim of a look, a word, a moment of boredom. The woman stubbing out her cigarette was a kind of minuscule adolescent, despite being in her sixties. Her husband, a former ambassador, was a tall, heavy man who, all the while he was listening (that is to say, pretending to listen) was raising his eyebrows in greeting to people over the heads of his interlocutors, then rejoining the conversation, diving in with a glancing remark. There was another woman, a high priestess of Parisian culture with a masculine profile and a voice like iron. Her very thin body, the expression in her eyes, and the movements of her chin seemed to be full of militancy for some cause. Below her short-cropped hair, her neck with its almost childlike delicacy, the last refuge of her femininity, belied this militancy and even she may not have been aware of its beauty. His eyes slid over yet another woman, an absolutely classic blonde who smiled and whom one had the impression of having already met a thousand times, until one penetrated through this gilded, smiling carapace to an unknown stranger. Finally, the young man who had just been speaking about the "phantom country." He was young at fifty and always would be. Black jeans, a white shirt widely unbuttoned to reveal a pale chest, an artist's mop of hair, elegant round spectacles. More than from this style of dress, the illusion of youth derived from his knack of always being up-to-the-minute. What he actually said mattered little, for during his long life as a teller of truths he had been a Maoist, a communist, an anti-communist, a liberal, an anti-bourgeois living in the most bourgeois district possible; he had defended every cause and its opposite, but, above all, he knew what you had to say to be perceived as a controversialist, a revolutionary, someone who could think the unthinkable, even while uttering banal propositions he would strenuously oppose the next day. At that moment the thing to do was to denigrate the phantom country. He was a master of the sound bite.

As I was leaving I was stopped by a journalist I had met at one of these gatherings. "I'm going to cover your president's visit here with a Russian journalist. Maybe you know her, she's called . . ."

Walking through the night streets I told myself that the chances of discovering you again under a Russian identity were virtually nil. Especially alongside "our" president. However, it was the only means I had left for eliminating one by one the women who were not you.

The epithet "phantom country" haunted me for some time, like a tune you get on your brain but can't identify. And so did this regret: I should have intervened, tried to explain, told them that . . . Later, in the night, I thought about the phantom pain an injured man can feel after an amputation. He has an intense physical awareness of the life of the arm or leg he has just lost. I told myself that it was the same for one's native land, for one's country, lost or reduced to the state of a shade. It comes to life again within us, as both desolation and love, in the deepest throbbing of the severed veins.

"I should have talked to them about . . ." But what came into my mind was a silent image: that woman, alone, amid the immensity of the steppe, her gaze lost in the last glow of the sunset. I pictured this same woman, younger, at the start of the war, a nurse in a hospital in a little town beyond the Volga. Wards crammed with wounded, dying, dead. Surgeons operating day and night, collapsing with exhaustion. The earth resonating underfoot, thanks to the bombing, like a broad slab laid over a cavity. Trains arrive, discharge their cargoes of bodies, sticky with blood, mud, lice. Arms numbed by the weight of all these men who have to be carried, turned, lifted. In the tumult of cries one can no longer make out which mouth is calling out. Pain makes all look alike. And this is happening in a country in which both of the capital cities are under siege, the army is routed, the towns laid waste. A phantom country.

She had never called it that, had certainly never said to herself, "I am a foreigner, this country isn't mine, I don't have to suffer the extreme fate of this people." During a bombing raid a piece of shrapnel had maimed the fingers of her right hand. Since then she had worked from dawn till dusk and often through the night sorting men in transit at the switching yard among the trains setting off for the front and returning from it.

I remember that, as I was taking my leave of the people with whom I had spent the first part of the evening, I heard someone remarking that the price of real estate ("in central Paris, in any event," the girl-woman qualified) was about to go up again.

The winter night was warm, the rain at the open window split up the city's glow into an infinity of twinkling lights. Myriads of luminous dots spread out before me, a crude symbol of human dispersal: to discover a lost person all you would have to do would be to visit each of these sources of light, one after another, over the whole planet. Often in my despair this infinite sifting of the lights seemed to me achievable.

I could remember very precisely the day I told you about Sasha, about the woman who suddenly appeared to me, all alone in the immensity of the steppe.

In our jargon we called them "Peeping Toms."

That day, in the furnace of an African city, there was nothing left but the shreds of the two opposing armies, exhausted soldiers who no longer even had the strength to hate one another. A few citizens besides, lying low, deafened by explosions, watched over their dead. And, finally, the Peeping Toms, professionals in the pay of arms manufacturers, specialists who observed the fighting from a reasonable distance, took photos, noted the performance of weapons, filmed death. People who bought guns were no longer satisfied with advertisements or demonstration firings at mickey mouse rifle ranges. They demanded the real conditions of war, evidence obtained under fire, real bodies being blown to pieces instead of dummies with holes shot through them. The Peeping Toms' telephoto lenses would capture the outline of a tank with a torn-off turret, from which blackened human carcasses were emerging, or achieve a well-composed shot of a group of soldiers cut to ribbons by an assault grenade.

They were our reason for remaining in the city. We had contrived to approach them, get to know them, help them out, make sure we would be able to pick up their trail in Europe. Then, when the smoke from the fires had begun to interfere with their filming, we had watched them leaving: a helicopter slipping by against the russet hills, so light that it looked like a tourist flight.

Moving from one hiding place to another, we had found ourselves on the top floor of a hotel dominating the port area. The first five or six floors were blackened with soot and had no glass left in the windows. An iron spiral staircase leading to the terraced garden on the first floor had been ripped away by an explosion and now swung like an enormous spring, pointing up into the void. The top floor was occupied by a panoramic restaurant that in peacetime revolved slowly, enabling tourists to contemplate the sea, the colorful crowds swarming in the market, the ocher shapes of the mountains. Now that the dining room was still and without air conditioning, we felt as if we were in a glass cage. Not a breath of air was admitted by the double glazing, which even deadened the sound of the shooting. The tables were laid, the napkins stood there like little starched pyramids. The silence and the stale air were reminiscent of an empty museum

on a July afternoon. A great swordfish, mounted on the wall above
the bar, added to this impression of being behind glass in a museum.
From time to time bursts of gunfire could be heard at the bottom of
the building, then on the floors above, climbing higher. One night
the electric current returned for a few seconds: tinted glass lamp-
shades spread a soft light the color of tea, the fans above the tables
came to life. And next to the bar came a sighing sound from a cassette
player: two or three phrases of a blues number that faded almost
immediately as the darkness returned.

By day we could observe virtually the entire city from the
curved windows. Often two groups of soldiers, rebels and government troops, would be advancing blindly toward each other, separated by a block of houses, and would suddenly come face to face,
dive into porches or onto the ground, and kill each other. Occasionally a lone man would be moving along, hugging the walls, his gun at
the ready, and from our glassed-in refuge we would see his enemy
proceeding with a stealthy tread, just around the corner of the house.
Seen from above, war revealed its whole nature: that of a comic and
ruthless game. Watching the two soldiers as they drew closer, not
yet having seen each other, we knew what was going to happen and
both our vantage point and this superhuman prescience distressed us,
like a prerogative usurped. In the distance, several miles away from
the burning city, we could make out the gray rectangles of the American camp. They were waiting for the fighting to end before they
intervened.

Our thoughts and our words had a hard, decisive clarity during
these days of confinement in our rooftop refuge. Perhaps because
we were seeing the battle from a great height, as if on a model, and
realizing that, in the end, all you need to do is to climb up ten floors
for human folly to be laid bare. Or else it was because our own situation was only too clear and irrevocable: watching the Peeping Toms
take off we could no longer hope that, as in the past, a heavyweight

combat helicopter would come thundering down to land alongside the blazing houses and lift out the remnants of the forces still stubbornly serving the empire. The latest confused and improbable news that had reached us from Moscow spoke of shooting in the streets and civilian buildings being bombarded. Chaos that very clearly spelled out the end.

And to underline it all, the war appeared so transparent. Despite the smoke from the fires, despite the amount of blood spilled, despite the tangle of commentaries the newspapers wrapped it up in. Its logic was very simple. A change in the governing team had been decided on by the Americans a million miles away from this city. What they would gain from this was the halving of the price of a barrel of oil. The new team would sell oil to pay for the arms already delivered. These would need to be regularly renewed, in accordance with the advice of the decision makers. And, in order to get the right choices made, the advisers would project the videos filmed by the Peeping Toms, showing the weaponry in totally authentic combat conditions.

You began talking to me about this transparency a few minutes after a soldier's death. We had heard him running up the stairs, shooting at the men pursuing him. The door to the restaurant was not barricaded—we knew this would have infuriated any attackers and deprived us of a slim chance of survival. There had been the crackling of several bursts of gunfire, magnified by the echo from the various floors, then an explosion. It was impossible to know if the hand grenade had been thrown by the fugitive or his pursuers. In any event, they had not climbed any higher and the soldier lay dead on the landing outside the restaurant. I no longer recall which side he was fighting for. I was simply struck by his youth.

We had covered his body with a tablecloth and it was then that you talked about the people in their New York or London offices dressing up these wars with all the trappings of news stories, articles, broadcasts, in-depth surveys. They pretended to forget about the price of a barrel of oil. They spoke of ancestral enmities, humanitarian catastrophes, the shackling of the democratic process.

"Just you wait. They'll blame this carnage once again on the rivalry between Bantu and Nilotic peoples," you said. It was such a bitter gibe that I did not recognize you.

"But I thought they were all Bantu in this region."

"Some tame anthropologist will discover as many ethnic groupings as are needed. And they'll be taught that they've always been sworn enemies and all they have to do is kill each other. Or someone will remember that the president they don't want made a visit to Qaddafi or Fidel twenty years ago. And across all the screens in the world, on every radio station, he'll be portrayed as a bloodstained terrorist. And the firm that organizes this blitz will have its fee paid thanks to the reduction in the price of oil. What was it old Marx said? 'Offer a capitalist a three hundred percent profit and there's no crime he won't commit.' It's still topical."

In silence we contemplated this model of a city that looked, in the dusk, like the fires of a nomad camp. The two armies, entrenched in their positions, were waiting for morning. In the distance, above the American contingent, one could see the shafts of light beamed toward the ground by helicopters already swallowed up in the darkness. I believed I could guess your thoughts and, to distract you, I began to tell you about my meeting in Milan with one of these P.R. virtuosos. His tongue loosened by drink, he claimed that his firm could create a political personality, give him a profile, have him acclaimed, and then within ninety-six hours demolish him and present him as a total villain, without public opinion being aware of having been manipulated. "Yes, ninety-six hours, four days," he had boasted. "But on one condition. It must happen on the weekend. That's when critical faculties are at a low ebb. Besides, every break in routine makes it easier to reshape the collective memory. And as for the summer vacation, believe you me, there's enough time then to get public opinion used to the idea of Saddam Hussein being the next president of the United States."

Instead of smiling I saw your face grow tense, you closed your eyes and shook your head slightly, as if to suppress a sudden pain. You were already a long way away from this city, from this war, at once so real and such a sham. You were away in some past and I did not know if your pain was derived from an excess of sorrow or too great a joy. I drew you to me and it was at that moment, as if by some stupid and aggressive mockery, that the lights came on again. I rushed to the light switches—through the uncurtained windows our silhouettes would have been visible all over the city. But the tape deck hidden at the back of the bar remained connected and in the darkness we listened to the ebb and flow of a saxophone in a melody that, for its part, had nothing aggressive about it. It was a gust of weary notes that occasionally slid, as if along a razor blade, to the brink of a fall, a shout, a sob, then returned to a deep and rhythmic breathing, painting a picture in the darkness of the end of a long race, the end of a struggle, the weariness of a man on the night of a lost battle. The melody broke off but for a time in the darkness we went on hearing its silent rhythm.

That night I told you about my last meeting with Sasha, her solitude in the middle of an endless steppe, about that moment when her story had reached its conclusion, leaving me with a picture of a mother and father bowed over their child one night in the Caucasus.

Shortly before sunrise a shell hit the wall of the hotel; in the bar a row of glasses slid down one by one and smashed on the counter. The bursts of gunfire were already penetrating into the foyer on the ground floor, and moving toward the upper floors. I broke a window in the kitchen, then another on the landing, hoping to find a fire escape. But there was only an old, dry bird's nest that crumbled away from a cornice and fell among the soldiers milling around and shooting. We knew from experience that ropes, drainpipes, staircases leading onto roofs, and other lifesaving devices only existed in adventure films. The acrid smoke swirled around the banisters, gradually filling the dining room of the restaurant.

Time vibrated, taking its cue from the renewal of the attacks, the tumult of the explosions, and the deafening silence of the brief lulls. Our eyes fastened upon a table, the place settings, the little bouquet of artificial flowers, the sun and the sea outside the window—the tranquillity of breakfast in a hotel—and for a second it was difficult to imagine that a few stories below a soldier, his legs riddled with bullets, was crawling along the corridor to hide in a bedroom. During one of these pauses we tried to leave via the terraced garden and, just when we were close to the spiral staircase, encountered gunfire. It was the last of the old regime's troops. They thought it was an attack coming from the upper floors. We retreated up the staircase now reverberating with gunshots. I had an eyebrow nicked by a ricochet. You turned as you ran, saw my forehead all bloody, but I had time to intercept your look, to calm it with a wink. The bullets fired at us provoked a new round of gunfire. In the end the attackers had the building surrounded.

During the course of that day, amid all the flurries of our sudden dashes for survival, our eyes would collide with a quick glance, without words, grasping in a flash all that our life was and all that awaited us. These glances, when our eyes met, comprehended everything up to the very end. But translated into thought, words whispered inside one's head, this comprehension became improbable: "This woman who is so dear to me will fall, die within an hour, within a couple of hours."

They were already fighting on the staircase outside the restaurant door. What could be heard in the shouting was the hysterical ferocity of those who are certain they have won. The bursts of gun-fire were shorter, people were being finished off. They were no longer fighting, they were hunting down, flushing out, finishing off. The smoke now smelled of the steam from water poured on flames. Outside the window night was falling, encouraging the soldiers to fight it out as fast as possible before dark.

For a few instants our weariness, our remoteness, made us invisible. The soldiers streamed into the dining room, riddling the nooks and crannies with bullets wherever darkness and smoke lingered, transforming the kitchen into a long cascade of shattered glass. And yet there we were in front of them, by the broken window where one could breathe, standing pressed against each other. For us everything came down to this embrace, to a few words guessed at through the gunfire, from the movement of our lips.

An instant later they discovered our presence. The barrel of an automatic rifle began to poke me in the back, a butt struck us across the shoulders, as if to separate us. Then they drew back, noting the distance necessary for the execution, to avoid getting themselves sprayed with blood. After three days of siege and three sleepless nights the world outside our bodies was blurred, flaccid. The mind floundered, trying to grasp the hardness of death amid this softness and, without growing alarmed, fell back into somnolence. The only fragment of lucidity was the soldier's arm, seen in a sidelong glance, when I lifted my face from yours for an instant: he was wearing a slender leather bracelet on his wrist. "This one won't shoot," I thought with irrational conviction. "No, he won't shoot us."

Like us, they noticed the sliding beneath their feet. For some time now the electric current had been restored and the restaurant was revolving. The picture window framed the fire in the port and, a moment later, the minaret and roofs of the old town. The tape deck struck up again the same flow of weary notes. Its breathy rhythms isolated us even more. We were alone and for a little time still remained in this life, but already felt detached from our entwined bodies, which the yelling soldiers were manhandling. They needed two ordinary condemned people, two bodies standing with their faces to the wall. Our embrace made them uneasy. For them we were a couple of dancers on a tiny island defined by the tea-colored light, the table with a bunch of artificial flowers, the saxophonist's breathy notes. The brassy swaying of the music suddenly took off into a dizzying flight: it was simultaneously laughter, shouting, a sob. Anyone who followed it, in its madness, could only have fallen to his death from this vibrant cliff. There was a click from a magazine being engaged. You raised your eyes toward me, very calm eyes, and said to me, "Till tomorrow, then."

His voice, disdainful and very sure of itself, cut through the bawling of the soldiers. Later you referred to him as an "extraterrestrial." My first impression was precisely that: a cosmonaut captured by the denizens of some planet. He was a GI, escorted by Africans, who made his way into the dining room. His equipment surpassed even what could be seen in films about intergalactic warfare: a helmet with a built-in microphone and a transparent visor, a flak jacket, and a belt that looked like a chastity belt, for it extended down at the front to protect the genitalia; thick padded leggings that covered his knees, gloves with ringed fingers; and, in particular, an infinite number of little balls, capsules, and bottles attached to his webbing, or thrust into the innumerable pockets of his jacket. No doubt these were all the possible antidotes and serums, all the flashlights, all the filter pumps. He stood a head taller than his indigenous escorts, who surrounded him respectfully and watched him as he spoke. Confronting our perplexity, they all began shouting at the same time, demanding a reply from us. It was simply their din that now stopped us understanding. And I heard myself exclaiming, still a stranger to myself, "Look, first tell your bodyguards to keep quiet!"

I saw you smiling, realized what an absurd expression I had used, and laughed as well. "Bodyguards" had just slipped out.

Later on we often found ourselves picturing this military novelty: the intrepid American warrior flanked by a dozen bodyguards, a new method of going to war. And, in truth, the United States was terrified of the idea of having to send body bags back to America, especially during presidential elections.

These long underground passages of our remembered past would often open out onto the smiling banality of the present and, on that day, onto a reception room and a woman trying unsuccessfully to dislodge a tiny pastry, a petit four topped with a drop of cream, which she was being offered by a waiter. While tormenting this pastry, which was stuck to the others, she went on talking to me and her voice, already smoothed off by the triviality of social conversation, became completely automatic: "It was, you know, so moving. And awfully well documented . . . All those clips from the archives . . ." What brought me back from the past was not her words but the glass in her left hand that was tilting and on the brink of spilling its contents. I grasped her hand. She smiled at me, finally succeeding in capturing the petit four. "You know, there's a great deal in what he says. It's, you know, incredibly powerful!" Her mouth rounded as she spoke, and her tongue slipped out delicately and captured a morsel from the petit four. At last I realized where I was, in this room next to a woman praising a film that had just been shown in preview. Back in the underground tunnel of my memories I was still seeing the soldier who had been shot a moment before and whom we covered with a tablecloth; the smell of that African city in flames was still in my nostrils; and in the deepest galleries, in the most remote years, other cities appeared, other faces frozen by death. The woman seemed to be waiting for me to reply. I agreed with her, echoing her last remark. I must return to the present.

To get my bearings again in this Parisian present, all I needed to do was to identify old acquaintances in their new guise. The blond woman talking to me about the film was always the same blonde. I had encountered her a hundred times at gatherings like this, where I hoped to discover traces of you. Since our previous encounter she had simply grown ten years younger, altered the color of her eyes and the oval of her face, lengthened her nose, altered her name and profession. She was a different person, of course, but still a perfectly formed specimen of this golden feminine type, smiling and so vacuous as to be almost agreeable. A little farther off, in a polite scramble around the tables, I saw the ex-ambassador, that massive, graying man who on this occasion was an ex-minister. He had less hair and had adopted a more nasal, but still ironic, voice. Making deft use of a pair of tongs, he was serving his wife as she held out her plate. He was making jokes and the people around him were smiling, even as they struggled to slip their forks through the bobbing and weaving of arms to obtain their slice of cake or their portion of salad.

I once again located the young man of fifty, the intellectual with a hot line to the truth. He was now older than a couple of weeks ago and, instead of the black curls he had last time, he had chosen a sleek ash gray hairstyle, but what he was saying could have been said, word for word, by his double who had held forth about the "phantom country." He had already filled his plate and was in conversation now with a very corpulent man sporting a ponytail and dressed in black, the maker of the film that had just been screened. Sitting in a little circle of guests, the two of them unintentionally formed a variety double act, the thin one and the fat one, and their remarks corresponded to this physical difference: the thin one, the intellectual, modulated and elaborated on the fat one's deliberately crude remarks based on his "gut feelings." The fat one, the artist, was apt to begin his sentences by saying, "Personally,

I don't give a damn for the official history" before going on to explain how "you have to swallow the archives raw." It was a remark from a woman that drew me toward their circle. Tall, bony, with a masculine profile (I recalled the literary journalist who had played the role of this Parisian type last time), that evening she was an official of the Ministry of Culture. "You should show your film in Moscow. They ought to know these facts as well," she said to the filmmaker with the authority of one who provides subsidies.

"In Moscow . . ." I was used to picking up these Russian references. But more crucial still than this reflex was the desire to see the face of the person who could have made that film. From where I was I could only see his very broad back and the ponytail dangling over his black silk shirt. I went up to them.

The film was called *The Price of Delay* and was black and white, for it consisted mainly of archive film from the Second World War. During the opening minutes it showed Soviet soldiers, eating, coming and going, laughing, sitting and smoking, dancing to the sound of an accordion, washing in a river. Then Stalin loomed up, tugging at his pipe, looking both jovial and cunning, and, in the tones of a verdict being delivered, the commentary declared that this man was guilty of . . . (here there was a pause) . . . slowness. The advance of his armies was much less rapid than it could and should have been. The result: thousands and thousands of deaths in the camps, which could have been liberated much sooner by this army that had moved at a snail's pace. The archive film moved on to piles of bodies, lines of barbed wire, squat buildings with their chimneys belching out black smoke. And again, without transition, one saw the soldiers with their broad laughing faces, a close-up of a smoker blowing elegant white smoke rings in the air, another of a soldier, with his fur *shapka* pulled well down over his eyes, sleeping under a tree. And a few images further on we again saw the living skeletons in their striped pajamas, their eyes distended with suffering, naked, emaciated bodies which no longer looked like human beings. The commentary began adding up figures: the delay accumulated by these lazy soldiers, the number of victims who could have been saved. . . . There were several ingenious technical devices in the film. At one moment the screen was split in two. On the right-hand side the scenes were shown in slow motion, focusing on the soldiers moving at a sleepwalker's pace. And the left-hand side, with speeded-up film, showed a mass grave being rapidly filled with corpses in striped clothing. In the final sequence these two juxtaposed realities faded and the image came through of the armored vehicles and the American soldiers sweeping in, as liberators, through the gateway to a camp.

I should not have intervened. All the more because I knew how useless it would be. Or at least I should have done it differently. I talked about the front that extended well over a thousand miles between the Baltic and the Black Sea, about the forced march offensives Stalin launched to save the American troops defeated in the Ardennes, about the crude arithmetic of the numbers of soldiers who had to die in their thousands every day just to shift the front line a few miles farther west.

At this moment the fat filmmaker, deeply ensconced in his armchair, crossed his legs and knocked over the glass the woman next to him had put on the floor. He roared with laughter and apologized, the woman gave him a paper napkin with which he patted his splashed pants bottoms, and everyone stirred, as if liberated by this interlude. And it was in the tones of a cocktail party argument that he exclaimed to me, gruff and ironic, "Look, I don't give a damn for all that official history, Stalin, Zhukov, and all that claptrap. What I do is open an archive like a can of beans. I wolf it all down. And then I spit it out onto the screen, just as it stands."

He must have realized that, after having "wolfed it down," he could not then spit it out just as it stood, and quickly corrected the image in more aggressive tones: "Don't tell me you're going to come out with all that old stuff about twenty million Russians killed in the war!"

The intellectual with the ash gray hair elaborated with, "The great trump card of nationalist propaganda."

The conversation became general.

"The German-Soviet pact," interrupted the ex-minister.

"If it hadn't been for the Americans Stalin would have invaded the whole of Europe," said a woman, still young, who spoke like someone reciting a lesson.

"You know, those twenty million must have included everyone who died of old age. Over four years that's quite a crowd!" wise-cracked the ex-minister.

"The Katyn massacres . . ." chimed in the official from the culture ministry.

"Our duty to remember . . ." added the intellectual.

"Repentance . . ." intoned a man who a few minutes earlier had collided with a woman at the salad table and had made an apologetic face: exactly the same as now when speaking of repentance.

"Listen, it's very simple. In the archives I slaved over in Moscow it's as plain as the nose on your face. If the Russians hadn't dragged their feet in Poland and Germany at least half a million men could have been saved. Hold on, it can't hurt to do a bit of number crunching."

The filmmaker took a daybook out of his pocket with a cover that opened out onto a little pocket calculator. Several people leaned forward to follow his explanations better. I could hear my own voice, as if from outside myself, booming away above these bowed heads. I tried to say that, when liberating a camp the soldiers could not use artillery or assault grenades, and that often they had to go in without shooting because the Germans sheltered behind the prisoners, and that out of two hundred men in a company only a dozen were left at the end of a battle.

The ringing of a telephone buried in someone's bag interrupted these wasted words. People began patting their pockets, rummaging in their bags. In the end the filmmaker grabbed the machine out of his own jacket pocket. Cursing, he swung his body out of the arm-chair and moved away a few paces. Without him the conversation split up into couples and was lost in the general hubbub of the room.

I made my way through the crowd, seeking to rid myself of a feeling of nausea at having said too much. But the words I had just spoken came back to haunt me in increasingly irreparable tones: "Without artillery . . . With their bare hands . . . Human shields . . ." In the looks I encountered I felt I was sensing the ironic tolerance people have for what is, at the end of the day, a harmless gaffe. It struck me that I should have found it easier to make myself understood by that Wehrmacht officer barking out his orders on the square in the Brest Litovsk citadel than by these people sipping their drinks.

Stopping in a recess in front of the window, beside a piano pushed against the wall, I studied the room for a moment, the little gathering around the tables with the remains of the food, the circle I had just left, other groups. The filmmaker, whom I had not at first noticed, was seated near to me on the piano stool. He was shouting into his telephone while swinging round in little abrupt half turns that reflected the vehemence of his replies: "No, listen, I'm not a charity! It's already costing us an arm and a leg. Okay, but they should lower their commission. No, keep your hat on, I'm not holding a gun to anyone's throat. . . . Nor to anyone's head either, I mean . . . You'd have to be the biggest dumbass in the world to offer them a million and a half. Yes, but it was figured in, pal. Hold on, I can tell you that right away. Provided we keep the rate that was quoted, all in all what you'll get is . . ."

He laid his daybook-cum-calculator on the lid of the piano and began doing his numbers and communicating the result to his inter-locutor. If he had looked up he would have seen a kind of admiration in my eyes.

At that moment the memory of the soldier came back to me. Surrounded by his comrades, he paused on the brink of what must once have been a narrow river, and was now stagnant, clogged up with human ashes and corpses. After a few seconds' hesitation he walked into the yellowish liquid, the others following him, soon wading in up to their chests, and emerging covered in sticky scum. And they began running toward the rows of barbed wire, toward the watchtowers.

It now came to me that in the absurd discussion after the film I should simply have spoken about that soldier. And especially about those few minutes between the moment when he plunged into the brown porridge containing a thousand dead people in suspension and the second when, still conscious, he raised his hand to his face, half blown away by shrapnel. Yes, I should have explained that it was the sight of that water that had slowed down the soldiers' advance (oh, that Russian slowness!). Nothing could amaze them any more, not blood, not the infinite diversity of wounds, not the resistance of bodies that, though dismembered, mangled, blind, still clung to life. But this beige scum, these lives reduced to dust . . . The soldiers hesitated, as if on the brink of what reason could not conceive.

At that moment, in front of the almost bare table, I saw the filmmaker turning a glass upside down, no doubt to see if anyone had been drinking from it. A young woman (the one who had announced that Stalin could have invaded Europe), obliged to shout because of the noise, was speaking to him with her mouth close to his ear, directing a whole pantomime of gestures at his ear as if this organ could see. Beyond the swaying of heads the intellectual with the ash gray hair was holding forth, surrounded by the figures of women, and his hands were making hypnotic passes. In the circle around the ex-minister and his girl-wife they were roaring with laughter.

The idea of telling them about the soldier suddenly seemed unthinkable. No, I had simply to imagine his mute, invisible presence somewhere in this room, where the aromas of sauces and wine spilled on the carpet lingered. I should observe his gaze—first at the sequences of the film, then at these mouths, eating, tasting the wine, smiling, talking about the camps. The soldier's gaze did not judge, it focused on things and beings with a wry detachment and understood everything. It understood that the people in the room who spoke of millions of victims, of repentance, of the duty to remember, were lying. Not that the victims had not existed. The soldier still had their ashes stuck to his hands, to the folds in his tunic. But at the time of their martyrdom and their death each of them had a face, a past, that not even the serial number tattooed to their wrists had succeeded in obliterating. Now they were conveniently assembled into these anonymous millions, an army of the dead that was constantly being paraded about in the great bazaars of ideas. The soldier had no difficulty in grasping that the sinister building in the film, belching forth black smoke and producing human ashes, had become a real family business for the filmmaker and his friend. And, like good salesmen, this fat man with his pocket calculator and his thin friend with his dogmatic voice, they and their countless ubiquitous doubles uttered deafening rallying cries, hurled abuse at the indifferent, cursed the incredulous. They did not allow the millions of dead a moment's peace, reviving their torture in front of cameras, on the pages of newspapers, on screens. Every day they had to find something new. First it was the spuriously contrite face of a bishop collapsing into repentance. Next the police, like inconsolable penitents, asking forgiveness for the errors of their colleagues half a century ago. Then one day this brilliant notion! Why not accuse the soldiers who liberated the camps of being too slow? The thin men and the fat men were indefatigable in invoking the memory, but, curiously enough, the fuss they made provoked forgetfulness. For they talked about millions without faces, like those cascades of zeros that appeared on their pocket calculators.

I knew that the soldier would not have taken the trouble to deny or debate. His gaze would have been silent. He would have observed the room and would no doubt have formed a single impression that summed up everything: ugliness. Ugliness of words, ugliness of thoughts, ugliness of the shared lie. The extraordinary ugliness of that young woman's face, leaning toward the filmmaker's ear, her young body, tall and lithe, contorted with the hypocrisy of the words the man was listening to with paternal indulgence. Ugliness of all these faces and these bodies, smooth through careful grooming, rubbing shoulders in the agreeable coziness of the in-crowd. The infinite ugliness of that France.

No, the soldier would not have been thinking about all that. His silent presence would have placed him far away from these well-nourished bodies, these minds well versed in the conventional wisdom, far from the hypnotists of memory and the dealers in millions of dead. In this faraway place there was the barbed-wire entanglement on which he had fallen, transforming his own body into a bridge for those who followed him. Beyond his death, there was that instant when, in the liberated camp, the echo of the last shot fired faded away, those blurred minutes when the soldiers who had survived were roaming among the barrack huts with their gaping doors, among the bodies, disposed according to the whims of death, long minutes when they were getting used to feeling they were alive, to seeing the tranquillity of the sky, to being able to hear. In those first instants there was a wounded man, wearing the uniform of a penal company, a young soldier crumpled up against the wall of a hut, his hands pressed against his belly and filled with blood. He cried out, asking for water. But the others, still deafened by the last of the explosions, did not hear him. As the burning pain increased, it seemed to him that no one in the universe heard his cry. He was wrong. A man was coming toward him, very slowly, for he was afraid of falling. This man without flesh, without muscles, clad in striped rags, was moving like a child learning to walk and all his equilibrium was derived from an old bowl filled with water clutched in his hands. It was the water he had gathered from a drainpipe's tiny drips. Water that had already saved life. The wounded soldier saw the prisoner, saw his eyes sunk in his emaciated skull and fell silent. There was nothing more in the world, just these two pairs of eyes slowly approaching each other.

Thinking about that prisoner gave me a feeling of joy I could not explain to myself. I told myself simply that his look was not recorded by any pocket calculator adding up the millions, nor inscribed in any official martyrology. No one was forcing me to recollect him but he lived in my memory, a remarkable being in all the grievous beauty of his gesture.

Threading my way toward the exit between the groups of guests, I passed the girl-wife. Through the noise I could only grasp the last part of the remark she addressed to me: ". . . really enthralling!"

"Yes, it was extremely interesting," I said, echoing her tone of voice.

She shook my hand, tugging on it slightly, which obliged me to lean over a little.

"It was quite true what you said about the German-Soviet pact," she said, screwing up her eyes as a mark of complicity.

"Well, it wasn't actually me who . . ."

"And then that . . . what was it you were saying? Katyn! What a story! Mind you, I've never trusted the Poles."

"Yes, well, but, it was really the Russians there, who . . ."

"My daughter has a Russian friend, you know, a delightful young woman, very cultivated. She speaks three or four languages. She's been everywhere. You must meet her some time. She plays the violin as well."

After hearing this detail I listened to the rest of the story distractedly. The violinist used to remark, "Scratch a Russian and you'll find a Tartar underneath." This turn of phrase delighted the girl-wife. Listening to her, I was waiting for a pause in the rhythm of her breathing that would enable me to take my leave. But the reserves of breath in that puny chest seemed inexhaustible. "Scratch a Pole, you know, and you'll find a . . . ," she drew me toward her to round off her verdict. "Oh, but some of them are not like that at all!" I protested vainly.

At that moment among the groups of couples behind the girl-wife, I saw a man's face in profile that seemed to me both familiar and unrecognizable. I stared at him. The profile seemed to be smiling at someone other than the person he was talking to. I taxed my memory but before I could fix on either a name or a place, the face disappeared behind the moving throng of guests.

Between the end of one story and the immediate start of the next I succeeded in slipping in a brief word of good-bye and dove back into the crowd, wresting my hand away from the storyteller's grasp. The pact. Katyn. The terrible reputation of the Poles. This drawing room farrago, I told myself, was an indirect response to the lies of those hypnotists of memory. I saw them together, the film-maker and the intellectual, a little apart from the others. A snatch of a sentence from their conversation cut through the din: "We'll get Jean-Luc's write-up tomorrow and then on Thursday . . ."

In the concierge's lodge the television was flickering with the last minutes of a match. Standing on the threshold the man looked both weary and still buffeted by the excitement of the game. "Four one! I've never seen anything like it!" he exclaimed, noticing my glance at the screen and in no doubt that one could hardly fail to be surprised by this score. I realized that the match had been broadcast during the screening of the film.

Near the exit a knot of people gathered, the one that forms at the end, the most talkative one, the slowest to disperse. I was waiting for these guests to slip, one by one, through the bottleneck of the door. Suddenly, disturbingly, for the second time I caught sight of a man's face, that discreetly smiling profile, whose smile, it was now clear to me, seemed aware of my presence. Like me, the man was waiting for the crowd to depart. I took a few steps toward him. He turned his head slightly. It was Shakh.

"There must be a stage door somewhere." Shakh spoke these words softly, as if to himself, and, avoiding the throng that was still blocking the exit, he began to climb a staircase at the end of the foyer. I followed him.

We found ourselves on the balcony of a glass-enclosed mezzanine floor that circled the room, which was already half empty of guests. The voices floating up sounded like those of vendors at the end of a street market, pointlessly loud and shrill among a mere handful of shoppers. You could also hear a series of suction-cup sounds, good-bye kisses accompanied by meows of politeness. The staff were moving the tables, rearranging the armchairs. As he walked along, Shakh looked at the room then turned, and I saw a weary expression on his face that seemed to be saying: "It's a hopeless case!"

No doubt he knew this other exit that led us out, as is often the case with cinema buildings, into a nighttime street in which it is difficult at first to recognize the building fronts. "I listened to your speech for the defense just now," he said, when we were settled in a brasserie. "And I was certainly the only one listening," he added with a slight smile. We sat for a moment without speaking. Outside the windows of the brasserie groups of young people were parading past, celebrating their team's victory with loud chanting and the waving of brightly colored flags.

"Yes, I listened to you, but I'd actually come to meet one of the film's sponsors . . . Would you like to guess who?"

"Some official in the Ministry of Culture who finances pseudo-documentary rubbish like this with the French taxpayer's money?"

"No, you're not even close."

"A former left-winger who's become a press magnate and is still campaigning against Soviet imperialism?"

"Not that either. I can see that, after years of idleness, you're losing your touch. Next guess."

"No idea. Someone I know?"

"A man you've met and who in those distant days used to be called Mr. Scalper. We always used to joke about how well the name suited him. Do you remember? Well, you knew him better than I did."

"Yes, it all comes back. Ron Scalper, the arms dealer with almost artistic tastes. He used to leave two or three days before the killing started. It was as if he could smell the blood. And he had the habit of saying to the Peeping Toms who stayed behind to film the performance of his guns, 'Get some black-and-white pictures for me, with Africans in them. That generally turns out best.' We really wanted to scalp him. So has he moved into arts sponsorship?"

"Well, he's been hugely successful since then. He runs a big American firm with several arms factories, a research institute, and some specialist journals. For rocket launchers he's one of the best in the world."

"But that film? Is he trying to redeem himself or what? I can hardly see him shedding tears, not even crocodile ones, over the mass graves in the camps."

"No, the film is simply high-class publicity. They have a department that looks after all this agitprop. The competition's very fierce in the arms trade, as you well know. It's no longer enough to show films shot by the Peeping Toms intended for a few officials. You have to work in-depth on public opinion in a country. Get people used to the idea that it's always been the Americans who came to the rescue and that these days the Russians can't even make a decent saucepan. The whole of Eastern Europe is going to be reequipped with American arms. Contracts worth tens of millions. Very soon the Americans won't have a single man on welfare. So it's worth financing a few films and running a few little wars, here and there, just to test the product."

"And all that high society who were there just now. Do you think they'll remember anything about the film tomorrow?"

"Ah, products like that aren't designed to make people remember but to make them forget. Forget the battle of Moscow, forget Stalingrad, Kursk. I've talked to the sponsor: the next episode's already in production. It's going to be called *The Soldiers of Liberty*. El Alamein, battles in the Pacific, the Normandy landings, the liberation of Europe—and that's the whole of the Second World War. And above all, not a word about the Eastern front. It never existed. Furthermore, and he told me this in all seriousness, 'El Alamein was the first great victory, the real turning point in the war!' In their war, that is."

Shakh lowered his voice, smiled at me, and added in apologetic tones, "There! I've started repeating your speech for the defense." He fell silent, then, doubtless not wishing to leave the impression of a man who had lost his cool, continued in tones where no rancor could now be heard, "You know, when all's said and done, this trafficking in the past may also be a way for them to avoid thinking about it. I grumble because I've seen tank tracks covered in ground meat at the battle of Kursk. I remember the rainstorm beating down on those thousands of tanks that evening, the water boiling and rising up from the burning steel in clouds of steam. But dinosaurs like me will soon be gone. As for the new generation, try talking to them about Kursk. It would spoil their joie de vivre. Look at that idiot, he's going to get himself run over."

In the street the soccer fans with their flags and bottles were marching along among the cars, which honked as they swerved to avoid them.

"And in order to pass their exams they'll repeat what they've been taught: once upon a time there was a wicked man called Hitler who didn't like the Jews and killed six million of them and would have killed more if the Americans hadn't come down from heaven with their jeeps and their chocolate bars. And the hardest thing will be for them to learn the names of the camps by heart. But they'll invent some mnemonic device. That's how we learned the names of the Great Lakes of America: Erie, Michigan, Huron, Superior, Ontario. There's a kind of jingle to it, no? They're sure to find one for Buchenwald."

In the feigned levity in his voice, I sensed the desire to keep at bay the questions we could not avoid. I stared at his face, which had aged the way the faces of men of action age: the dangers overcome are transformed into an outward appearance of steadfastness and lines of force expressing strength. And it seemed to me increasingly unlikely that within the next few minutes this man might tell me where I could find you.

Shakh must also have noticed that we were talking about the film in order to avoid speaking about what our meeting had suddenly revealed. He fell silent and cocked his head a little to one side. Then, gazing out of the window, he remarked, "That said, at the sight of all the Parisian glamor this evening, I was remarking to myself, as I often do when I come here, that our friend Jansac—you remember that agent we negotiated with in Aden who died shortly after the hostages had been released—yes, I was saying to myself that, instead of repatriating his body, the Legion would have done better to bury him down there, in a tomb cut into the black rocks looking out toward Aden, across the Strait of Bab el Mandeb. I find it hard to picture him living or dying here in this country, such as it has become."

I waited no further and asked him about you. I knew that the initial tone of his voice would already tell me a great deal. He gave me a quick, hard look, probing me with an unspoken question, as if to say, "It's me you're asking?" But what he said dispelled this air of reproach immediately.

"I don't know what's happened to her. I would certainly never have met up with you again in order to tell you of her death. Condolences from relations and friends was not her style. But, for your own sake, think carefully. It's often easier to live in vague hope. As long as you don't know . . ."

"But that's it: I want to know."

Shakh gave me another hard look, then he confided to me, as if reluctantly, "Her last identity was German. A German who'd lived in Canada for a long time and returned to Europe. So you can forget your Russian quest. Don't waste your time. All you'll find among these Russian women living in Paris will be violinists from Saint Petersburg, Ukrainian prostitutes, and Muscovite wives. Sometimes all combined in one person. I'll be coming back through France in ten days' time and by then I think I'll know which country you need to look for her in."

Before our next meeting I had time to take stock of what had changed in Shakh. It would have been easy to say he had aged. Or to explain the bitterness that showed through in his words by the disappearance of the country he had served for so many years. But there was something else. He was now working without any protection, like a trapeze artist whose safety net has been taken away, and worst of all, if he were caught, without the slightest hope of being traded for a westerner, as they used to do in the old days. I mentioned this to him when I saw him again. I said that in Moscow they were thinking more about opening Swiss bank accounts than spiriting away agents. He smiled. "Sooner or later, you know, we shall all be spirited away by the good Lord."

That evening, on the day of our second meeting, we were indeed talking about those years when everything in Moscow had turned upside down. The years when the Kremlin was turning into a swollen Mafia tumor whose cancerous spread undermined the whole country. The years when, as in the panic after a lost battle, they were abandoning former allies, writing off wars, dismantling the army. The period when the collapse of the empire was tearing apart, link by link, the intelligence networks woven during the seventy years of its existence. The period when we never knew if an agent who failed to keep a rendezvous had been intercepted by the Americans or sold down the river by our own people. The period when one day I had watched you disappearing into the crowd at Frankfurt airport after a few deliberately inconsequential words of good-bye.

Shakh made me talk about your departure, about the months preceding it, about the colleagues we saw at that time. I told him how we had been besieged in that revolving restaurant in the middle of a blazing city, and, going back in time, about the weeks spent in London, and, still further back, about the disappearance of the couple who were supposed to replace us, Yuri and Yulia. Your remorse at not having been able to protect them.

"What was he like, this Yuri?" Shakh suddenly interrupted me.

"Fair-haired, quite hefty, an engaging smile."

"That I know. I've seen the photos. Have you heard him speak English?"

"Er—no, why?"

Shakh did not reply, stared hard at me, then rubbed his brow.

"What's almost sure is that she spent a certain amount of time in America. I have the address, the contacts. But after that there was this great upheaval at the Center and a good deal of disruption in the departments and it's from that moment on it's difficult to keep track of her. We can talk about it at the end of the month, if you like. I guess I'll have a clearer picture by then."

Shakh had come to our meeting with a suitcase that still had baggage labels on it. As he set this bag down beside our table it reminded me vividly of the nomadic life you and I had led, a life this man was still leading, in an endless round of cities and hotels, of winter mornings in empty cafés where the coffee machine hisses and a customer, leaning on the counter, talks to the barman who nods his head without listening. And that suitcase. He caught my eye and announced with a smile, "The most precious item is not in the suitcase but here." He gave a little pat to a leather briefcase that lay on the bench. "Two million dollars. That's the price they want for this pile of papers. The complete technical documentation for a combat helicopter. A marvel. I wonder how the engineers, who haven't been paid for months, can go on making machines of this quality. Beside it, the American Apaches are flying tin cans. But Russia remains true to herself. The engineers get nothing and the mafiosi who organize the leakage buy themselves villas in the Bahamas. This briefcase will return to Moscow tomorrow, but, you know, the craziest thing is that I don't know if the people at the Center will be really pleased to have it back. It's quite likely that the very person there who takes delivery of it was actually hoping to be paid a commission for selling it."

Guessing what his work was now, I thought again of the trapeze artist without his safety net. I knew from experience that in extreme cases this total lack of protection could become a great advantage. Doubtless Shakh was playing it that way. The void that was all that lay between him and death freed him. He no longer had to take account of death, nor to master fear, nor to check parapets or fire exits in advance. He met people taking briefcases out of Russia crammed with secrets for sale, he passed himself off as an intermediary for an American arms manufacturer, negotiated, asked for time for an expert opinion. The sellers, he knew, were no longer agents of the old school, with their well-honed tactics and refinements like lethal umbrellas. These people thought little and killed quickly and often. It was his indifference to death that confounded them, they took this indifference as a guarantee of his all-American respectability. And he was successful because he surpassed all the degrees of risk imaginable.

I remarked to him, ineptly and in absurdly moralizing tones, that this could not last. At that moment the waiter set down our cups and inadvertently stubbed his toe against the suitcase placed under the table. Shakh smiled and murmured at the man's retreating back, "He should have been more careful. This case is mildly radioactive. Yes, I've actually been transporting the components of a portable atomic bomb in it. I'm not joking. You can't imagine what they manage to smuggle out of Russia now. I sometimes tell myself they'll end up by dismantling the whole country, or what's left of it, and shipping it to the West. But this bomb is a delightful toy. Total weight sixty-four pounds, length twenty-seven inches. A dream for a petty dictator who wants to command a bit of respect."

He took a drink, then continued in more somber tones, "You're right, one can't play the way I'm playing now for long. It can only work nine times out of ten. But, you see, if I still thought we could win I don't think it would even work once. Maybe the real game begins when you know you're going to lose. And we've lost already. This helicopter in my briefcase, it's still going to land in America, by another channel, a little bit later, and they'll have it all the same. Just as they'll have all the talented research scientists who are starving in Moscow. As one day they'll have the whole planet under their thumb. With Europe it's a done deal. Those are not separate nations anymore, they're hired help. If the Americans decide to bomb some transgressor nation tomorrow, with one voice all those lackeys will respond 'yes sir, no sir, three bags full, sir.' Of course they'll be allowed to keep their national folklore. You know, the way each girl in a brothel has her speciality. The French, true to tradition, will write essays about the war and lend their palaces for negotiations. The English will assume an air of dignity; the brothel madam always has one girl with a bit of class. And the Germans will be the zealous whore, trying to ensure her past errors are forgotten. The rest of Europe is a negligible quantity."

"And Russia?"

I asked with no ulterior motive and certainly with no desire to cut him off, but that was how Shakh must have taken it. He fell silent, then continued with an apologetic air, "Forgive me, I'm rambling. I've played the role of the American tycoon shopping for secrets so many times that I've ended up loathing him. A basic and visceral anti-Americanism, as the Parisian intellectuals would say. No, one shouldn't be a bad loser. You know I once told . . . our friend about Sorge's death. I expect she thought I was giving her a patriotic propaganda lesson, maybe I went about it the wrong way. But I quite simply wanted to say that in that last moment on the scaffold he, the loser, with the noose around his neck, achieved victory. Yes, by shouting out words people would find laughable today: 'Long live the Communist International!' Who can tell what'll carry more weight in the balance between good and evil: all the victories in the world or the raised fist of that agent everyone had betrayed."

"And Russia?"

I repeated it in a neutral voice, intentionally abstracted, leaving him the possibility of not replying. But his reply amazed me by its confessional tone.

"Several times I've had the same dream: I'm crossing the Russian frontier by train. It's winter, white fields as far as the eye can see, and I know there will be nothing but these infinite snows right up to the end. It's twenty-two years now since I went back there. The last person I knew there, who's still alive, is our friend: you'll find her again in the end. The other Russians I have all known abroad. As for those who come here to sell me helicopters on paper, they're a new breed already. The ones who are going to run the show down here after us."

He looked at his watch, leaned forward to pull out his suitcase, and, already poised to leave, remarked with a wink, "Since you're burning with curiosity to know what's in this case, I'll tell you the scenario. This evening two fine specimens of the new breed are coming to stay at the same hotel as me. They'll wait until it's night and break into my room. Not finding me there, they'll attack the suitcase. The vigilant French police will already have been alerted. The specimens will be deported to Moscow and met at Sheremetyevo airport. And there will be an attempt to plug the breach through which these combat helicopters and other toys dreamed up by our hungry engineers keep flying away."

He ordered a taxi and, as we were waiting for it by the door, we heard the swirling torrent of news blaring out above the bar; a mixture of strikes, wars, elections, sport, deaths, goals scored. "Nothing amazes me any more in this world," said Shakh, staring at the gray, rain-soaked street. "But for the German aircraft bombing the Balkans to have had the same black crosses on their wings as they had at the time they were bombing Kiev and Leningrad does seem like a really bad joke."

"It'll be easier to talk about her over there."

I already knew what he was going to say. I had sensed it from his voice on the telephone. Then from his face. From his silence in the car. At moments the pain of what I was going to learn still seemed remediable—as if all it needed was for us to do a U-turn, dash to an airport, land in a city where your presence, even if under threat, even if improbable, could be divined at one of those addresses I could completely reconstitute from memory: the street, the house, the traces left by our presence there several years before. A second later I realized that Shakh was going to tell me about a death (for me your name and your face were not yet associated with this death) that had happened some time ago.

He talked about it as we walked along a country road between two rows of bare trees, their trunks blue with lichen, engulfed in brambles. Someone who did not know him would have thought he was weeping. From time to time he wiped from his cheeks the melted flakes of the snow that had surprised us on our journey. But he spoke little and in a toneless voice. When his words broke off I again began to notice the whistling of the wind and the tramp of our feet on the sodden path. The pain made the world less and less recognizable. I saw myself walking beside an old man miles from any-where, among lackluster fields, a man I knew to be on the run, at the end of his tether, who was at home nowhere, a man who was telling me, as he mopped the trickles of water from his face, that he now knew almost the exact date of your execution. But this precision only served to make more improbable the death he was announcing and the need to connect this death with you, still so intensely alive the previous day and now separated from us, separated from this cold spring morning by a year and a half of nonexistence. The path itself, which ran beside an old stone wall, was marked by unreality, for, according to what Shakh had just said, we must picture you passing this way more than twenty years before, at the start of your life in the West. What was also unreal was the notion that this very spot could have helped him to break the news.

He told me the date of your death and now it was no longer possible to avoid linking you with this loss. The world became empty, thunderous, hollow. A place where your name rang out repeatedly, like the echo of a vain incantation. By a hasty reflex in the face of death, in deference to the proprieties, the image of a coffin surrounded by wreaths and weeping faces flashed into my mind. Shakh's voice began again, as if to sweep away the vision of this funereal pomp. He spoke of a death preceded by interrogations, tortures, violations. And of burial in a mass grave, among anonymous bodies.

At that moment we emerged into a vast courtyard in front of an old farmhouse converted into a restaurant. I walked behind Shakh like an automaton, crossed the yard from one end to the other, passed very close by the crowd gathered around a bridal pair. I saw the guests with a clarity that hurt my eyes: a woman's hand, with veined fingers clutching a little patent leather purse; the bride's bare forearms, her skin rosy and covered in goose pimples; the closed eye, as if in sleep, of the young man filming the ceremony with a little camera. Everything about this gathering seemed so necessary and so absurd, as it moved slowly toward the restaurant's open door. Everything had a point, both the old fingers gripping the black leather, and the youthful arms shivering beneath the icy drops. And nothing could have been stranger. Just for a moment, in a notion that verged on madness, I thought it might be possible to join them, very simply to tell them of my grief. A man emerged from the crowd and seemed to be urging us to go in more quickly, then realized his mistake and adopted an air of offended surprise. The path continued around the farm building and led back into the avenue where Shakh had left the car. As we passed, a large gray bird stirred among the branches and launched out obliquely in a low, irregular flight over the emptiness of the fields studded with raindrops. I suddenly thought that to plunge into this springtime void, to vanish into its indifference, would be a salutary step so easy to take. A body crumpled up behind the bushes, the temple brown with blood, the arm flung out by the recoil from the gun. Shakh stopped, looked in the same direction as myself and seemed to guess my thought. His voice had the firmness you adopt when addressing a man who has drunk too much and needs to be reprimanded. "If she had talked we would not be here. Neither you nor I." Still drowning in the torpor of the void, I felt I was closer to that body than to this man speaking harsh words to me, closer to that imagined suicide than to myself. He swung round, started walking again and said in a muted voice, "I have the name and address of the man who turned her in."

The death of someone close to you affects not the future but that immediate past you realize you have been living through in the futile pettiness of daily routine. Sitting next to Shakh, I noticed on the back seat the briefcase which several weeks previously had contained the technical documentation, whose market value he had told me with a smile. I remembered the tone of our meetings, their deliberate lightheartedness, the triviality of the days that had preceded and followed them. My fruitless speeches for the defense during the course of those social gatherings, the fat man peddling his cinematic trash, the business with Shakh's suitcase, the suitcase-bait that had amused me like something from a spy novel. These snatches must now be measured against your absence, against the impossibility of finding you anywhere in the world, against the infinity of this absence.

Nor, doubtless, was it lost on Shakh that death is this infinite unit of measurement. Speaking to me of the man who had betrayed you, he mentioned a droll detail but pulled himself up at once. "He lives in Destin, Florida," he was saying. "I hope he doesn't speak French: a name like that would be enough to make you superstitious." He broke off, regretting his tone, and finished drily, "His office, by the way, is in a place called Saint Petersburg. You should feel at home there."

Your death did not affect the future, for this imagined time, I now realized, was compressed into a single, very simple moment I had carried in my mind for years: in the crowd at a station, in a passing throng of faces, I met your eyes. I had never pictured any other future for us beyond that.

From now on there was also my vision of an inert body slumped behind the bare thickets next to a country road. I could see myself like this and the comfort of such a way out was especially tempting because of its practical ease. One evening the agreeable weight of the pistol was cradled in my palm for a long time. Next morning, as I consulted my watch, it occurred to me that in these days emptied of meaning, only my meeting with Shakh at noon would mark a time, a date, and give the rest of this life a semblance of necessity.

He spoke. His voice conjured up the little town of Destin, Florida, then a man, a former Russian who called himself Val Vinner, an ordinary turned agent, whose only distinguishing feature was to have betrayed you. His profile was coming together like a jigsaw puzzle from which several pieces were still missing. Prudent, ambitious, very proud of his success. Working for American intelligence, he ran the network that dealt with the transfer of scientists from the East. He had managed to persuade his new employers that importing a scientist whose head is crammed with secrets was more profitable than sending agents to glean the same secrets on the spot. Listening to Shakh, I had the strange impression that the incomplete mosaic formed by Vinner's life was becoming my own life, that this still-blurred shape was giving me a future.

"He travels all the time as a procurer, especially in Eastern Europe," explained Shakh, "but there's a chance that during the spring break he'll spend a few days with his family. You should go the day after tomorrow at the very latest. Try to see him right away. He's very suspicious. You'll say you've come on behalf of one of his best friends. I'll give you his name. This friend is currently in China on a mission, virtually incommunicado. That gives you at least four days. If he resolutely refuses all contact, mention his mistress in Warsaw. In America that can be persuasive—"

He broke off and stared at me, screwing up his eyes slightly.

"Unless you've decided quite simply to liquidate him?"

This question dogged me during the night. I did not know what I would do when I met Val Vinner. Extort a confession from him, blackmail him and so force him to justify himself at length, pitifully. See him tremble, humiliate him—or, as Shakh put it "quite simply" kill him? A pistol with a silencer, my armed hand concealed behind a map of Florida, the appearance of a lost tourist. Vinner, who is sitting in his car, agrees to help, opens the door, leans toward the map. "Yes, you're on the right road." Then he throws his head back and freezes in his seat. I lock the door and close it—he's sure to have smoked glass windows! During the course of that sleepless night there came a time when my brooding on all these methods of vengeance suddenly laid bare a hidden motive, the one I was trying to conceal from myself. In every night there comes a moment of great lucidity, of ruthless sincerity, from which one is generally protected by sleep. This time I had no protection. My thoughts were brutally exposed. There was nothing I could do against the admission that came back time and again, more and more clearly: I was going to America in the hope of hearing Vinner say that your death was not the long torment that Shakh had spoken of. That it was . . . an ordinary death. And that, in any case, I could not have prevented it, even if I had been at your side. That you had not suffered. That I was not answerable for this death to . . . To whom?

I got up to interrupt the flood of these admissions. But their sharpness now acquired the force of a living voice: "You want to see this unfrocked spy in the hope that he'll grant you absolution. Like a good old-fashioned Orthodox priest."

As the night was ending I dozed off into a sleep that retained the extreme clarity of that forced confession. But its lucidity turned into light and the edge of my grief into ice. The cold of a snowfall on a winter's day, of snow slowly chilling my brow. I saw again the wooden house you had often told me of, with its low front steps, whence one could see, beyond the fir branches, the shores of the frozen lake. After waking, I continued for a long time to experience the coolness of that day you had told me about, white and tranquil. In the aircraft, as I mentally fitted together all I knew about Vinner, playing over like chess moves all his possible reactions, I found myself from time to time far away in a fit of forgetfulness, on the shores of that lake, surrounded by the measured slumber of the snow-clad trees. At one moment, in a brief excess of grief, I thought I had grasped something which, expressed in words, faded and only told part of the truth I had sensed. "We could have lived together in that winter's day!" No, what I had just grasped went far beyond that imagined possibility. The moment I had glimpsed was shattered by words into shards of regret, remorse, hatred. I turned my thoughts once more, and with malicious joy, to the doses of mounting fear I should contrive to inject into my visits to Vinner. Then I accused myself of seeking exoneration, of secretly hoping for the account of a gentle death from him, even of wanting to kill him so as not to hear what he knew. Finally, to put an end to this verbal torture, I went back over my chess moves one by one.

I recalled that, before leaving me, Shakh had uttered this sentence, of which only the first part had seemed helpful at the time: "If you don't get a grip on him instantly, during the first ten minutes, you've lost. From what I've been told, he's an eel." The rest of his words now came back to me and seemed even more important: "But whatever happens, don't forget that for . . . for her, it's all the same. The die is cast." Calling these words to mind, I told myself that, ever since that walk with Shakh along a path winding around an old farm, I had had the impression of living in some obscure afterlife.

6

In my mind I had fashioned the town where Vinner lived out of the dark and humid stuff of the Parisian spring. I pictured the man himself dressed in an overcoat, his face clouded by rain and suspicion. Exhausted by sleepless nights, by my anticipation of our first meeting, I had not given a thought to the sun over the Gulf of Mexico. As we touched down, the light and the warm wind came surging into my imagined town, and the man in the somber overcoat was me. Traveling to Destin along the coast, I sensed the very particular atmosphere, at once carefree and nervous, of southern towns preparing for the holiday season. It could be detected in the noise made by a workman taking beach chairs out of a shed, in the smell of paint from the fresh lettering that promised a fantastic reduction for those dining early. At the hotel I rid myself of my Parisian clothes, like shameful and ridiculous witnesses beneath this clear sky.

I went out at once, not so much from fear of missing Vinner (I did not even know if he was at home) as in order to forestall a new wave of doubts. I followed Shakh's advice to go directly, without telephoning, without wasting time on normal reconnaissance in the area. Certainly the atmosphere of beach resorts, where everything is designed to lighten the load of things, contributed to the ease with which, half an hour later, I found Vinner's house on the corner of a street. Not a grayish structure, the impregnable fortress my imagination had constructed from the damp stone of Parisian apartment buildings, but a small one-story villa, set back in a garden dominated by several clumps of young palm trees. Behind the metal gate, to the left of the narrow path that led to the house, there was a parked car with an open trunk, which a man, who had his back to me, was cleaning with a small vacuum cleaner, reminiscent of a watering can. I pressed the bell. The man turned, unplugged the machine, left it in the trunk and, instead of coming toward me, which would have seemed natural, walked over to a little sentry box made of pale bricks, which stood beside the gate and was almost entirely hidden beneath the leaves of a creeper. I heard his voice very close to my ear on the intercom and at the same moment noticed the dark, flat eye of the surveillance camera. The voice was slow, thickly American. As I explained who I was, I was hardly aware of what I was saying, dazed by the comical vision I had just seen: a fifty-year-old with close-cut hair, a corpulent man rendered almost square by a white short-sleeved shirt open to his chest, this man who had been running his vacuum cleaner over the carpet in the trunk and who was now greeting my explanations with long drawn-out "Okays," this man was Val Vinner! An almost mythical being, given the evil he had wrought and the scale of what he had, negligently, destroyed, and here he was parading himself in all the banality of this little paradise beneath the palm trees, in the domestic peace of a holiday morning.

Patiently, and giving a very good imitation of the dull-witted amiability Americans devote to the explanation of details, the one-time Russian continued to question me about our mutual friend, now traveling in China, about the purpose of my visit. Suddenly what I saw beyond the gate eclipsed our conversation through the wall. A child, a boy of six or seven, walked around the car and came toward the entrance, clung to the bars, and stared at me curiously. His brother, not yet very steady on his feet, crossed the yard to join the older child. I was to learn later that the older child was the son of Vinner's wife but, seeing these two children, I felt like an emissary from a bygone age, an age since when this renegade had had the time to Americanize himself and found a family at least eight years old.

It was then that a man appeared on the front steps of the house and called to the children. I looked up. It took me a few seconds to overcome the improbability of this face under such a name and in this location. Then I recognized Yuri.

He came to the gate, took hold of the little one and detached him from the bars, despite his protests. The square man in the white short-sleeved shirt (a caretaker? a bodyguard? a gardener?) emerged from the sentry box and began to repeat the information he had gathered, mispronouncing my name, trying to make himself heard above the squeals of the child. But already Vinner was speaking to me in Russian and let me in through the door next to the sentry box.

"I'm really sorry but today I'm taking these two rascals to Miracle Strip Park. I've been promising them this since Christmas. Do you know this park? It's full of attractions for kids. There's even a giant roller-coaster, I don't know how many feet high. So is our friend well? China just now must be quite something. I think he's told me about you. Dave, quit shoving him or you won't get to come with us."

He uttered this threat in English, in that good comprehensible English that gives foreigners away, and threw me a glance in which feigned severity mutated into a father's smiling pride. I noted that his face had changed very little and that his eyes had even kept that youthful brightness that had so touched you in the old days. It was his body that had matured a good deal: he had a belly now and his fore-arms filled the short sleeves of his T-shirt with the flabby bulk you see in athletes who have given up exercise. A tall, fair-haired woman came out of the house, went in again at once and reappeared with a large red thermos. She came toward us, Vinner introduced me, she shook my hand, and I had time to notice that her face showed signs of morning-time distraction, that withdrawal women regularly

permit themselves to inflict on their families. The children were
shouting impatiently and pushing their father toward the car. I still
had the map of Florida under my arm and a loaded pistol in my bag.
With one hand I slung this bag over my shoulder and pushed it
behind my back, just as one hides a sharp object from children.

Vinner proposed that we should meet again the next day.

That night, recalling his facial expressions, I realized that his
features, even though attached to a hated name, had brought the
sound of your voice back to life for me, the calmness of your gaze, a
few days in our old existence, some of those moments of happiness
lost among the wanderings and the wars.

Then, recalling Shakh's warning, in which he had given me the
first ten minutes to attack and win, I recognized my defeat. I had a
vision of Vinner's two children, hurtling down the roller-coaster. In
any case, I was finding it harder and harder to define what victory
might have been.

Contemplating the beach that stretched away a few yards from the
terrace on stilts where we sat, Vinner had the proud and smiling air of
the cocreator of this sun-drenched panorama. Rather as a Parisian,
when showing a foreigner the Arc de Triomphe or the Louvre,
always feels a little bit as if he were the architect, or at least one of the
stone masons. He recited his commentary, pointing into the distance
with his fork, and reeling off the names of fish and shellfish, gave a
little laugh and threw me a wink at the sight of a pretty girl in a
swimsuit walking past the terrace. And when a group of young men
in bathing suits rushed toward the waves, shouting at one another as
they ran and tossing a big beach ball back and forth over the heads of
the vacationers, he smiled indulgently and explained that these dis-
turbers of the peace were, alas, inevitable during the period of the
"spring break." He pronounced this phrase with evident pleasure.

"It makes a change from the rain in Paris, doesn't it? And those
anemic Europeans. I remember one day on a beach somewhere

near . . . La Rochelle, was it? I'm probably getting mixed up. It was so depressing, all those appalling bodies, it looked like a museum of degeneration. Especially the women. And here, you can see, these young ones are bursting with health. And even the not so young, they're in good shape. And the air. Just smell it! Not an atom of nicotine. No one smokes. After two days in Europe I'm coughing and spluttering like an old man. And in Eastern Europe, forget it. It's worse than Chernobyl. . . . She's not bad, that one. No, the other one, under the shower. Yes, maybe a bit too much, you're right. But the women here are all very athletic. Very healthy. In fact, you know that new man our propaganda promised us: here's where he's in the process of being born. Stalin thought he could forge him through a schizophrenic mix of terror and heroism. Hitler, via biological messianism. But here they don't need brainwashing. Everyone understands that, as one of my friends says, it's better to be healthy, tanned, and rich than a Russian research scientist in Moscow."

When he spoke of America Vinner sometimes said "they," sometimes "we." I interrupted him two or three times to ask, " 'We' is who? The Russians or the Americans?" I did it from annoyance but also to avoid confusion between the "we" who were "putting a little order into this whorehouse of a world" and the "we" who "are only good at begging for handouts from the West, instead of getting on with the job." Smiling, he accepted the correction and, for several minutes, paid careful attention to his use of pronouns. The good "we" were fulfilling their onerous mission, as masters of the world, by punishing the guilty and defending the righteous, but above all by demonstrating, through their example, that the formula for universal happiness had been found and that it was within everyone's reach. A moment later the confusion returned and the bad "we" had embarked on "drinking, behaving hysterically like something straight out of Dostoyevsky, begging for dollars."

There were, it is true, many beautiful bodies on the beach's extremely pale sands. Both their youth and the relaxed insolence of their movements swept aside any attempt at criticism. The happiness was too evident, it was on their skin, in their muscles, in the stream of cars coming from the north to spill out these tanned bodies onto the sand and the terraces, or to carry them on toward other pleasures. Their exuberant vitality seemed to be saying: "Go ahead and grumble as much as you like. But we're the ones who are right!"

In any case, what Vinner was saying was more or less his regular recruitment test number, a well-worn speech for sounding out the opinions of research scientists he enlisted in Eastern Europe. He knew that you learn more about a man, not by letting him talk, but by talking to him and observing his reactions. Instead of objecting to it, I was trying to imagine the objections of previous listeners. What could they have said, faced with Vinner's guided tour of this paradise? Some of them, no doubt, nodded their heads for fear of displeasing their benefactor. Others, remembering their post-war Soviet childhood, would have embarked, with the aid of nostalgia, on a defense of poverty, which, it appears, promotes loftiness of thought. Yet others, the most ungrateful and generally the most independent, thanks to their scientific clout, would have dared to remind him that this oasis of the American Dream had its price and, with typically Russian exaggeration, would have begun talking about slavery, Hiroshima, napalm in Vietnam, and sometimes, in a fit of rage (what Vinner called "hysteria straight out of Dostoyevsky") rebelled, crying out, "Yes, of course you're the richest and the strongest! But that's because you pillage the whole world. Your damned America is draining our lifeblood! Do you think you can buy everything with your dollars?" At such moments Vinner would remain silent. He knew only too well the explosive but forgetful temperament of his former compatriots. But above all he was convinced that one really could buy everything. And that the hysteria was only a passing symptom on the part of a person he was in the process of buying.

It struck me that a further objection could be added to all of these: the wars started in order to test new weapons and those ended in order to lower the price of a barrel of crude oil. And a good many other negative aspects of things besides. But I let Vinner finish his performance, as one lets a guide complete the tour of a site of no interest. He did not have a coffee but some extremely frothy milk drink. And his concluding comments (he was speaking of the success of the "melting pot": "In the sun all cats are brown, isn't that so?") were accompanied by rhythmic gurgling and sucking noises. I reflected that the only counterargument in harmony with the genial tone of our meeting would have been to criticize the obesity of some of the vacationers around us. Vinner looked at his watch and hastened to bring matters to a close.

"I'll see what I can do. I can't make any promises. You know, we have plenty of doctors here and then some. But I have a friend who may be interested in your experience as a doctor in Chechnya. I should get a reply within—um—let's say four or five days."

That was the story I had quickly concocted with Shakh: an army doctor on the run from the Caucasus via Turkey, who had landed in America. Very sketchy, it had the advantage of corresponding to my former profession and being relevant to Vinner's. "Four or five days," that is to say not before the return of his colleague from China. I had an urge not to wait, to tell him who I was and why I had come. The obese woman next to us stood up and, as in a gag on television, almost walked away with the plastic armchair stuck to her backside. Vinner threw me a wink while noisily inhaling the rest of the froth from the bottom of his glass.

I needed words that would have eclipsed the sun, obliterated the whiteness of the sand, stilled the shouts and the peals of laughter. Words that would have been night, the dark, damp granite of cobbled streets, solitude. I realized that I had never left that night and that Vinner's seaside paradise was a future age into which I had strayed by mistake, and that in four or five days I would have to go back into my night.

"He forgot the sugar. I'll go and ask him for it."

I got up and went to the bar at the other end of the terrace. I had to wait for the barman to emerge from a cupboard where he was noisily stacking empty bottles. The ornamental pillar that extended upward from the counter to the ceiling was covered in small pieces of mirrored glass. One of the fragments gave a view of the table I had just left, as well as the one behind it, occupied by a young man reading a newspaper. Throughout our lunch I had been aware of the rustling of pages. Now, reflected in the mirror, I could see his face clearly. He had lowered the newspaper and was talking, without seeming to address anyone in particular. Vinner was turned slightly toward this mouth talking into thin air. A few seconds later he gave a little nod of his head. The man reading the newspaper picked up a bag placed under the table and left. His face, reflected on the pillar, jumped from one square of mirror to the next.

So Vinner was taking my appearance more seriously than all his chat about the new man and the melting pot on the beach might have suggested. I found my own reflection in one of the fragments. I had no idea if he could have recognized my face with these gold-rimmed spectacles and beard. I had no idea what those years now meant to him that lay between him and the dust and heat of that African capital on the verge of war where we had seen him for the first and last time. For him, certainly, it could only be a past he had suppressed, voluntarily wiped from his memory, relegated to the dull prehistory of his own life before his glorious present. Nor had I any idea in what manner the fact of having betrayed you was preserved, carried with him, tolerated in the brief moments of truth and solitude he could not avoid.

"Watch out for sunstroke," he warned as he left me. "And thieves. They can smell foreigners five miles off. Especially the young blacks and the Latinos, too. What a crew!"

"I see, I thought the melting pot . . ."

"Now, look, that's just between the two of us, as one Russian to another. Don't repeat what I said or you'll get yourself lynched."

★

That evening the taxi moved along slowly, often held up by cars try-ing to park near restaurants, and by the crowd of young vacationers embarking on their night of celebration. There was a fine, warm drizzle. The tanned skins of these very skimpily dressed young passersby shone with a dark gloss. Even more than on the beach one sensed their lust for life, their nonchalant insistence on happiness. As I had asked him to, the driver left Destin, following the coast. There was much too much traffic in those streets for it to be clear if I had been awarded an escort. I took a last glance through the rear window and asked for us to return the way we had come. I was aware that it was of no importance to understand what Vinner knew or did not know and how he might be preparing to respond to my appearance. I had neither to protect myself nor, above all, to imagine how my life might be after this trip to Destin. All that remained for me to live through was concentrated in the here and now.

The taxi dropped me in a quiet, narrow street, a street of small villas that already seemed fast asleep. One could hear the rain, heavier than a moment ago, and somewhere in the depths of the thick vege-tation the voices from a television set, probably the dialogue from some science fiction film portraying a civilization in the twenty-fifth century. All that remained of the sparkle at the town's center was a halo of faded brightness in the sky. As I walked along, the sound of conversations between men of future centuries gradually passed out of earshot and I could only hear the rain. I recognized Vinner's house from the wrought-iron ornaments on the gate.

The darkness was punctuated by bluish areas around the street lights. The alternation between this harsh glare and the dark foliage transformed my arrival there into a strange negative of my first visit, the day before, in the morning sun. Everything was repeated so pre-cisely that it left me the leisure to observe brief gaps of absurdity and silence between words and actions.

The caretaker appeared, dressed in a windbreaker, looked at me through the gate and disappeared into the sentry box. The intercom hissed, I spelled out my name, then the name of the man who had recommended me. The caretaker's drawling questions came back at me, unchanged since the day before, as if in the rhyming refrains of a children's game. Vinner came out onto the front steps, a cluster of small lights flashed on, marking the curve of the path that led toward the gate. He came up, blinking in the drops of rain, and saw me. He smiled, rapidly erasing a slight twitch of annoyance or alarm that remained lurking in one of the lines of his forced grin. Before he could reach the gate a powerful but completely silent dog interposed itself and reared up at me, the whole of its long, muscular body seething with barely contained energy. Vinner invited me in, still smiling, like someone who has been disturbed just as he was nodding off for the night.

"Over here in the West you know, arriving like this at ten o'clock at night without warning is the best way to give your acquaintances a heart attack. Try doing it in Paris or London. Ringing the bell on the off chance and when the door opens announcing, as we used to do in Russia, 'It's like this, I was just passing in the street and I saw your light was on. So I decided to come up.' A cardiac arrest guaranteed! Well, that's a slight exaggeration. Come in, I've got some good whisky."

I realized that within a few more seconds this tone would again make it impossible to say what I had to say. Vinner's words had the same anesthetizing effect as his gurglings with a straw in the frothy milk of his glass, and the efforts of that obese vacationer standing up with the plastic armchair clamped to the rolls of flesh on her haunches.

"I forgot to give you something," I said in a very neutral voice, feeling in my bag.

The dog tensed even more and uttered a throaty, menacing growl. I went on speaking in Russian with the slightly sheepish air of an absentminded person.

"I expect your dog is trained to react to nervous gestures. I won't make any. I have a gun with a silencer and I shall shoot through the bag at the slightest refusal on your part. For a start, tell the caretaker to go away and take the dog with him."

He complied. His voice remained cheerful, but he could not conceal a quavering note nor, in particular, his Russian accent, which was suddenly more marked. The caretaker grasped the dog by its collar and disappeared to the bottom of the garden. The dotted line of lights along the path went out and Vinner's face was now only lit by the bluish haze coming from the street lamps. He tried to smile, started to speak . . . and fell silent, hearing his wife's voice through an open window, gently reprimanding the children.

I told him the name I had been using at the time when we first met. I reminded him of the arrival of the two of them, Yuri and Yulia, their naïveté, so well feigned, their disappearance. I spoke of you, your remorse at not having been able to protect them, of your attempts to find them again. I realized that in fact I had very little to say to him. My ringing cry, long since prepared ("You betrayed her, you bastard!"), which was to be followed by the gunshot, seemed unbelievably false and did not fit this man in beach sandals, with a drop of rain suspended from the end of his nose. His wife's voice became clearer. "No, you're not going out, Dave. I said 'no,' do you hear me? First of all because it's raining and look at you. You're in bare feet. No. Go find your slippers." I saw Vinner's eyes glance toward the lighted window of the house for a second. I broke off, as if preparing my final peroration, but, in reality, not knowing how to end this monologue that was telling him nothing new. He threw a similar rapid, oblique glance at my bag, still open with my hand in it, pretending to be looking for a lost object. We saw one another for a moment with a total reciprocal understanding, with a sharp awareness of what we both were, standing here in the rain, sharing a past that made our lives logically impossible and at the same time perfectly ordinary, like his beach sandals, like my bag bought the day before at the airport.

At that moment there was a brief pause in the hissing of the raindrops, a second of complete silence, and from the damp, still depths of the darkness there emerged a faint yawn, a woman's sigh, followed by the grating of a window being closed. We looked at one another. Instinctively I lowered my voice. I surprised myself by talking to him about what I had not intended to say, about what it seemed to me unthinkable to tell.

"Near the harbor there were docks where they crammed in all the opponents of the regime, mixed up together with several who were under suspicion. She was among them. As she had admitted nothing, the Americans had handed her over to the local rulers, those paramilitary choppers-off of heads. A week later, when one of their chiefs had the idea of trading her in negotiations with the government forces, he didn't dare show her. A week of rape and torture. She no longer had a face. They preferred to kill her."

"I didn't know."

He said this in a dull and broken tone of which his voice had seemed to me incapable.

"Yes, you did. You knew very well. During that week you were listening to interrogations taped by the Americans. Interrogations of her."

"I didn't know."

"What interests me is what you do know. Everything you know about those days. To the very last word. You were a methodical man. You even kept certain objects that belonged to her, isn't that right? Photos . . . Everything you know, written down. To help you, I'll ask you questions. Yes, an interrogation, you're quite used to them."

"But I kept nothing! I remember nothing!"

We turned. In the silent respite between two onslaughts of rain the gravel grated beneath footfalls, like the crunch of broken glass.

Vinner's wife seemed not to notice my presence. Upright, with an air of ruffled dignity, she stopped a few yards away from us.

"What is it, Val?"

Her tone of voice and a slight raising of her chin summed up the whole of their life as a couple: sure, I have a husband with a strange past, whose profession is pretty hard to explain to our friends, but my tact and my remote serenity make it all perfectly acceptable.

"I forgot to give your husband this scientific journal which he'll need tomorrow," I announced, taking a magazine from my bag.

She smiled distractedly, as if she had just noticed me in the darkness, and moved away, saying good night to no one in particular. In the middle of the path, beside a little lamp, she bent down to pick up a small plastic spade left there by the children. The fabric of her dressing gown, very fine, like satin, revealed the line of her back, the breadth of her hips. In a quite unreal vision I found myself thinking about the night they would spend together, the nights he always spent beside this beautiful woman's body, their pleasure.

"Don't complicate things," I said to Vinner, moving toward the gate. "I have nothing to lose. But you have a fine life ahead of you. That's worth a few admissions. Tomorrow I'll wait to hear from you. And don't forget that I'm working in tandem, as the marksmen say. If I'm waked up by the police at four A.M., my colleague will be forced to wake you up at four-thirty. Sweet dreams."

He phoned me at nine and proposed that we should meet in two days' time at his office in Saint Petersburg.

In the foyer of my hotel there was a bookshelf squeezed between two plants with broad glossy leaves: from it I took down three or four volumes at random to occupy those two rainy days, to stop me thinking about Vinner. I tried to identify with the characters in these American novels, to believe in the lives of an honest, warmhearted horse breeder, or a naive young woman from the country ensnared by the big city. But in a roundabout way my mind kept returning to our nocturnal conversation. I vaguely envied those authors who knew everything about the slightest mood swings of their heroes, who guessed their intentions, even when "after that, without knowing why, Hank always avoided taking the North Falls Road." I felt I could understand the attraction of these pages, turned by so many hands, all these fictional worlds. It was the comfort of omniscience, the vision of chaos vanquished, pinned down, like a hideous insect in a glass case.

Thinking about Vinner, I did not even know whether, during our conversation in the rain, he had been afraid, had felt guilty, had believed me really prepared to shoot him and his wife. I did not know if the change in his tone of voice was assumed or not. I did not know his order of preference for ways of getting rid of me: the police, a contract killer, an amicable outcome. I did not know if he was particularly perturbed by my appearance. In a nutshell, I had no idea what was going on in his head.

I closed the book and pictured Vinner going back up to his house after my departure, shutting the door, going through all the little rituals of bedtime hygiene, lying down beside his wife. I sensed that these daily gestures verged on madness. But what would be real insanity would in fact be for me to picture Vinner lying beside that beautiful woman's body I had recently glimpsed through the satiny fabric of her dressing gown, to picture him caressing her, to picture them making love. For it was quite possible that everything might happen in precisely that way: the trivial hygiene routine, their bedroom, their bodies. I told myself that a real book should have copied this improbable sequence of real actions. A man learns what Vinner had learned, goes up to his house, washes, goes to bed, draws his wife to him, squeezes her breasts, caresses her thighs, enters her, faithfully following all the small singularities of their sexual ritual.

My two days' wait was spent between this phantasmagoria of imagined actions and snatches of reading and an increasingly clear mental certainty: whatever happened, I would leave without having learned what Vinner, to use the language of the novels filling that hotel bookshelf, felt in his heart of hearts.

He met me in front of the entrance to the building. A third Vinner, I thought, recalling the first one, the charismatic guide to the seaside paradise, then the second, a man in sandals disturbed on a quiet evening at home. And now this businessman in a dark suit who wove together into a single swift sequence a cold smile of greeting, a thrust against the copper of the revolving door, and this warning, expressed as a brief, uncompromising statement: "We will have to leave our bags at the desk. They've installed a metal detector." He was already handing his own to the attendant.

As he walked into his office he made a quick sign with his head in the direction of two men who were in the process of shifting bulky cardboard cartons around. "Sorry about the mess, but we're in the middle of moving offices: I hope their presence won't disturb you." I recognized one of the movers as the reader of newspapers I had seen reflected in a fragment of mirror on the pillar at the restaurant the day we had lunch. The cartons were placed just behind the armchair Vinner offered me. The speed with which he embarked on this meeting smacked of a well-prepared operation. He had doubtless managed to contact our alleged mutual friend in China, or else the man had already returned. Furthermore, over two days he had been able to verify that I was in Destin on my own. Glancing at the cartons, I noticed that some of them were big enough to hold a man's body.

"I owe you something," he said, opening a drawer in his desk. "The journal you gave me so as not to alarm my wife. Here it is back, but with something extra."

Vinner handed me an English newspaper. He had certainly envisaged a theatrical effect but could not have been aware of the force of the shock. There were various articles on the arms traffic controlled by the Russian Mafia. Photos, statistics. And suddenly this headline: "Death of one of the barons of the nuclear network." Very clearly in the photograph I recognized the face of Shakh.

I did not take in Vinner's opening remarks. He was probably asking me if I had known the man in the photograph well. I gave no reply, still blinded by the expression of the eyes, the movement of the lips I sensed behind the immobility of the photo. All the article did was to list the usual components of the criminal web: dubious contracts, the leakage of military technologies from a Russia in decay, exorbitant commissions, rivalries, the settling of accounts, the death of an "arms baron." As I was skimming through these paragraphs I caught up with Vinner's voice. Curiously enough, it sounded the same vaguely contemptuous and triumphant note as the style of the article.

". . . a strange character. I only met him once and that was for highly technical reasons. And he could find nothing better to do than talk about the war. His war, that is. It was so beside the point that I almost asked him if he'd driven a tank himself. I thought that would bring him to his senses. And then—"

I noticed that the two men behind my back had stopped their commotion but were still in the room. I interrupted Vinner, "He would have told you he had. First of all in the Leningrad area, then in the battle of Kursk."

"In the 'Saint Petersburg' area, you mean? Ha, ha . . ."

"I don't know if we should start pronouncing it in the American way."

"That'll come in time. Anyway, what an irony of fate! He who struggled so valiantly with the arms traffickers is shot down and labeled as a Mafia man. What an end to his career! It's true that he didn't have the good fortune that you have of working 'in tandem,' as you put it. A loyal companion can always come to your aid or, if need be, rehabilitate your honor posthumously. But in his case . . ."

He went on talking with an increasingly disdainful smile. I was sure now that on the evening of our meeting in the rain he had been very much afraid and much too uneasy to think about his wife's beautiful body, and that he had spent the past two days in humiliating anxiety, which he was attempting to dispel through this contemptuous conqueror's tone. I also understood that I was highly unlikely to be leaving that office alive. The two men behind my armchair were no longer even pretending to move the cartons around. But Shakh's death had thrust me into a strange remoteness whence I viewed Vinner: his face resembled a twitching mask. I interrupted him again, and, as I was speaking, I became aware of his tenseness as he listened to me and also the tautness of my own lips.

"You promised me some notes on . . . on you know who."

"I haven't been able to get very much together but . . . here."

He passed a folder to me, held shut with elastic bands. There was a somewhat mechanical precision about his gesture, as if he were afraid I would refuse it, as if the sequence of actions in this office were dependent on the precision of this handover. Without taking my eyes off his face, I took the folder, put it on my lap. Vinner stared hard at me, then threw a rapid glance at my unmoving hands. I guessed he was waiting for me to lower my gaze, to start tugging at the elastic bands. Everything was geared to this moment of distraction. A floorboard creaked behind my back. I began talking very softly so as not to upset the unstable equilibrium.

"I would like to pass on to you the greetings of a person who is very dear to you, who lives in Warsaw. I could also offer you some documents recounting the story of your loving relationship but one folder wouldn't be enough. There are cassette tapes, films. I suggest we meet tomorrow morning at nine A.M., on a pretty beach near Destin, far from all those metal detectors. You will come alone, with your reports under your arm. I imagine what you've given me today is a bunch of virgin sheets."

I opened the folder: a single photo had been slipped in between the blank pages, it seemed to be all part of the presentation. Out of the corner of my eye I intercepted a signal with his head that Vinner gave his men. They started work again.

As I went out I gave one of the cardboard cartons a kick. "Thanks for giving me the chance to see my own coffin." Actually, this little dig occurred to me as an afterthought, when I was back at the hotel. At the moment of my departure all there was between us was the banal awkwardness of two men who cannot shake hands.

That evening, when I was back in Destin, I read the page from the English newspaper that had published the photo of Shakh. Weariness, disgust, and fear now flooded in on me with the delay of a shock wave. But the strongest of these delayed emotions was surprise. I could not bring myself to believe that Shakh was dead. Or rather, granted that they had succeeded in killing him, I nevertheless pictured him alive and living a freer life than my own, one I sought vainly to understand. It now seemed to me like the lives of those soldiers in the war, protecting an army's withdrawal and sacrificing themselves, knowing that their deaths would enable the retreating troops to gain a few hours. I thought of the strange existence of such men in that interval, consciously accepted, between life and death. A few hours, perhaps a day. A fresh intensity in their eyes and a relinquishing of everything that only yesterday had still seemed important.

As long as one stayed on the bench that was half sunk in the sand one did not notice the wind's force. In that sheltered space behind the dune the first light of the morning already made it seem like a fine sunny day, idle and warm. Only on getting up did one feel the breeze that had made the sea white and stung one's face with tiny pricks of sand. But, even as I sat there, I could see whirlwinds arising on the ridge of the dune for a moment, then settling again with a dry rustling sound as they collided with the tall tufts of tangled plants. Two or three times, launched from the beach, a kite sliced the air above the ridge then disappeared, swerving in a tensed, hissing trajectory.

I had risen well before dawn, without having really slept, and, as I approached the sea, I had caught it still in its vigilant, nocturnal sluggishness. I had swum in the midst of a darkness rhythmed by long silent waves, gradually losing all awareness of what awaited me, all memory of the country massed behind the coastline ("America," "Florida," a perplexed voice within me proclaimed), all connection with a date, a place. Occasionally a livelier wave rose up out of the blackness, covered me with its foam, disappeared into the night. I recalled the man I was going to see again (an involuntary memory: Vinner's cheek with a fine scratch left by the razor). I was surprised to realize that my hatred of this man was the very last link that still connected me to the lives of those who lived on this sleeping coastline, to their time, to the multiplicity of their desires, their actions, their words, that would start up again once it was morning. Vinner's face faded and I returned to that state of silence and forgetfulness that one day, without finding the right word for it, I had called an "afterlife," it being, in fact, all the life that was left to me to live out, in what was now a bygone age, that past I had never succeeded in leaving behind. I had remained sitting on the sand for a long time, leaning against the hull of an upturned boat. The night above the sea formed a deep, black, vibrant screen, like the restless darkness behind closed eyelids. Against this nocturnal background the memory drew faces from long ago, a figure lost among those ruined days, a look that seemed to be searching for me across the years. You. Shakh. You . . . The ghosts of this afterlife did not obey time. I saw people I had hardly known, people who had died well before I was born: that soldier, his glasses spattered with mud, carrying a wounded man on his back; that other one, lying in a field plowed up by shellfire, his lips half open, and a nurse holding out a tiny mirror toward them, hoping, or not hoping, to capture a slight trace of breath. I also saw the one who had told me of these soldiers, a woman with silvery hair, at rest in the endlessness of the steppe, gazing at me across that plain, across time, as it seemed to me. A man, too, with a face of quartz, a strip of bandages around his forehead, who smiled as he spoke, defying the pain. Shakh walking along in a crowd in an avenue in London; he was keeping our rendezvous, but had not yet seen me and I surprised him in his solitude. You, at a dark window lit by the ruddy glow of fires in neighboring streets. You, your eyes closed, lying beside me one night after the fighting was over, telling me about a winter's day, the forest silent under the snows, a house one could discover by crossing a frozen lake. You . . .

I had stood up when I noticed that the sand was beginning to be colored by the first glow of the morning. The night, still this negative that sheltered me, was going to evolve into the sunlit shades of blue of a day by the sea. It would fill with tanned bodies and shouts, imprint itself as a happy holiday snapshot. I had hurried to extricate myself from this snapshot in the making, gone up onto the dune (from the top of it, in the distance, one could see the first houses and the terrace of the café where Vinner was due to join me in two and a half hours' time), and taken my place on this bench, sheltered from the wind that was already blowing the tops off the waves.

The sun-drenched silence of the place, sheltered by the dune and, behind it, the scrub, filtered out the sounds one by one: now a shout coming from the beach, now a car passing beyond the trees. These sounds seemed to come from very far away, isolated by distance, like signals from an alien world. This world, another holiday morning, was waking up all around me, routinely genial in its ways, making my presence here more and more incongruous. I was a man who had come from a forgotten age to demand satisfaction from a vacationer who, but for my arrival, would have been playing with his two children, making sandcastles or catching shellfish. One could hear voices more frequently and more distinctly, carried up from the beach by the wind. The hum of vehicles was becoming more continuous. There was a tone of triumphal tranquillity in the rhythm with which the sounds of the day were gradually coming together. I was a ghost whose presence could make absolutely no difference to it.

But a brief jolt in these cadences drew me out of my drowsiness. The sound of a car stopping and driving off again at full tilt. It all happens so quickly that I am not aware in what order the noises come. "Someone's opened a bottle of champagne," suggests one thought numbed by the sun. But before this dull pop, suddenly matched by a burning pain in my shoulder, before this pain there is a leap: two adolescent boys come running down the dune, preceded by their kite which, buffeted by the wind, struggles on the slope, climbs again, then hurtles straight at me. I lean to avoid it. It tangles me up in its nylon threads. It is at this moment that someone opens a bottle of champagne behind the trees. The boys rush toward me, yelling apologies, and disentangle me. Their "sorry" is said in tones of: "Gee, we're sorry, but you'd have to be a total idiot to be sitting on that bench. It's bad enough with all those people getting in our way on the beach." During their maneuvering I have time to reconstruct the sequence of noises. First the appearance of the kite, grazing my head. The man who just fired at me (with a silencer: the "champagne"), aiming from his car that had stopped behind the trees, was put off his aim by the appearance of the boys. He did not fire a second shot. A professional would have had to do it, even if it meant bringing down a couple of kite flyers. I slip my hand under the beach towel around my neck. Fingers have a memory of old gestures on the bodies of the wounded: a flesh wound, nothing more, already a lot of blood. Mustn't frighten the children. They scramble off up the dune. The wings of their kite flap in the wind. They have noticed nothing.

At the hospital reception desk it took me quite a long time to prove I was creditworthy. The receptionist explained to me in detail what type of medical insurance I needed in order to be admitted. The towel on my shoulder was no longer holding the blood and this was trickling down my arm. I managed to get her to accept my credit card. She telephoned a superior for reassurance. On the walls I looked at the photos showing off the most high-performance equipment the hospital had at its disposal. While she was talking the receptionist was wiping my card with a Kleenex tissue to remove the bloodstains, then she wiped her fingers with a swab soaked in alcohol.

In the corridor where they made me wait I came upon a whole row of young cooks in their white uniforms, some of them with their hats on their heads. Each of them, all in identical postures, was holding an injured hand wrapped in an emergency bandage. They looked as if they were the victims of a mad killer bent on exterminating all kitchen staff. Tiredness at first stopped me realizing that these were simply accidents at work. Hundreds of restaurants along the coast, knives that cut a finger at the same time as a slice of steak. As I awaited my turn I thought again about Vinner's stinginess in hiring a killer who was not really professional, a cheap contract for the easy prey that I was. I recalled the receptionist explaining to me with faultless logic why I had no right to medical attention. This whole world, with its triumphal air, seemed to me quite simply pathetic, like an account book someone had tried to brighten up with a few picturesque seaside views.

The nurse who came to fetch me thought I had lost consciousness. I was sitting motionless, my eyes closed, the back of my neck against the wall. In the questionnaire the receptionist had told me to fill in I had just discovered, at the very bottom, this form of words: "Person to contact in case of emergency." I had replied to all the other questions and I was getting ready to put a name beside this one. . . . The name of a relative, of a friend. I thought of you. Of Shakh. In a flash of memory I pictured a white-haired woman at the heart of the steppe. . . . I realized that you were the only people whose names I could have written on this line in the questionnaire. The only ones among whom I still felt alive.

That night at the hospital I took out of my overnight bag the folder with the sheaf of paper Vinner had handed to me. Then the English newspaper; the photo of Shakh, the caption: "One of the barons of the nuclear network." That photo, that stupid caption. There would be no other record of his life.

Opening the folder, I came upon a snapshot Vinner must have slipped in as bait. I studied it, recognized it. Long ago, after more than three years of our life abroad, I was spending two weeks with you in Russia. It was in February, the abundance of light already heralded the spring. Intoxicated by these days of sunshine, for a moment we believed we could live a life like other people, quietly accumulating memories, letters, photos. I had bought a camera and, to try it out, I had taken a first test shot, aiming the lens low. That had produced this strange photo: the ground covered in snow, a section of an old wooden fence, two shadows on the white surface, dazzling in the sunlight. We did not keep the photos taken during those two weeks. In the event of a search they could have betrayed us. Only this shot, with no identifying marks and no date, had come with us on our travels (you sometimes used it as a bookmark), indecipherable to other people.

"No other record of her life." I silenced this thought before having really formulated it. Too late, for the truth was there, unstoppable. Soon everything would be reduced to that winter snapshot,

243

from which I alone could still call to mind your features, picture one of the days of your life.

My own disappearance, which for Vinner was only a question of organization, suddenly appeared in quite a different light from these cloak-and-dagger games. Dumbfounded, I saw myself as the last person who could speak about you, tell your real name, give you an existence among the living, if only through the ludicrous means of recollecting the past.

Feverishly I set about seeking for some glimpses of our old life, glimpses of cities, of skies, moments of joy. They surfaced and quickly disintegrated under the touch of memory. I needed a more solid fact, a particle of you whose evidence would be beyond dispute. A certificate of civic status almost, I thought, with stupidly administrative but irrefutable information on it, like place and date of birth.

Place and date of birth . . . I repeated these details that must surely hold your life back from the brink of oblivion, and recalled the day when I had learned them. A rainy day in Germany, on a journey that had exasperated me because of its lack of objective, when suddenly this objective arose. The story you told me.

It was several months before the end of the nomadic life that had been ours for so many years. You mentioned a town to me in what, until recently, had been East Germany and we set off, soon crossing the abolished frontier. The contrast was still visible: "A tourniquet has come off," I said to myself, "and the benefits of the West will now flow into the limb constricted for so long. The benefits or maybe the poison. Both, probably." We could already observe the start of this transfusion process. Roads were beginning to be mended, housefronts were being cleaned. But the rain that day was eliding the changes under the gray light of autumn, mingling the two Germanies with the same question: "How can they live in these dark, damp little towns that go to sleep at six o'clock in the evening?" In one street a window facing out onto a dirty, noisy crossroads gave me a glimpse of a very white lace curtain, a flowering plant, a crowd of little china vases and figurines—all of it only three yards away from the huge trucks thundering up a viaduct. And further on, in the low doorway to a tavern, men were gathered in folk costumes and their laughter mingled with the sounds of merry, strident music.

This trip toward the east was becoming more and more painful to me. Before we set off you had vaguely explained to me that we had a contact to pick up in one of these towns I was in a hurry to drive through. Their ugliness and the poverty of the bare forests made the purpose of our trip uncertain in advance, held in suspension in the glaucous air of this rainy day. Absurd, like all our work now, I thought, recalling my first visit to Berlin, then still divided by the Wall. Your silence, the silence of someone who knows where she is going, weighed on me. It was when I saw the lace curtains and heard the din of the folk music that I began to speak, with assumed irony.

"I know I've become suspect in your eyes and Shakh's. Heavens above! I've dared to question the value of our heroic mission. But, even as I crumble under your mistrust, I think I have a right to know what we're doing in this moldy little hole."

My tone was simply a fresh attempt to provoke a real explanation, to make you voice the doubts I sensed in you. You looked at me as if you did not understand and all you answered was, "I don't know." Then, since I looked nonplussed, rousing yourself from your reverie, you added, "We're looking for the exact place where I was born. It can't be far away. It could be on the road out of this village. They've done a lot of building since then. I thought you might be interested. And as we had three hours to spare . . . It must be here. Under those warehouses. A pretty place to be born. Shall we walk a bit?"

The outskirts of a town, corrugated tin warehouses, a terrain of withered grass where I parked the car. We took a few steps in driving rain and, as we studied the gray fields beyond the sheds, you told me about those long hours of sunlight, one fine day in March 1945.

*

It had happened on that same road, narrower in those days and broken up by tank tracks. The warm steam rising from the fields in the dazzling sun mingled with the brief gusts coming from the patches of snow piled up in the shadow of the bushes. The place was empty: the Germans had withdrawn during the night, the main body of Russian troops was held up by fighting farther north and would only appear on this road toward evening. For the moment all one could see was these two clouds of dust, two groups of civilians advancing painfully toward one another. One, stretched out into a faltering line of some twenty people, was traveling toward the west. The other, more compact and less stricken with weariness, was walking toward the east. The first, survivors of a camp liquidated at the approach of the Russians, had been taken before dawn to a railroad station, from which they were to be sent farther west into the depths of the country. Halfway there, their guards had learned that the station was already under enemy attack. They had abandoned their prisoners and made themselves scarce. The prisoners had not altered the direction of their walk, they had simply slowed their pace. The others, those who were going toward the east, young women and a few adolescent boys, were members of the labor force rounded up by the Germans from the occupied Soviet territories and sent to Germany. Guessing the outcome of the war, the peasants, for whom these young people had been working, had got rid of their serfs, and were themselves fleeing west before the Russian offensive. One of the women was pregnant. Her master had stooped to inseminate an inferior race. She walked along, wailing continuously, her fingers joined beneath her enormous belly.

The two groups drew closer to one another, halted near the crossroads, stared at one another in silence. Only a few minutes earlier the young women walking east had been convinced they had touched the extreme limits of misery: several days on the road without food, bitter cold at night, a burst of gunfire that morning from a

German truck. Now no moaning could be heard in their group any longer. The pregnant woman, too, had fallen silent, leaning against the slatted side of an abandoned trailer. They stared in silence and simply had no conception of what they were seeing. The beings in front of them could not be recognized according to conventional attributes: Russians or Germans, men or women, living or dead. They were beyond such differences. You could meet their eyes only for as long as it took to perceive in them, as it were, the first steps of a staircase descending into darkness, although these eyes contained it in its entirety, down to the very depths. One who was lagging behind the line of prisoners had just fallen. He was carrying a strange wooden box solidly fixed to his forearm.

The young women stare and do not understand.

These prisoners are scientific material. That is why they have been spared. There are those among them whose faces are burned with liquid phosphorus: methods of treating the effects of incendiary bombs were being studied. The women have been burned by X rays: experiments in sterilization. Some prisoners are infected with typhus. Others wear striped garments that conceal experimental amputations. The medical case history of each one corresponds to the subject of a thesis, which the people conducting the experiments had counted on having time to complete. The man who has just fallen over is burdened by a box attached to his forearm filled with malarial mosquitoes. The Reich might have been called upon to fight the enemy in infested areas.

The young women observe them, meet their eyes, catch sight of the first steps of that staircase descending into black night and turn their gaze away, like children who will only venture a little way down a staircase into a cellar.

On a road at right angles, coming from the north, a long dusty streak appears: a company sent on reconnaissance. A light armored car and a four-wheel-drive, soldiers already jumping down and running toward the crowd gathered at the crossroads. The young women begin weeping, laughing, embracing the soldiers. The prisoners are silent, still, absent.

The child will be born under the spring sunshine on a great canvas cape, which the officer spreads out beside the road. The cord will be cut by a bayonet rinsed in alcohol, a blade that has been plunged so many times into men's entrails. When the young mother ceases crying out there will be a moment of silence poised in the lightness of the spring sky, in the scent of the earth warmed by the sun, in the coolness of the last snows. They will all gather round the square of canvas: the young bondwomen, the prisoners, the soldiers.

This moment will endure, set apart from human time, apart from the war, beyond death. There is still no one in that sun-drenched space to give history lessons, to do the accountancy for the suffering, to judge who is more worthy of compassion than the others.

There will be these young women who, on returning to their country, will be regarded as traitors until the day they die. These soldiers who on the following day will continue on their road to Berlin and half of whom will not see the end of the war. These prisoners, who will soon be dragooned into the ranks of the millions of anonymous victims.

But at this moment there is only silence around the mother and her child, wrapped in a broad, clean shirt, which the officer has taken out of his knapsack. Where the roads cross there is this prisoner lying dead on the verge, with a box on his forearm in which mosquitoes buzz about, sucking the blood of the lifeless body. There is this woman with cropped hair and huge eyes in a transparent face, she who has helped the mother and who now raises her eyes toward the others, eyes in which they can see, as it were, a slow return from the pit of darkness. There is the child's first cry.

We drove back through the little German town, traveling through it in the opposite direction: the warehouses, the tavern, the viaduct, the window with lace curtains. Watching the procession of housefronts washed out by the rain, you murmured softly and without emotion: "I quite likely have cousins who live in these parts. Maybe even my father. The world is such a small place."

On that return journey you told me about the house in the north of Russia where you spent the first years of your childhood. About the clock with its weights and the chain that your mother often rewound, for fear that the knot in it should stop the march of time. Your mother had died when you were three and a half. Your only memory of her was of that winter's day with the flakes dreamily swirling, the forest slumbering beneath the snow and the lake no one dared to cross, on ice that was still too thin, having just begun to spread over the water's brown surface. And, in the midst of this calm, a faint anxiety lest that knot in the chain might at any moment interrupt the passage of the snowy hours.

I wrote down your name and the name of the German town near which you were born. And I realized that the sheet of paper came from the bunch Vinner had given me. Never before had the traces of our past seemed to me so derisory and fleeting. I remembered how, several years previously, in talking about our past, you had said to me, in tones that seemed wistful about the elusiveness of all testimonies: "It must be possible to tell the truth one day. . . ." The truth was there on that sheet of paper. A message destined for no one, with no hope of convincing anyone. Like all the ghosts we carried within ourselves. The soldier in front of the lines of barbed wire, his hand raised to his face, smashed by a splinter from a grenade. The couple in their mountain refuge surrounded by armed men.

The shuffling feet slipped along the corridor, and stopped outside my door (a nurse? someone sent by Vinner? such anxious thoughts would be inextinguishable until death, thanks to a survival reflex). This reminded me uselessly of the brevity of my reprieve. Strangely enough, this period of time under threat now seemed very long, almost infinite. Sufficient for telling the truth that needed no other addressee than you, one that would be told without my needing to argue a case, offer justification, convince. It was very simple, independent of words, of the time that was left for me to live, of what others might think of it. This truth corresponded to a saying I had heard long ago, whose haughty strength and humility had always appealed to me: "I have not been called upon to make you believe, but to tell you." I did not think this truth, I saw it.

I saw the soldier who had just fallen, a hand reaching out toward his smashed face. I saw him not at the moment of his death but in the early light of a morning that no longer belonged to his life but was still his life, the very sense of his life. I saw him sitting beside other soldiers on the benches of an army truck. Their eyes watched the road through the open tarpaulin at the rear. They were silent. Their faces were serious and as if illuminated by a great pain finally overcome. Their tunics, bleached by the sunlight, bore no decorations, but at chest height retained the darker traces left by medals that had been removed. The truck passed through the still-sleeping suburbs of a great city, stopped in a street shrouded in half-light. The soldier jumped to the ground, saluted his comrades, followed them with his gaze as far as the corner. Adjusting the knapsack on his shoulder, he walked in through the entrance to a building. In the courtyard, in that stone well with echoing walls, he raised his head: a tree that seemed to be the only thing awake at the dawning of this day and, above its branches with their pale foliage, a window at which a lamp was shining.

The truth of the soldier's return was undemonstrable, but for me it had the force of a life-and-death wager. If it made no sense nothing made sense any more.

I also saw, within me and very remote from me, the man and the woman standing motionless in the night on the bank of a watercourse. The outlines of the mountains were incised into the air's resonant transparency. The current of the stream carried the stars along, thrust them into the shadow of the rocks, into shelter from the waves. The man turned, looked for a long time at the half-open door of a wooden house, at the ruddy glow from a fire dying down between the heavy stones of the hearth and the tall, straight flame from the candle on a fragment of rock in the middle of the room.

It was not a memory or a moment lived through. I simply knew that one day it would be so, that it already was so, that this couple were already living in the silence of that night.

You know, I shall have to go soon. But before leaving I shall have enough time to tell you what is essential. The winter's day I can see, which one part of me is beginning to inhabit. A muted day, traversed by slowly eddying flakes. A time will come when everything is like that moment in winter. You will appear amid the snowbound sleep of the trees, on the shore of a frozen lake. And you will begin walking on the still-fragile ice; every step you take will be deep pain and joy for me. You will walk toward me, letting me recognize you at every step. As you draw closer you will show me, in the hollow of your hand, a fistful of berries, the very last of them, found beneath the snow. Bitter and frozen. The icy steps on the wooden stairway will give off a crunching sound that I have not heard for an eternity. In the house I shall remove the chain from the weight-driven clock so as to undo the knot. But we shall no longer have any need of its hours.